ONE LAST

ALASKA AIR ONE RESCUE | BOOK ONE

SHOT

ONE LAST

ALASKA AIR ONE RESCUE | BOOK ONE

SHOT

SUSAN MAY WARREN

Revell

a division of Baker Publishing Group
Grand Rapids, Michigan

© 2024 by Susan May Warren

Published by Revell
a division of Baker Publishing Group
Grand Rapids, Michigan
RevellBooks.com

Printed in the United States of America

ISBN 9780800745479 (paperback)
Library of Congress Cataloging-in-Pulication Control Number: 2023050161

This book is a work of fiction. Names, characters, places, and incidents are either
products of the author's imagination or used fictitiously. Any similarity to actual
people, organizations, and/or events is purely coincidental.

Scripture quotations are also taken from the Holy Bible, New International
Version®, NIV®. Copyright© 1973, 1978, 1984, 2011 by Biblica, Inc®. Used by
permission of Zondervan. All rights reserved worldwide.

For more information about Susan May Warren, please access the author's website at
the following address: www.susanmaywarren.com.

Published in the United States of America.
Cover design by Emilie Haney, www.eahcreative.com

24 25 26 27 28 29 30   7 6 5 4 3 2 1

For Your glory, Lord

ONE

BOO COULDN'T THINK OF A WORSE WAY TO die.

The kid was buried under tons of snow, lost in a crevasse, the snowy mountainside simply opening up to gobble the ten-year-old skier whole.

Yeah, no. "I'm going down there." Boo slammed her ice axe closer to the edge, testing the snow near the side of the crevasse where she sat. Overhead, the sun gleamed, no help at all to forestall the peril on the backside of one of the Copper Mountain resort ski area bowls. Just a little more heat and the entire snowpack might release.

And of course, kill them all.

But that's why she was here. And frankly, hanging off the side of a mountain beat sitting in front of a warm hearth, watching reruns of *Chicago Fire.*

Boo looked over at Axel, her fellow rescuer and the man holding her on belay. "I need you to rig up a rappel system."

He sat also, his feet dug into the snow, harnessed and anchored with three points, his expression grim. He wore a wool hat, a pair of snow pants, a bright red Air One jacket, helmet, and gloves. "I'm not sure this entire crevasse won't collapse if you do that. For sure, that snow bridge won't hold you."

"It won't have to. I won't step on it. But Macie is frozen in fear. No matter what I say, she can't get that harness on. And I can guarantee you that she can't climb out on her own. So she needs help. Me."

"Wait for the chopper, Boo." This from London. The female climbing expert had set up more anchors above them in case, indeed, the snowpack decided to let loose and career down over them all. Avalanche.

That's what happened when you went skiing outside the boundary only a day after the Alaskan sky dumped fresh powder on already melting snow. A slippery, unsecured foundation that could turn lethal.

Macie's parents refused to leave, of course, and they stood with Shep, the team lead, some fifty feet away, out of the slide path. Shep barked into his walkie, arguing with Moose, piloting the Air One chopper. So far, no joy.

She'd heard Shep's dispatch on the radio only moments ago. "The winds are still too high for him to come in, and if he does, he's going to loosen this pack up with the rotor wash."

She'd never been great at waiting anyway. So they needed to get creative.

Crying found her, despite being muffled thirty feet down in the crevasse where Macie lay, her leg twisted. They needed a splint, and a litter, and frankly, luck.

Because beyond the snow bridge, into the depths of Copper Mountain, the crevasse fell thousands of feet. And that snow bridge could give way any moment.

Boo looked at London. "Either rig up a rappel system, or let me go and I'll climb down—"

Screaming cut off her words. Boo rolled over and peered down into the hole.

Macie's ski careened down the never-ending spout only to land at an angle some hundred feet below.

"Macie!"

"I didn't touch it—it just fell!" Her voice shook.

Her other ski remained on her twisted leg. Bindings too tight, clearly, but worse, she had a precarious hold on the edge of the bridge.

What was a ten-year-old doing out here in uncharted territory?

Probably following her parents. Or maybe they'd given in to her whims, because according to Mom and Dad, Macie was some sort of youth champ on skis.

Now she was just a terrified kid.

"Give me slack. I'm going down there."

"London—give me the descender." Axel held out his hand. London was working through the gear slung on her webbing, over her shoulder.

"Too late. I'm climbing down." Boo stood up even as Axel fed out slack. "London, Axel, get ready to pull her up. You can feed the rope back to me—I have ascenders."

Axel was shaking his head, but she ignored him, got up, and even as he held the rope, she stepped over the edge, holding tight to her ice axes.

Her crampons bit into the snow, and she looked down.

Oops, bad idea. But she was in it now.

Improvise. Adapt. Overcome. She blew out her breath and stepped over the edge.

Her feet dangled while she kicked for purchase. The rope held her, but she didn't want to dislodge the snowpack and drop it on Macie.

One in ten people who fell into a crevasse died, buried under snow.

She hung from one hand and moved her other ice axe down, found a hold, then lowered herself onto it. Dangled from that while she chipped into the ice on the side of the chute.

Found another hold, then slammed her crampons in and eased her weight onto the two points. She secured her other foot, then held on to the ice axe as she rerouted her other hand.

She was Spider-Man, climbing down a wall of ice and snow. *Please don't let the girl slip.* The prayer sort of just slid out, but frankly, she needed more than luck.

Below her some twenty feet, Macie whimpered.

"Hang in there, sweetie. I'm coming for you." She moved down the wall, steady, sure, and then stopped about a foot from Macie. Here the walls were only four feet apart. She kicked her foot in above Macie, standing spread eagle over her. "Okay, honey, I'm going to put this harness around you, then clip you into me. Don't move. Let me do all the work, okay?"

Macie nodded. Cute kid. Dark brown hair in braids, blue eyes— reminded Boo of her sister, Austen. She leaned down, then slid the harness around the girl's waist, clipped it, then snapped the webbed line onto her carabiner.

The knot in her chest eased, just a smidgen. But no way could Axel hold her weight and Macie's. Okay, maybe he could hold it, but he couldn't haul them both up.

"How are you doing up there?"

London had probably created a haul system by now. She'd seen the woman at work in training over the past few weeks, and no one understood ropes and climbing and rescue systems like London. Not her real name, but given her accent, it seemed right. Boo had asked a few questions and discovered that London had served on some European rescue team.

"We have the ratchet system set up—ready to haul her up." This from Axel, who bent over the hole. Clearly he'd anchored in the rope and taken her off belay. "Can you attach yourself to the sides while we pull her up?"

"Yeah." She took an ice screw and angled it in, then attached webbing to it and that to her harness via another carabiner. Then she unhooked from the line. "I need to get her ski off!"

Macie's eyes widened. "But—"

Boo turned to her, her crampons still jammed into each side of the walls. "Macie, we need to haul you out of here. But we can't do it with your ski on."

"Will it hurt?"

Boo met her eyes. "Probably. But I'll be fast. Do you know a song?"

"Um. I . . . maybe . . . 'Let It Go'?"

"Sing it. Really loud."

Macie started in. "Let it go, let it go—"

Boo reached down, grabbed the ski, held it steady, then pressed down on the binding.

Macie got louder. "Can't hold it back anymore—!"

"That's right, Mace." The ski snapped off and Macie screamed.

"Let it go! Let it go!" Boo said, grabbing Macie's shoulders. "C'mon, Macie."

Tears burned down Macie's cheeks, but she nodded and started singing again.

"Okay, Axe. Haul her up!" She directed Macie up, holding under her arms, then under her backside, as Axel and London hauled her up.

"Almost there, Macie!"

The girl was still singing.

Axel appeared over the edge and reached down. Next to him, Shep appeared, and together they pulled Macie up and out and onto the snow.

Boo blew out a breath.

And that's when the shelf above her, where they'd just hauled up Macie, broke.

Snow thundered down over her, hit her helmet, slammed against her anchor, and took out the snow bridge below her.

It fell into the yawning blackness.

She grabbed her ice axes, shaking.

Oh, this was a great way to die. Her legs tremored, sweat trickling down her back. It seemed her ice axes as well as her anchor were holding, but who knew for how long?

"Axel?"

Nothing.

"Anyone?"

"Hey, Boo? The edge gave way—" This from Shep.

"No duh."

"We're not sure it'll wait for you to climb up. I think we need to pull you out."

"Fine. I'm just hanging out here, Shep. Wouldn't mind, I dunno, a rope?"

"Demanding."

She smiled. She liked Shep. He did his job and left her alone on her off time. No invitations to buddy up with the crew after work at the local Tenderfoot Bar and Grill or hang out at the boss's house. And sure, she liked Moose, and Shep and London and Axel, but she wasn't looking for camaraderie, and if she needed family, she'd visit her cousins at Sky King Ranch.

She'd come up here to hide, thank you. And that didn't mean palling up with her teammates. But it also didn't mean giving them a reason to start asking questions about her past. Maybe do some googling.

So yeah, she'd let him tease her a little.

"I'll just be chillin' out here, then, while you all tidy up on top."

A rope fell, smacking her on the head. A Prusik knot was tied on it, with a sling for her foot. She took the rope, created some slack, twisted it twice, and pulled a loop through, creating a figure eight on a bight. Then she clipped an extra length of webbing from her harness to the bight, and finally unclipped from the anchor.

"You got me?" Her gaze went to the darkness below.

The line tightened.

She put her foot into the Prusik sling and eased her weight onto the rope.

Please let the lip hold.

She unscrewed her anchor, then, "Haul me up!"

She still hadn't released her ice axes and now used them to anchor herself as she was hauled up, walking with them up the side.

She reached the overhang, and the snow began to dribble down, breaking, falling.

"Just hold me! I'll climb out!" She flung one ice axe out over the top, then the other, and began to haul herself up.

But her arms had turned to rubber and she had no purchase.

Hands gripped her harness, and in a second, Axel and Shep yanked her out of the hole. She fell on her knees in the snow, breathing hard.

"Bravest thing I've ever seen," Axel said.

She rolled onto her back. "Please. Don't patronize me. The only reason you didn't go down there is because you're a moose."

Axel's blue eyes widened. "Hey? I'm not the moose in the family."

"Right." Moose, the boss of this little rescue team, outweighed his brother by a good twenty pounds. Wider shoulders, taller.

But Axel was no slouch. Now he held out his hand, gripped hers, and pulled her up.

Away from the crevasse, Macie lay in the snow, London affixing an inflatable splint to her leg. Nearby, a ski patrol sled waited with Copper Mountain patrols, ready to ferry her down. Her mother held her hand, weeping, her dad behind her, holding their skis.

High overhead, a chopper came into view.

"Now he decides to save the day," Boo said and tromped over to London. She knelt beside Macie in the snow. "Great job, kiddo. You were super brave."

London had clearly administered some painkiller because Macie was smiling more freely now. "That's because you said you wouldn't leave me."

She had? She didn't remember that, but it sounded like her. "Yeah, well, that's what rescuers do." She winked.

"Let's get her down the mountain," said one of the ski patrols, and Boo stepped back while they lifted Macie onto a litter and then onto the sled.

Her parents strapped on their skis, following.

Boo tromped back over to Axel, now winding up the gear, re-stowing it. She worked out the ice anchors. Dropped them into the duffel bag.

Moose had set down the chopper on a flat outcropping some one hundred yards away. Shep tossed her the snowshoes, and she fixed them on, then grabbed a gear bag.

They set out in silence, heading toward the big red bird, adrenaline still thick inside her veins. She could use a workout, sluice off some of the rush.

But how she loved a good-outcome rescue. Lived for it, actually.

After all, she had nothing else.

Oaken Fox never slept on planes, which today left him groggy, crabby, and in need of a nap.

Mostly, it didn't bode well for his upcoming demise.

Because he wasn't a hero, and no amount of trickery by the camera was going to make him one.

Goldie had sold the producers a bunch of Who-Hash about

country star Oaken Fox being a hero, and apparently it was up to him to deliver.

Most likely, he'd plummet to his death in front of millions. At least it would be epic. And hopefully painless.

His manager really should have warned the camera crew not to stand too close to him lest they be hit by lightning because, yep, it was that bad.

But clearly no one but him was paying attention to the fact that God had it out for him.

Oaken pulled his wool cap down over his ears, tucking his chin into his parka. Probably—and it only took one look at the dour gray skies and the hidden but white-capped Alaska Range to the north to conjure this thought—he'd freeze to death on his way down, so maybe it didn't matter.

His body would be entombed in layers of snow and ice, never to be found again. Or at least, not until the thaw, when his remains could be picked over by bears and wolves—

"Okay, the sound levels are right. We're nearly ready." Huxley Shaw, the associate producer, gave Beto Gomez, the cameraman, a nod as he trained the camera on Oaken. She stepped away and addressed Oaken. "Don't forget to smile. Your fans love your smile."

Then she flashed Oaken a thumbs-up, like she might be one of those fans.

Oaken shoved his gloved hands into his parka, the snow lifting off the semi-frozen lake behind Huxley into the pellet-gray horizon. A different day, different circumstances, and Oaken might not hate fifty hours alone in the woods of Alaska. Even maybe at a tiny, remote log cabin like the one behind him. Although he'd prefer one less ramshackle, with the roof intact, and maybe running water and an outhouse that didn't list to one side.

Still, the moment the chopper from Anchorage settled them down on the shore, the snow crusty and thin, melting after a snowstorm dumped five inches on the mountains two days ago, the moment he breathed in the thick pine-scented air, the sense of wild lurking in the dense forest surrounding the clearing, he felt it . . .

Peace. Or maybe just the hint of it. Still, maybe here—

"Okay, we're rolling, so anytime." Huxley stepped back, her gaze on him behind her mirrored sunglasses. She wore her dark hair in two short braids, a white cap, a yellow parka, mukluks, and a sense of ease in this rugged landscape. But maybe that was the byproduct of standing in the shadows, filming the wild adventures of Mike Grizz and his victims.

No, not *victims*. Celebrities who were crazy—or maybe desperate—enough to take the fifty-hour challenge.

He fell into the desperate category. *When you find yourself in a hole, best stop digging . . .*

Thanks, Dad.

He smiled into the camera, the red light blinking, and took a breath. "I'm standing here on the shores of a lake I can't name, in the middle of breathtaking Alaska, not sure why I agreed to this."

Huxley grinned and nodded.

"Except that I grew up on a ranch, and I love the wilderness, and who doesn't want to hang out with the legendary Mike Grizz for two days, right?" He leaned into the camera and lowered his voice. "I'm actually supposed to be working on a new song, so maybe I'll be inspired, right?" Now he winked.

That should get him some social-media love.

He took a step back. "I'm pretty much waiting for a bear or wolf to run out of the woods, and it looks like a blizzard might be heading my direction, but then again, it's April. In Alaska. And not Anchorage but a hundred miles into the bush. In fact, that's Denali behind me." He turned and pointed to the fuzzy outline of a rugged chain of mountains, just over his right shoulder. "And it's freezing." He pulled his hat down, just for emphasis.

Huxley was motioning him to continue, so he looked over his left shoulder. "Behind me is my only escape—a chopper from a local rescue team who dropped me off so I can wait for Mike to pick me up." He waved to the chopper pilot, a big guy who ran the rescue company they'd hired the chopper from, and then the executive producer, Reynolds Gray, who waved in return, now climbing back in after dumping a couple packs onto the ground.

"Honestly, I'm looking forward to pushing myself. I expect it to be crazy, off the hook, and wild." He leaned in again and this time waggled his eyebrows. "I just hope I live through it."

Then he winked again, and Huxley gave two thumbs up as she walked up to the camera and paused it.

"Great job. I'll stick around until you get on the chopper with Mike, then you'll be on your own."

And that would be the part where he plummeted to earth.

"Don't worry—Mike will tell you what to do. You'll be fine." She disassembled the camera from the tripod, packing it up and strapping it to her pack.

Oaken just stared at her. What, could she read minds?

"You've got the pre-jump look. You should have seen Winchester Marshall. He was ashen."

No wonder they'd made him sign a couple thousand waivers. But what did he expect? Mike's shows were all about survival, epic adventure, and crazy feats of bravery.

This might be the stupidest thing he'd ever done. Or maybe the second stupidest—

A hum burred the air, and he looked up to see another chopper clearing the tree line. Blue, it looked similar to the chopper that had brought him up from Anchorage this morning.

"That's my cue," Huxley said. She stepped up to Oaken and checked his chest-mounted camera, the one strapped over his shoulders. "This has enough battery life for all fifty hours, so just keep this running the entire time. We'll edit it later."

Then she picked up her pack and ran over to the first chopper, now firing up the blades. She climbed on, and in a moment, the red chopper took off, moving over to the lake, where it hovered.

Oaken stepped back, holding up his hand to protect his face from the snow that whisked off the lakeshore, and watched as the blue chopper settled where the other bird had landed earlier. A man sat on the deck, dressed in a ski jacket and thermal pants, worn hiking boots, and a helmet, and waved to him.

Oh boy.

He waved back.

Mike Grizz. Former Navy Seal, survivalist, free climber, brand icon, and now celebrity trail guide. A bona fide hero.

Oaken just hoped he didn't look like a complete idiot next to him. *Please just let me keep up.*

Mike jumped out, ducked, then ran over to Oaken. He was lean, chiseled, and wore a bit of a beard—every inch the picture of an action hero.

And here it began.

Already Oaken felt like a chump in his black Cloudrock hikers, his fleece-lined jeans, the oversized parka. He wore a slight beard but only because he hadn't had a chance to shave this morning in Anchorage, still trying to survive jet lag.

Yep, he was murdering Goldie next time he saw her. *Go to Alaska, be a tough guy, generate some social-media love.*

Write a song.

Land an album.

Forget about the last horrid eight months.

Yeah, whatever. The hole seemed to be getting deeper.

"Hey, Mike!" he shouted and held out his hand. Mike gripped it.

"Ready for this?" Mike bore a bit of Montana drawl, although he'd lived all over.

"Not even a little." But Oaken grinned as Mike clamped him on the back.

"Alrighty, let's get this started." Mike pulled a topographical map contained in plastic and folded into a square from his leg pocket. "We're here," Mike said, pointing with his glove. "The road is here"—he ran his finger along a thick black line to the west—"and we're starting here." He tapped a circle maybe ten miles from the road, at the base of a mountain, according to Oaken's quick glance at the legend. "But we need to get to this river tonight. If we can, we'll cross. If not, we'll camp on this side. Tomorrow, we will cross it, camp at this old fire shelter. Then we follow the river and finish at the Bear Lake Inn. It's about fifteen miles total haul, and there's a steak waiting for you, if you can make it."

He clamped Oaken on the shoulder, gave it a squeeze.

"And we need to do it all before the blizzard sets in, so let's not waste the sun!"

Blizzard? Aw—

Mike ran over to the two backpacks, then lifted one and held it out to Oaken. It contained leg loops and a chest strap.

Oaken fixed on the rig, snapping it tight as Mike donned his, then handed him a helmet. "Let's fly!"

Ho-boy.

"Stay low!" Mike grabbed him and they ran out to the chopper. Mike secured him to the deck with a carabiner on a line and then settled in next to him. The pilot looked back. Dark hair, gray-green eyes. A copilot with braids sat in the other seat.

"You good?" the pilot shouted.

Mike gave him a thumbs-up.

They lifted off, and in a moment the cabin on shore turned small, the lake a mirror of the sky, now shimmering with the muted sunlight. Despite the cold, they had nearly fourteen hours of sunlight today.

Across from them, Mike waved to the other chopper, Huxley still filming. Oaken did too, giving two thumbs up. *Good grief.*

Mike turned to Oaken, shouting over the rotor wash. "So, Oaken, ever jump out of a chopper before?"

"I've tried to keep my legs and hands inside the flying vehicles."

Mike laughed. "Okay, so we have a saying—pull high, don't die. As soon as you get out of the chopper, pull the rip cord."

"Where's the rip cord?"

He patted the pack near the bottom, and Oaken put his hand on it.

"Now, if it doesn't deploy, here's what you do. Put your arms out."

Oaken held them out.

"Now move them up and down."

Oaken started to move, then got it, shook his head, and put his arms down. "You're hilarious."

"You got that faster than most!" Mike was grinning. He pointed to the bag. "Here's your cutaway, and here's the reserve chute. But if you run into trouble, I'll be there. I won't deploy until you're good to go."

They had climbed, the bushy green forest below, shadows between the trees, left Denali to the north behind, and now flew east, into the smaller Copper Mountain range. Still rugged. Still deadly.

But brutally gorgeous. He took a breath, the air thinning as they rose, fragile and frigid. Mike leaned out, then came back in, grinning at him.

Below, a river jagged in and around granite walls, trees, even muddy washes where it chipped out snow. Alaska, in the throes of awakening.

Maybe it wouldn't be terrible. So he'd tromp around nature, learn some skills, and maybe even get out of his head for a while.

"There's our drop!" Mike said, pointing to a clearing far, far below. He grabbed a pack that sat between them, stood, and then heaved it out of the chopper.

It fell, and in a second, the chute deployed. For some reason, a fist released in Oaken's chest.

Alrighty then.

"We're going to climb down onto the chopper skid and drop from there," Mike shouted. "You're going to love this! Don't worry—you're in safe hands. There's nothing like jumping out of a plane to figure out what you're made of!"

Okay, maybe. Cool. Oaken almost wished the other chopper had stuck around, because he felt like Jack Powers, the action hero that Winchester Marshall played onscreen, as he climbed out after Mike onto the skid, then dangled off it.

"Don't let your rigging catch on it!" Mike strained his voice over the wind. "Live big! Live wild! The best is yet to come!"

Whatever. Out here, the air turned brutal, frigid, thunderous in Oaken's ear.

"Release!"

He let go, falling, and in a moment, found his rip cord. Pulled. His chute deployed, jerked him up, and suddenly he was floating.

His heart still hammered, nearly in his throat, but the rushing died to a whisper, and only the glorious frontier beauty of the Alaskan wild remained. He spotted a cabin to the west, settled on a lake, and recognized it as where they'd taken off. And to the south, the gray-blues of the river that Mike wanted to cross. He even caught a glimpse of a fire tower. The road ran perpendicular to the river, and along it, he spotted a lodge.

But mostly, towering pine, rugged cliffs and rushing mountain rivers, the snow-topped granite mountains. So much wild beauty it swept him up, hollowed him out.

Dumped out of him everything from the past eight months, just like that.

Who knew that breaking free of his past simply required leaping out into nothing?

He looked around for Mike and spotted him, higher, his chute white against the pale sky. The chopper had veered away, now disappearing into the horizon in the east.

So maybe he shouldn't have pushed against Goldie so hard. Clearly his manager knew what she was doing.

He could almost, maybe, hear a tune forming in the back of his—

Mike simply fell from the sky, right in front of him. What—?

The lines tangled around Mike's pack, and he fought to cut them away from his ripped and flapping chute. The trees had begun to take shape, the forest coming into focus even as Mike struggled.

C'mon, Mike!

If he had a clue what he was doing, maybe he could cut away and . . . what? He had no time, no air—

Mike's torn chute spun away, and in a second the emergency chute flared.

Not enough. The chute arrested his corkscrew into the ground but only enough to slow it to a bone-crushing landing.

He landed in the field but lay motionless, crumpled, as Oaken fought with his chute handles. He'd learned to jump solo on a dare from the guys in the band during a tour in California; certainly he could figure out how to maneuver into the field.

Pulling down on the right toggle, he got the chute to move left. And then right, and suddenly he was driving, the earth rushing up at him.

Fifty feet. Ten. Five.

Oaken pulled down hard on the handles, and the chute luffed. He landed, almost running, then fell, hit his knees, and skidded to the earth.

Wanted to grab the tufts of sodden, lifeless grass and hang on.

"Mike!" Oaken rolled up, not bothering to unhook his chute, and ran over to him.

Please let him be alive. Mike lay on his side, his arm clearly dislocated, barely breathing. Blood trickled from his mouth. Oaken pressed fingers to his carotid artery.

Thready, but alive. Oaken let out an audible moan of relief.

"Mike. Buddy. Wake up."

Mike didn't move. Oaken didn't roll him onto his back—he knew better. They couldn't stay here. He searched Mike's jacket and found the walkie.

Crushed.

Perfect.

He leaned back on his heels, looking around for the pack, then up at the sky, now a darker gray, the taste of menace in the wind.

And even as he got up and started to run to the pack, he knew the worst.

Apparently, God had found him.

TWO

I F SHE CLOSED HER EYES, BOO MIGHT BE BACK home in Minnesota, sitting around the family table in the middle of the raucous Kingston sibling chatter. Sure, the log lodge of Sky King Ranch here in Alaska didn't exactly possess the Victorian charm of her family's King Inn, but it bore its own cozy aura, with the open-concept great room and the massive stone fireplace that rose two stories. And nothing could compare with the grandeur of the Alaska Range, white and majestic, rising from their backyard—although today storm clouds hid it, the sky a bleak gray.

Even the Alaska Kingstons resembled her own family—her uncle Barry almost the spitting image of her father, her cousin Dodge like her bossy oldest brother, and Larke, the oldest of the Alaska Kingstons, reminded her of her sister, despite the eighteen-month-old on Larke's lap.

But they *weren't* the Minnesota Kingstons. Her cousins in the far north weren't judgmental and bossy, and as far as she knew, Dodge and Larke and Uncle Barry didn't know about . . . well, the Great Betrayal.

And all the splinters of pain that went with it.

So yeah, maybe heading up from Anchorage to Copper Mountain and the ranch for the day to hang out with Dodge and his wife, Echo, along with Larke and Riley and baby CeeCee, eat a homemade meal, and catch up with her cousins could be a sort of healing. Not quite redemption or forgiveness, but maybe a cool balm on the wound.

At least for today. And maybe, if she kept her cool and didn't make a mess of her current gig, she'd figure out a way, someday, to go home.

"This is amazing chili, Echo," Boo said, reaching for a slice of freshly baked bread.

"It's a family recipe." Echo ran a hand over her expanding belly. "Although I think I need to cut down on the chili powder." She made a face. "Heartburn." She wore her dark hair down and pulled back in a loose braid, and one of her husband's sweaters, maybe, because despite being at the middle of her second trimester, it seemed to swallow her.

"I remember that part," Larke said, then leaned down and kissed her baby, her blonde hair wispy white and curly.

"Me too," Riley said.

"Please." Larke gave him a look. "You were barely home."

"The perils of the Navy." Riley reached over and pulled Cee from her lap, set her on his own.

"No, the perils of being an active-duty SEAL." Dodge grabbed his bowl and filled it with seconds from the pot in the middle of the table. "How much leave do you have left?"

"A couple more weeks." Riley's attention, however, had gone to his daughter as he bounced her on his knee, clapping her hands. Cee squealed with laughter. He looked up at Boo. "So, you're out for good? Didn't even go into the Reserves?"

"No. One tour was enough. Uncle Barry, you want more chili?"

Her uncle's gaze on her seemed fuzzy and he nodded. Dodge had filled her in on Uncle Barry's macular degeneration a couple months ago, after she'd arrived in Alaska. Tough end for a bush pilot. But Uncle Barry still helped with dispatch for Air One Rescue, the Sky King Ranch branch.

Boo scooped up the chili and set it in front of him. Tried not to watch as he found his bowl and spoon. How she hoped that the hereditary disease didn't touch her father.

"You still a probie?" Uncle Barry asked now, stirring his chili.

"For another month, according to Moose," she said. "But I've already passed my paramedic certification in Alaska."

"Moose says she's the best EMT he's had on the rescue team," Dodge said.

"That's because of her steely nerves from deploying with all those jarheads," Riley said.

"You really deployed with the Marines?" Echo said.

"I was their attached corpsman, so yes."

"So that's how you did it," Larke said.

Boo frowned.

"Lasted so long on *Survivor Quest*."

Oh.

Quiet around the table. She swallowed. So, clearly they knew too. So much for dinner or healing or—

"What's *Survivor Quest*?" Echo asked.

Dodge was also frowning.

"It's a show—like *Survivor* meets *The Amazing Race*. Except you make your own teams, trying to stay alive," Larke said. "Every week, one person gets cut, voted out by the others along with input from the viewing audience." She had finished her chili, now pushed it away. "Boo lasted almost to the end. Got cut by her partner."

That was one way to say it. She met Larke's gaze.

Larke's eyes held a touch of compassion.

Aw, that might be worse than the brutal truth.

"It was after Cee was born, and Riley was gone a lot . . . You did great, Boo."

Okay, that was enough. "I need to get back to Anchorage before it gets dark."

"Sun doesn't set until nine thirty now," Uncle Barry said.

"It's a two-hour drive, and it's nearly seven," Boo said. "And I think the weatherman might actually be right this time. That storm cloud doesn't look good."

Dodge looked up, considering the view. "Any word from Mike Grizz?"

She had pushed away from the table, picking up her bowl. "Who?"

"Mike Grizz—from the show *Go Wild with Grizz, the Celebrity Challenge*? Fifty hours of survival?"

"I know who Mike Grizz is—but why would I hear from him?"

"He's filming a show here this week. Moose and I brought his team to O'Kelly's cabin yesterday. He met Oaken Fox."

"The country singer?" She set the bowl in the sink, then came back to the granite counter.

"Yeah. He jumped out of my chopper yesterday with Mike over near the Copper Mountain River. We saw both their chutes deploy, and Mike gave us the okay before we veered away. They have a route along the river, all the way back to Bear Lake Inn. I think he's going to cross the gorge."

"I've seen that show. Mike makes them eat grubs and rappel and sleep out in the open," Larke said.

"Air One is contracted for transportation and any emergency extraction," Dodge said. "I'm not sure he's supposed to check in— maybe he can't. But with the blizzard coming, I'm hoping they're hunkered down somewhere."

Boo came back to the table. "Wasn't Fox the guy who got in a fight with a fan at a concert?"

Blank looks around the table.

"Maybe that's a different guy, but I thought that was him. Some guy threw a beer at him at a state fair event and he lost it. Jumped off the stage, beat the guy up."

Riley raised a shoulder.

"Sounds fair," Dodge said.

"Yeah, well, I think he got sued."

"That's rough. No wonder he's doing this gig with Mike." Riley handed Cee back to Larke and picked up his wife's bowl, his own.

"How's that?" Dodge asked, also getting up. He grabbed Echo's bowl.

"If they survive all fifty hours without tapping out, they get 50K for a charity of their choice." Riley brought the bowls to the sink. "Lots of good social media there."

"Poor guy," Larke said. "The internet remembers everything."

"Which is why we live off-grid," Echo said. "The last thing anyone needs is the internet reminding you of your greatest mistakes."

"Like you have ever made any mistakes, Echo," Larke said, laughing.

Echo gave her a small smile. "Everyone makes mistakes. It's how you recover that matters."

Right. And on that, "I gotta run. Thanks, Uncle Barry."

He held out a hand and Boo grabbed it, then bent to kiss his leathery cheek. He even smelled like her dad, and that rattled her for a second.

Then she hugged Larke and Echo and raised a hand to Riley and headed to the door.

Dodge followed her all the way outside.

"Something on your mind, cuz?" She stopped at her Nissan Rogue.

He had always been a sort of hero in her mind—just a few years older, but bold and courageous, living up here in the last frontier. They'd spent little time together growing up, but her dad had kept her informed of the family's wild exploits, a sort of whimsy in his voice when he did.

Probably that whimsy seeded her own.

"Your mom would be happy to see your survival gear in the back," he said, obviously glancing through her cargo window.

"Minnesota winter driving rules. Can't escape them."

He laughed. "Yeah." Dodge folded his arms, his dark blue eyes meeting hers. "I just want to know how you're really doing," he said. "I got you into this mess—"

"Hardly. I needed a fresh start. Your email came at exactly the right time. I was going nowhere in Minneapolis. Now . . . I live here." She held out her hands. "Fresh air. Wide spaces. What more could a woman want?"

Dodge drew in a breath, his gaze not faltering. "I wasn't lying— Moose says you're fantastic on the job, but that you haven't really connected with the team. And that's an issue. He is all about team unity—"

"What is he talking about? I *share a house* with London."

"You don't go to the team events."

"At Moose's fancy lake lodge? To roast marshmallows and play broomball, sing Kumbaya? Um, no, thanks. You don't have to pal with a team to do your job."

Dodge nodded. Looked away. "Yep." He looked back at her. It seemed he was struggling for words until, "Just don't let the past wreck your future."

Whatever that meant. "I'm good, Dodge. Thanks for this gig. I won't let you down."

"Drive safe," he said and closed the door behind her as she climbed in.

He stood, hands in his pockets as she pulled out of the long drive.

Okay, maybe there was more likeness to her family than she wanted to admit.

Shoot.

You don't have to pal with a team to do your job.

So maybe she had turned down the last three—okay, all—of the team events. She didn't need friends. She liked being alone.

Alone meant no one got inside her heart to tear it to shreds. Betray her.

Derail her entire life. Especially on national television.

Nope, not taking that chance again, thanks.

She turned on the radio to a country station and turned up the heat. The sun still hung high over the western ridgeline, the days lengthening with every sunrise.

Alaska had started to awaken from its winter slumber too, with much of the snow receding, patches of dry greensward poking through the crusty layers. The air still bore a chill at night, but daytime temperatures had soared to a balmy forty-five for the last week.

Still, a flurry of snow started to brush her windshield, the storm crawling out of the high mountains more quickly than she'd expected. She turned on her wiper blades.

After crossing the river south of Copper Mountain, she put her car on cruise, turning up the volume. An old Ben King song played, and she sang along for a moment. "Hey there, pretty girl, let me sing you a song . . ."

Her phone buzzed on the seat, and the face of her sister appeared, her dark hair short and curly. She laughed into the camera. *Austen.* Boo popped down the volume and picked the call up through her car. "Hey. 'Sup?"

"I'm just sitting here on a beach, looking at the moon, wondering why you chose Alaska over Florida and trying not to take it personally."

"Ha. Because I needed a job."

"Plenty of EMT jobs in Key West."

"I'm tired of the ocean and boats, and did you know Florida has alligators?"

Laughter, and she could imagine her sister, dressed in shorts and a T-shirt, sitting on her charter boat in between gigs with Doctors Without Borders. "Yeah, but Alaska has bears."

"They're still in hibernation." *Probably.* "But I like it here." *Or was starting to.*

"I know. Listen—I talked with Doyle, and he said that Jack and Conrad are coming home for Mom's birthday. Even Steinbeck is going to try to get home. Doyle thought I could talk you into it."

She swallowed. "Oh . . . sis, I—"

"C'mon. You gotta forgive Jack sometime. And Mom misses you."

"Funny that she hasn't exactly called to say that."

"You were pretty rough on her. On everyone."

Boo drew in a breath. "I gotta go—"

"Sis—"

"Nope. Listen, Austen, I'm not ready."

"It's been months. You gotta forgive—"

"I have. It's over. But I'm not . . . Listen, my place here has a guest room. Feel free to fly up anytime."

"I just might do that. Swim with the whales or something."

Her voice untangled the knot that had formed in Boo's chest. "Sounds good."

"I'm going to keep harassing you."

"Get used to my voicemail."

More laughter. "So, how's Alaska—land of many men? Found anyone yet?"

"Wow, you're brave tonight."

"C'mon. It's a fresh start. Let yourself off the hook. I'm sure you can find a guy who can make you forget—"

"And we're done. Love you, Austen."

"Boo—seriously. Alaska is the one place where people don't live and die by social media. You're safe."

"Hardly."

"I just don't like to see you alone."

"Alone is better than betrayed. Or brokenhearted." *Aw.* "And this is why I don't like to talk about it. Listen, sis, I'm fine. And I'm not going to run into the perfect Alaskan man."

"If you do, please don't chase him away. Or, I don't know—shoot him."

"No one is dying on my watch. That's at least one thing I can promise."

A soft chuckle at the other end. "Okay. Love you, Boo. Be safe."

"Back atcha." She hung up, then glanced at her radio to readjust the volume.

Turned her gaze back to the road.

What the—

A man stood nearly in the middle, waving his arms.

She slammed her brakes, cranked her wheel. The Rogue spun, the snow turning the pavement a little slick. But she managed to right the car before it slid into the ditch. It jerked to a stop, and she grabbed the wheel, breathing hard.

The windshield wipers scraped the window, her heart in her throat.

A knocking on her side window made her nearly come out of her skin.

She turned, and the man stood there. Dressed in an orange parka, a wool hat, his face chapped, a scruff of whiskers on his chin, and his blue eyes just a little wide-eyed and desperate.

"What do you want?" Was that blood he'd streaked across the glass?

"Help!" He shoved his hands into his pockets. "Roll down the window."

Right. Um, never. She reached over to her glove box and opened it.

Pulled out her 9mm Glock 19.

The man put up his hands. Stepped back. "Hey . . . hey . . . calm down."

That's when she spotted the wound on his chin, the blood now crusty and dark. She rolled her window halfway down. Set the gun in her lap. "I'm calm. This is just in case you're a crazy person. What are you doing out here?" She didn't see a car in the ditch. "Where'd you come from?"

He turned and pointed east. "Followed the river. And I'm not crazy." He lowered his hands. "My name is Oaken Fox. And I need your help."

She blinked at him, took in the name.

And then, as she watched, he collapsed, right there on the highway.

He couldn't imagine this epic adventure into the wilderness going any further south, but as Oaken opened his eyes, staring up at the woman, all he could think was—

Gun.

And right after that—"Mike."

"Mike Grizz?" The woman knelt over him, her headlights shining across the shadowy highway even as he pushed himself up. Oh, his stupid jaw throbbed. That's what he got for scaling a cliff in the middle of the night.

Now, "Yeah. He's hurt."

"So are you." She had left the gun in her car, he guessed, and now seemed to be assessing him. "Hey, hey. Don't get up. You passed out."

"I'm just thirsty."

"Or you have head trauma. Where'd you get that cut?"

"I don't know. A rock." He pushed himself up, against her protestations, and then stood and reached out for the hood of her car, just to right the world a bit.

"I think you should sit back down."

He looked at her. "Do you have a phone?"

"Yes. But first, you . . . sit down. I have a power bar in my car."

He leaned against the hood. "And some water, maybe?"

She unlatched the back of her SUV, and in a moment returned with a power bar and a bottle of water. He drank the water down and ate the power bar in two bites.

She stepped back and pulled out her phone, and he got a good look at her. Dark hair, dark brown eyes, she wore a black parka, canvas pants, Ugg boots, no makeup, and a concerned look about her that made him take a breath.

So maybe running out into the middle of the road to stop the first—and only—car he'd seen in hours hadn't been a terrible idea.

"Moose. Hey, it's me. You remember that guy you dropped off yesterday?" She looked over at Oaken now. "Yeah, well, I'm standing on Highway 1, about forty miles south of Copper Mountain, staring at Oaken Fox. Minus Mike Grizz."

She looked at Oaken. Then handed him the phone.

He put it to his ear. "Hello?"

"What's going on?"

Sounded like the low baritone of the chopper pilot he'd met in Anchorage, what seemed like thousands of years ago. "Mike's chute failed. He's . . . really hurt. Walkie was damaged—I hiked out."

"Where is Mike?"

"I left him—I built him a shelter, but . . ." He looked up and met eyes with the woman. "We need to hurry."

"Give the phone back to Boo."

He handed her the phone and she stepped away, started to nod.

The sun had begun to drop behind the mountains, bleeding out red against the cloud cover that seeped into the valley. Flurries swirled in the air, down the neck of his jacket. The temperature must have dropped a good fifteen degrees over the past day.

Please be alive, Mike.

The woman—Boo—pocketed the phone. "Moose is on his way. Do you remember where you left Mike?"

Oaken shrugged. "Maybe. I don't know."

"That's okay. Moose will know."

Whatever that meant. "Mike's not there."

She looked up from her phone.

"I tried to carry him out."

She frowned.

"I couldn't just leave him out in the middle of the field." And yet—"I feel sick."

"Okay, okay, lean over, grab your knees—"

"I'm fine. I just . . ." He touched his hands to his forehead. "If he dies because of me—"

"Get in the car. Let's get you warm, and you can tell me what happened while we wait."

He stared east, from where he'd come, and finally nodded. "Okay. Yes. You have a map?"

"I have my phone."

He got into the passenger seat, and she closed the door, fired up the car, the heat, and turned on her dome light to scatter the shadows. Then she pulled up Google Maps and handed him the phone.

He closed his eyes, trying to remember the flight from the chopper. Opened them. Stared at the map. "I walked along this river." He traced his finger back along the river, away from the road. Widened the map, then turned on the topographical feature. "I fell somewhere in here, down this cliff. I'm not sure where—it was the middle of the night."

Her mouth pinched. "Was Mike with you?"

"No. I left him . . ." He followed the river, then away, near the scrub of foothills. "I dragged him to the cliff but knew I couldn't get down, so I backtracked and found a cave. I left him there."

He swallowed. Closed his eyes and handed her back the phone.

Silence.

"Okay, that'll help."

Please.

He looked out the window, shaking his head.

"We'll find him."

"I can't believe that Mike Grizz is going to die on my watch." He shook his head. "He's got a wife and a couple kids."

Silence.

He turned, and she was just staring at him. "What?"

"Nothing. I just . . . I heard you sing once. At a concert in Minnesota."

He blinked at her. *Really? A fan—out here?* His mouth tightened. "Oh."

"You were good. Some great love songs."

He gave her a look. "Thanks. I'm sure that's what everyone will remember. Not that I was the guy who killed Mike Grizz."

She flinched.

And now he was a jerk too. "Sorry. I just . . . my career is the last thing I care about right now." He gave a harsh laugh. "Except that was the whole reason my manager sent me out here—to get my creativity flowing again." He shook his head. "I think we can say goodbye to any fresh music."

"What happened?"

"Just a jump gone wrong, I guess. He picked me up and we went off the edge of the chopper. My chute opened—and then his. And everything was great, and then, just like that, his ripped and he was falling."

"Oh no."

"He was all tangled up in the lines and finally managed to cut them away. Another chute popped out, but he was really close to the ground by then. He landed really hard."

"But he was alive?"

"Yeah. His face was all swollen, though, and he had blood in his spit."

"What did you do?" She was glancing out the window, probably looking for the chopper. And maybe trying to keep him from going into shock.

He was painfully way, way past that. Now he was deep inside guilt, maybe some anger, and in the thick of regret. What had he been thinking, leaving Mike out there? To die alone. Good thing his video camera got crushed in his epic cliff fall. Last thing he wanted was the world to see his ugly fight with frustration.

They'd already gotten a glimpse once, and, well—

He could probably kiss his career goodbye.

"I debated not moving him for a long time. And then I realized that if I left him there, he'd be eaten. Or die of exposure. So I decided to make a backboard. I rolled up some of the parachute and made a sort of a neck brace then found a piece of thick birchbark and rolled him onto that. I used some of the parachute cord to tie him onto it. Then I made a litter with broken branches and the other parachute and secured him to that, inside the sleeping bag. Then I hauled him through the woods."

She just stared at him. "Seriously? Who are you—Daniel Boone?"

Um. "I mean, I couldn't leave him there. Until I got to the cliff. But I remembered seeing the river when we flew over it, so I figured it was only a few miles to the road. But then I fell and . . ." He blew out a breath. "It took longer than I wanted."

"We'll find him," she said. She gave him a tight-lipped smile.

And that only made him feel worse. "Listen, I didn't want to leave him. It . . . Trust me. If I could have done anything else, I would have—"

"Hey,"—she held up her hands—"no judgement here."

He stared at her. Something about her seemed suddenly, weirdly—"Have we met before?"

"As in before you showed up on the side of the highway like the Midnight Sun Killer?"

He blinked at her. "What?"

"It's a . . . Nothing. There used to be this story of a guy who flagged down women and then, when they stopped to help him, he'd assault them, then chase them down and shoot them like prey in the woods."

His mouth opened. "Now the gun makes sense."

"We're in Alaska. The gun always makes sense."

He lifted one side of his mouth. "How do you know I'm not him?"

She met his gaze without blinking. "Are you? Because you should probably know that I served with the Marines. You might be stronger than me, but it'll hurt you to hurt me."

Oh. "I was . . . That was a bad joke."

"Very."

"I'm . . . I'm just . . ." He leaned forward, his face in his hands. "I can't believe this is happening. I tried to tell my manager this was a bad idea, but she was all, 'Go to Alaska. Join Mike. Give money to charity. Win back your fans.'" He leaned back. "If Mike dies because I left him out there, my career is over."

She drew in a breath.

He looked at her. "And before you say that's a super selfish thing to say—I know it is. For the record, I care more for Mike than for my career. In fact, maybe I should just keep walking."

"Down the highway?"

"Away from my career."

"Oh." She drew in a breath. "Actually, that's what I meant about what happened. Why should we 'kiss fresh music goodbye'?" She finger quoted the phrase.

"You don't pull your punches, do you?"

"Life is short."

"Right. So I'm contracted to write some songs for an upcoming

Western, but I can't seem to wrap my brain around the music, or lyrics."

"I didn't know you were a songwriter too."

"Yep. Wrote all the songs on my first album."

"*Dedicated to Hollie.*"

"You know my debut album?"

"Two for one at the concert." She still didn't smile. "Not sure I get it, though. Who is Hollie?"

"Hollie Montgomery? She was a singer."

A pause, and he waited for the recognition to click in.

Softly, "Girlfriend?"

He looked at her. "She was ten years older than me, so no. She was my sister."

"I'm sorry."

"Yep. Thanks. But it was a long time ago."

Another beat. Then, "Fox is a stage name?"

"My dad's name. Mom was Montgomery."

"I'll bet your dad is proud."

"Dunno. We haven't talked for a while."

She nodded, her arms folded. "I get that."

He sighed. Looked at her again. Yeah, those brown eyes, the heart-shaped face, the solemn look. Something—"Boo?"

"Yeah?"

"So that *is* your name. Why Boo?"

"Because it's Boo, that's why." Her eyebrow lifted. And it was such a distinctive action, along with her words, it triggered something inside him. "I *know* I've seen you somewhere before. Have you ever been on TV?"

Her eyes widened. "Listen—"

"Oh, wait. You're with Air One Rescue." He pointed at the logo on her jacket. "I must have seen you when I got on the chopper in Anchorage. Or maybe a picture on the wall of the offices?"

"Yep, that's probably it." She flashed a thin smile.

It felt wrong, but whatever—it didn't matter because in the distance, the sound of a chopper thundered, shivering the nearby trees.

He got out of the car and stood, watching as the familiar red bird was set down on the highway. A second before he made to run for it, a hand grabbed him back.

Boo. "Head down."

She ducked and he followed her as they ran to the now-opening chopper door.

He followed her inside the deck, and the other rescue tech closed the door. "Strap in." The tech handed him headphones. Boo donned a pair also.

"Hey, Axel," she said and slapped his hand. Then she turned and showed the pilot—Moose, if Oaken remembered correctly—her phone. "He says Mike is about ten clicks east, on a cliff on the north side of the river."

Moose nodded. "It's getting dark out—let's get this done."

The bird lifted, and in a second, they flew up the river. Oaken leaned against the window, scanning the darkening shoreline, remembering his trek. His head throbbed with the beat of the rotors.

He spotted the cliff, wincing at the memory of the twenty-foot fall. Lucky he wasn't more injured. Then, "There. I left him over there."

Not much more than an overhang in the granite, but enough for him to shove Mike in, and as the chopper landed on the massive ledge, the lights illuminated the pocket.

Mike.

"Stay here!" said Boo, but hello, not on her life. He followed her out, ducking, and then ran over to Mike as they retrieved the litter from the chopper.

Mike lay still as ice, and Oaken whipped off his glove, pressed his fingers against Mike's carotid artery.

A faint heartbeat whispered against his fingers. He wanted to weep.

He leaned close even as Boo and Axel ran over to him.

"Don't worry, Mike. You're in safe hands."

Then he got up and backed away as they pulled Mike out and strapped him into the litter.

They secured him into the chopper, and Oaken followed him in, leaning back against the seat. Breathing. He closed his eyes.

And for the first time in thirty-six hours, he slept.

THREE

TOO CLOSE. WAY TOO CLOSE.

Mike Grizz had died, twice, in the chopper during the trip to Alaska Regional Hospital.

Boo paced in the hallway in the ER wing, arms folded, jaw tight, gaze flickering back now and again to the ER area where the docs worked on the television star.

"Good work, Boo."

She looked up to see the ER doors closing behind Moose, now coming toward her. He wore a baseball cap over his dark hair, a flannel shirt, a down jacket unzipped, a pair of jeans and boots, and carried a can of Coke.

"You got him here alive."

She nodded and glanced over at the chairs where Oaken Fox sat, his head bowed, hands folded, as if he might be praying. Or just hoping.

Poor guy had fallen asleep when they took off from the cliff.

Oaken had woken up when Mike flatlined the first time. And after Boo had brought Mike back, Oaken had appeared stripped, hollowed out, and horrified. Never mind the second time.

But she hadn't had time to consider Oaken and the tragedy playing in his mind, because she'd yanked Mike back from the white light just as they touched down on the helipad of the hospital. The ER crew had rushed out, loaded Mike onto a gurney, and taken over from there.

Oaken had gotten out and shuffled behind them.

She should probably go over and talk to him. Tell him he'd done well, keeping Mike alive. If he'd left him in the field where they'd landed, Mike *would* have died of exposure or, as Oaken had suggested, been eaten.

So the guy was a hero, and maybe, given his desperation when she'd nearly mowed him over on the highway, he should hear that instead of whatever voices currently played in his head.

But, *"I know I've seen you somewhere before. Have you ever been on television?"*

Oh boy.

Except, maybe he *had* recognized her picture from the Air One Rescue lineup, so she might be panicking needlessly.

Still.

Moose had walked over to a group of people standing in the lobby—a woman with shoulder-length hair and a yellow parka, a man with dark brown hair, in chinos, boots, a pullover sweater. He held out a hand to Moose and greeted him like he knew him.

Probably trail guides. Moose knew everyone who worked in the bush, and everyone knew him too.

Her stomach growled, and she glanced at the clock. Nearly midnight. She needed sleep. And food. Maybe not in that order.

What she really needed was a way to slough off the tension still stirring inside.

She glanced over at Moose and found his gaze on her. Then he turned back to the conversation, and for some reason, Dodge's words surfaced inside.

"You haven't really connected with the team. And that's an issue."

Maybe less of an issue, however, than a friendship with her might create. If people were smart, they'd just let her stay in her corner. Alone and unknown.

A male doctor came out of the ER doors, glanced around.

Oaken stood up. "I'm with Mike Grizz. How is he?"

"Are you family?"

She too had walked up to the doctor. His nameplate said Benson.

"I'm . . . yes. Sort of."

"He rescued him, Doc," Boo said now, and Oaken looked over at her, something of gratitude in his face.

"I'm sorry. I can't release any medical information."

"I was on the rescue crew who brought him in," Boo said. "I'm an EMT."

The crowd near the coffee machine had also walked over. The man in chinos reached out his hand. "Reynolds Gray. Executive producer of *Go Wild with Grizz*. His wife and kids are on the way. I'd like to give them an update."

Dr. Benson met his hand, shook it. Looked at Boo. "I'll have to wait on any specific information, but he has quite a bit of internal bleeding. We're going up to surgery now." He looked at Oaken. "I don't know how you kept him alive, but any longer out there and he wouldn't have made it."

Oaken swallowed. "Actually, *she* kept him alive." He glanced at Boo.

She held up her hands. "It's my job. Air One Rescue."

She caught a look passing between Moose and Reynolds even as the doctor nodded and headed back through the double doors of the ER.

"Oaken, I need to talk to you," said Reynolds. He and Oaken walked away, over to the corner of the room.

Executive producer, huh? She wanted to ask where the camera was, but that might be too cynical. And alert anyone with curiosity in their DNA to ask questions.

But no wonder the man had raised the tiny hairs on the back of her neck. *Note to self: Veer hard around Reynolds and, frankly, Oaken.*

Despite the fact that Oaken seemed to actually be a good guy. Not the kind of guy to leap off the stage and beat up a fan. So maybe another reason not to believe anything she read on social media.

Hello. She of all people should know that.

She turned to Moose. "Hey, boss, I need to go get my car. It's still sitting on Highway 1. I'm going to need a lift."

"I'll give you a lift in the morning. Let me drive you home," Moose said.

"I can take an Uber."

"At midnight?" He checked his watch. "C'mon, I need to talk to you anyway."

Fine. She glanced again at Oaken, who was now getting animated in the corner, his hands out, shaking his head. *Probably Reynolds delivering the bad news—show canceled. Of course.*

She shoved her hands into her pockets, nodded at Moose.

He tossed his Coke can into the recycling bin on the way out.

This far south, the sky arched clear and bright, so many stars winking down at her. Winter, however, still hung in the brisk air, the temperature in the low thirties. She zipped up her jacket and spotted Moose's F-150 in the parking lot under a streetlight.

As she got into the passenger side, her stomach grumbled.

Moose glanced at her. "I'll fix that."

She frowned but belted in.

Anchorage resembled a war zone during the thaw—muddy, crusty snow along the curbs, piled into the center of parking lots surrounded by skeletal, naked trees. A fog hovered over the sound. They drove past Merrill Field Airfield, the airport for small bush

ONE LAST SHOT

planes and the headquarters of Air One. The chopper was under cover in the domed Quonset hut, the rescue plane tied down on the tarmac.

Air One also owned a small arsenal of land units—a rescue-equipment truck modified to carry a couple litters, two snow machines with a shielded sled for towing victims, a handful of Polaris ATVs, and a four-wheel-drive command truck equipped like something out of *Mission Impossible*.

And for water, a sick-looking twenty-four-foot rescue boat.

Moose clearly meant business, and why not? Seventy-five percent of search and rescue in Alaska was done by volunteers or private organizations, a statistic she'd read in the orientation manual Moose had given her.

They passed the other commercial and international airport and then, instead of turning southwest to her cute, converted 1930s three-bedroom cabin, he turned north, drove one block, and pulled into the Skyport Diner.

"Moose—"

"Their midnight fried chicken will tame that grizzly in your gut."

"I have a box of Lucky Charms waiting for me at home."

"Stop eating like a two-year-old." He got out.

Two-year-old? She got out. "Moose."

"Consider this your two-month review."

"I get a two-month review?"

He stepped onto the curb, turned to her. "We need to talk." He opened the door for her, and it felt not unlike a prison door.

Perfect.

The Skyport Diner, open twenty-four seven, was everything Boo expected, with red vinyl booths along two walls, a few round Formica tables in the middle, and a long bar that extended the length of the place. A massive menu board hung behind the counter above the serving area, and on the counter sat an orders carousel and a bell. She could just imagine some beefy Popeye back there, dinging the bell with a gruff "Order's up."

A pie case hosted a few half-cut pies, and a massive coffeepot gurgled on the counter behind the bar.

A woman dressed in jeans and a white shirt covered by a long blue apron looked up. She smiled at Moose. "Hey there, Top Gun."

He smiled back and Boo looked at him. *What was that face? Interesting.*

He took a booth near the door, and she slid in opposite him. The waitress came over with a glass of water for both of them.

"Midnight chicken?" she asked. Closer, she seemed in her early thirties, pretty, and definitely a sweet smile for Boss Mulligan. Her nametag read "Tillie."

"For sure. And fries?"

"I'll have Kody put down a fresh batch." She looked at Boo. "Same?"

"Sure. Whatever."

"You won't be disappointed." She turned back to Moose. "Late night rescue?"

"Something like that."

"Everybody live?"

"So far."

"One chocolate shake coming up." She winked.

He watched her walk away for a second, then turned to Boo, who had an eyebrow up.

"Whenever I have a successful callout, Tillie gives me a chocolate shake. I'm not sure why."

"And if not?"

"A coffee. Black."

"Because she knows you'll be up all night trying to figure out what went wrong."

He lifted a shoulder but smiled.

"You like her."

"She's my favorite waitress." He leaned forward. "So, you did a great job tonight. And every rescue we're on, you're calm, you know what to say and do. Frankly, Boo, you're one of the best EMTs I've ever worked with."

Oh. She let out a breath. "I don't know why, but I thought I was in trouble."

"Not even a little." He sighed. "But Air One needs help. We've had a busy winter, lots of callouts."

"It's the world of cell phones. People calling in for things they don't need to."

"Yes. We've had our share of flat tires and panicked drivers in the ditch. But we don't charge for rescues, so the coffers are thin. We operate on donations, and our donors are generous, but going into the summer months . . . I'm worried."

So, this was about her job. "Are you laying me off?"

He raised an eyebrow. "What? No. I mean—I hope it doesn't come to that. But . . ." He leaned back as Tillie delivered an over-flowing chocolate shake, the ice cream dribbling down the side of the tall glass. "Thanks."

Tillie put a long spoon and a straw down on the table. "Of course." She looked at Boo. "You?"

"I'll stick with water. I don't want to eat like a toddler."

Moose gave her a look even as he dug in with the spoon. "This here is man's food."

"A man who burns two thousand calories in his sleep, maybe."

He laughed. "I like you, Boo. Maybe it was the Marine unit, but you aren't hard to be around."

She smiled back. Okay, so maybe midnight chicken wasn't torture.

He put the straw into the shake, then picked up the glass and wiped the ice cream from the table with a napkin. "You might have seen me talking with Reynolds, the executive producer of the Mike Grizz shows."

She stilled.

"So, actually, it was the last of a number of conversations with Huxley Shaw, his associate producer. Huxley approached me a while back after she contracted Air One for this gig. She and Reynolds had approached their network with the idea of an unscripted reality show about search and rescue."

Her stomach started to knot up.

"They were impressed with Oaken, and frankly, I was too."

"He kept his cool."

"He saved Mike's life. At least, enough to get him to help. And sacrificed doing it, too."

The memory of his distress on the highway stirred in her mind.

"Chicken's up," said Tillie as she set two plates of crispy chicken in front of them. And then in the middle, a pile of glistening fries. "Anything else?"

"Thanks, Tillie. We're good for now."

"I'll cut you a piece of cherry pie."

She walked away and Moose picked up a fry.

"No, seriously, where do you put all that food?"

He grinned at her. "I take the pie home. Eat it for breakfast. Try the fries—they're amazing."

Maybe, before she lost her appetite. She reached for a handful of fries and added them to her plate. She'd be eating chicken for breakfast, probably.

"Reynolds and Huxley would like to do a limited-run series with Oaken and Air One."

She stared at him, fry in hand. "What?"

"He'd join our crew for three weeks—a month, tops. We'd train him, and he'd go out on a few callouts—nothing too dicey. And . . . they'd pay us enough to cover our summer expenses and then some."

She washed the fry down with water. Then, "Are you serious?"

"As a bear in springtime. I need to get creative here, Boo. I have a fundraising event in the fall, but right now we need cash flow. This would help. A lot. I don't want to shut down Air One at the height of tourist season."

She picked at the chicken.

"The fact is, the emergency services are relying on volunteers and outfits like Air One more and more. Last summer, a group of campers was mauled by a bear, and they waited nine hours for rescue because the SAR troopers out of Anchorage were busy looking for lost hikers. Which they never found. Two of those campers—teenagers—died, waiting."

She leaned back, wiping her fingers on a napkin. "I get it. I do. And I agree Oaken Fox seemed . . . well, not your usual celebrity country singer. He's the real deal."

"I think so."

"Fine. Sign him up. Whatever. I'll help with whatever I can. I just don't want to be on camera."

He put down his shake. Met her eyes. He had dark, gray-green eyes, and they held a hypnotic sort of power, really. Made her still so that even her insides stopped moving.

"What?"

"That'll be hard since I want you to train him."

She blinked, her brain blank.

"You had a sort of chemistry—"

"There was no chemistry!"

"And you two already know each other."

"We talked for, what—an hour—in the car? I don't know him."

"And Huxley said that you would know exactly what to do—"

Oh no. No—

"Given that you've already been on a reality show."

She couldn't breathe.

"Boo?"

"Check, please."

50

He just frowned at her, and it occurred to her then that, "Wait—do you even know what show?"

"No idea. She just said you made it to the semifinals."

She closed her eyes. Wished she had that pie to bury her face in. "I was on *Survivor Quest*."

A beat. She opened her eyes.

He looked impressed. "That's a tough show."

"It's a brutal show. You not only have to survive in the wilderness or island or jungle or desert or wherever they drop you, but you have to reach a destination every day, like *The Amazing Race*. You compete individually, but you have to make alliances to survive. And then, despite your audience points, your own teammates can still vote you off the show."

"And you made it to the semifinals. What is that—three people left?"

Two cutthroat betrayers and herself. "Yes."

"Interesting." He picked up his shake again.

"What does that mean?"

He set it down, then signaled to Tillie, who came over. "Can you box up my pie? And a box for Boo and her chicken and fries."

"Of course." She walked away.

Moose looked at Boo. "It just explains a lot." He pulled out his wallet and then a card. "Must have hurt to get voted off, right near the end," he said softly. Met her eyes.

"It was a television show. A game. No. Big. Deal."

Except for the fact that it had shattered her life. Derailed her future.

Turned her into an internet laughingstock.

So there was that.

"Super. Then you won't mind taking Oaken Fox under your wing, training him up, and saving Air One Rescue from closing its doors."

And what was she supposed to say to that?

"What about London? She—"

"No. London won't work."

She just stared at him. He'd suddenly gone from friendly to scary. And for some reason, she didn't want to know why not.

Tillie returned with the boxes, but Boo left her chicken, the fries.

"What, no midnight snack for you?"

"Why, when I have a box of not-so-Lucky Charms waiting for me?"

"C'mon, Boo. Show off your amazing rescue skills. You might even have fun."

"I'm *not* going to have fun. What if someone dies? Like . . . *Oaken Fox.*"

"So don't let that happen. You're really not going to eat that chicken?"

"Knock yourself out." She pushed away the plate. "This is a bad idea, Moose. Really bad. You don't know—producers change footage, make it seem like you said things you never meant." She looked out the window, but it simply reflected back the inside of the diner where Tillie was boxing up his pie.

"I'll ask Huxley to let you review the footage."

She knew he was sincere, but that wasn't how it worked. Still . . . She folded her arms over her chest. She liked Air One. Wanted to stay. Build a life. "Okay. I'll train him and keep him alive. But no cameos, no digging up footage of *Survivor Quest*. And most of all—when this is over, we don't talk about it, ever."

He raised an eyebrow.

"And as of right now, I'm off probation." She raised an eyebrow.

"Done." He held out a fist.

A beat, then she bumped it.

Tillie brought over the pie and picked up Moose's card.

He gave Boo the slice. "Instead of the Lucky Charms."

She took it, because, "You're going owe me more than pie when this is done."

He grinned as he got up. "I'm right behind you."

She headed outside into the cold, holding her pie, looking at the stars. *Perfect. Just perfect.*

Because apparently, Boo Hoo Kingston was back.

Let the fun begin.

"She's my favorite waitress."

Moose's stupid words followed him home like a burr under his skin after he'd dropped Boo off. As he pulled into his timber-framed home seated on the banks of the Knik River, Axel's Yukon sat in the double garage. Moose pulled in and sat in the darkness, listening to his truck shut down.

Okay, maybe he did want to ask her out. Or at least have a longer conversation than simply an order of midnight chicken and small talk about his life.

Fact was, Tillie Young intrigued him—ever since she'd shown up a year ago on the night shift, her dark hair pulled back to reveal the tiniest red rose tattoo on her neck, and possessing a sort of demeanor that said she was more than the woman in the apron.

She didn't exactly flirt with him but simply looked him in the eyes, gave him a real smile, and somehow knew when he needed a chocolate shake or a piece of pie.

Weirdly, she felt like a friend.

He picked up his container of chicken. Still a little warm. He got out.

Closing the garage door behind him, he took the path to the side door of his home, went inside, set the containers down, took off his boots, and then walked, wool-sock footed, into the kitchen.

Added the containers to others already in the refrigerator. He should probably tell Axel that the chicken was up for grabs.

Silence, except for the hum of the refrigerator, told him that his roommate-slash-brother had turned in for the night. So much bundled up inside his brother, so much he'd carried home from the accident in Kodiak. Someday, Moose would unlock all of that, but for now, Axel did his job and stayed out of trouble, so Moose let him wrestle with his demons on his own.

They both did, really.

He walked over to the window, hands in his pockets. Just a sliver of waxing moon in the sky, the stars like eyes, watching. He drew in a breath at the memory of his words to Boo. *"I need to get creative here, Boo. I have a fundraising event in the fall, but right now we need cash flow."*

Maybe he shouldn't have said all that, but he'd done a little digging about her when Dodge asked him to hire her. Had seen enough social media to know what his ask could do to her. He hadn't known about the show, however.

Yeah, Boo was tough. She could handle this.

Honestly, he'd thought she'd turn him down.

But they did need the money. Because Alaska SAR did need Air One.

And maybe he needed Air One too.

He turned and headed upstairs to the master. The other bedroom, a mini-master, remained empty, Axel having taken up residence in the downstairs bedroom, turning the other into his office.

Such a big house. It needed . . . more.

Family, maybe. A wife. Kids.

Yeah, right. The last thing he wanted was something happening to him and leaving behind a widow and fatherless kids. Mostly, he didn't want to let anything slow him down, make him think twice about risking his life for a stranger.

He flicked on his light and it spilled across the pictures on his bureau. His mom and dad, and Axel, fishing. A picture of him and a couple buddies in his squadron standing in front of his Rescue Hawk.

And Aren, of course. He picked up her picture. Sixteen, and she sat with him and Axel around a campfire, squished between them, holding up a marshmallow, laughing. He'd dug up the picture from an online tribute and downloaded it. Kept it on his bureau because, well, reasons.

After a moment, he set it down and headed to the bathroom, brushed his teeth, then stripped down and donned pajamas.

Climbing into bed, he grabbed his tablet and pulled up an online newspaper, just to unwind. But his eyes went cross-eyed, so he turned off the light.

Then he lay there, Boo's words in his head. *"You like her."*

Yeah. Yeah, he did.

But that's where it ended.

He rolled over, slammed his fist into his pillow, and reached for sleep.

No, no, no, absolutely not, never.

Oaken stood outside the ICU unit, holding a cup of coffee, watching the sun arch over the Alaska Range, his body buzzing after just a few winks in the seedy hotel across the street. He'd had too many nightmares of things crawling on him, so he'd gotten up, showered, and returned to the ICU lobby.

He couldn't leave. Not until Seraphina Grizz and her two kids arrived.

Not until he knew Mike had made it through the night.

And not until he could get his brain around Reynolds's offer last night.

He closed his eyes, the conversation on replay in his head.

"You did an amazing job out there."

He hadn't expected Reynolds and Huxley to show up at the hospital, the show the very last thing on his brain as he'd watched Mike nearly die twice in the chopper.

Twice.

And twice, the pretty-but-tough EMT had brought Mike back. Yes, Boo was the real hero of the day.

He'd just been the desperate survivalist wannabe who'd managed, somehow, to find help. Oaken wouldn't call that heroic. Not when it took about eight cups of coffee to hold himself together.

Not when, every time he closed his eyes, he watched Mike plummet to earth.

So, no to Reynolds's uber-galling question, the one that'd come at the end of the way-too-leading conversation. He should have seen it coming.

"Unfortunately, the episode is a bust," Reynolds had said, coming up to him in the ER.

"You think?"

"So we need to come up with plan B."

Reynolds had then dragged him to the corner with Huxley, their group conversation quiet in the shadowed waiting room. Across the way, Boo and her boss, the chopper pilot Moose, were leaving, but he didn't bother to raise a hand. They were probably glad to be done with him.

He was glad to be done with this game. He'd known it would end in disaster—

"We'd like you to stick around Alaska and be our guest star for a pilot series we're doing."

He had barely heard Reynolds, so much clutter inside his brain, and should have probably stopped the man right then. But he wasn't catching up well, and Reynolds kept talking.

"We'd like you to join up with Air One Rescue for a month,

train with them, go on some callouts, and learn how to be a rescue tech."

He just stared at the duo.

Wait—"You're serious."

"Yes," Huxley said. "The Air One team has agreed to the terms and is willing to train you. It'll be a great show—"

"You're out of your mind." He gave himself a once-over, then glanced at the ER. "Have you not been paying attention at all? Mike was nearly killed—he might die. And I . . . I haven't slept in two days. I'm exhausted, I think my jaw is cracked, I hurt everywhere—"

"You'd have a few days off before we started filming," Huxley said.

He stood there, undone.

"Listen, Oaken," Reynolds said. "The thing is, you didn't technically complete the fifty hours, and . . . well, we can't pay out the 50K to Maggie's Miracle."

And right then, headlines played in his brain.

Oaken Fox Attacks Double-Crossing Producer . . .

Former Country Music Star Seals the Death of His Career . . .

One More Victim Joins Fox's Lineup of Accidents . . .

He took a breath, schooled his voice. "I think you could say that I fulfilled my contract—"

"Technically—" Reynolds started.

"I dragged Mike's body ten miles over tundra and bog and forest and mountainside, then I fell off a freakin' cliff on my way to get help! I nearly got run over by a car, I haven't slept in two days, I'm dehydrated, I'm starving, and I hurt everywhere. So, do you want to edit what you're about to say to me?"

Reynolds closed his mouth, pinched at the edges.

Huxley stepped in front of him. "Oaken, there's no doubt that Mike owes you his life. It's not a matter of deserving the 50K. It's . . . it's not there."

He just blinked at her.

"She's right," Reynolds said. "In order to secure the donation, we'd have to reach out to donors who would invest in the show, be part of the recognition for the donation. Not to mention advertisers. And now we have nothing."

Oaken ran a hand over his mouth, his stomach growling.

Reynolds put his hand on Oaken's shoulder. "How about if I take you out for breakfast and we—"

"How about if you just take a step back—"

"Okay," said Huxley, putting her hands up between the two men. "Here's our solution. You stick around Alaska for three weeks, maybe a month. We'll set you up in a nice Airbnb. You write some music, train with the Air One team, go out on a few calls, and let us inside the life of a training rescue tech, and in the meantime, Reynolds will get your money."

She looked at her boss. He nodded, his arms folded, mouth a grim line.

Oaken let a moment go by. Another. "I'll need to talk to Goldie."

"We'll work up a new contract. But I think Goldie will love it. Being a hero—saving others—now that is going to get you traction with fans. Even more than surviving fifty hours with Grizz."

Oh, how Oaken hated that his life decisions came down to likes on Instagram.

"We're all in the entertainment business, pal," Reynolds said. "It's part of the train ride."

Huxley looked at him. "You're not helping."

"Just saying what Goldie will say. You want to keep your career afloat, you keep smiling, keep your opinions to yourself, and make sure the fans are happy."

The words ground through Oaken. But Reynolds wasn't wrong.

And he wanted his fans to be happy.

"Get some sleep. Oh, and by the way, we got you a room for

the night at the Merrill Hotel across the street. The suitcase you left with us is at the front desk."

At least he could get his credit card and some grub.

"Talk to you in the morning," Reynolds had said.

And then they'd left him there, grimy, cold, and aching, the *No* stuck in his throat.

It was still stuck there now. *No. No. Never.*

He took another sip of coffee, watching the sunrise awaken the land. Denali, with her frosted peaks, jutted into a rose-gold sky. And in the distance, the deep blue of the Knik Arm of the Gulf of Alaska.

Reynolds, the smooth-talking jerk that he was, had a point—Oaken needed to stir up some love on social media if he wanted to resurrect his career. And never mind writing any songs—with Mike in a coma, he didn't have a hope of finding any creativity.

His conversation with Boo last night awakened in his head.

"I heard you sing once. At a concert in Minnesota. You were good. Some great love songs."

Yes, once upon a time, maybe, he'd been good. He'd like to be good again, but somehow the love of writing music and playing music had gotten cluttered up with performing and road tours and band squabbles and the ambition Goldie had for him.

Ambition she'd once had for Hollie.

He took another sip of coffee. *"Why Boo?"*

"Because it's Boo, that's why."

He didn't know what to make of her. Clearly capable. And brave. And calm.

But something about her did feel familiar and . . .

And if he stuck around Air One, he might figure it out.

And then there was the money—

His phone, picked up from his gear at the hotel, vibrated in his pocket. He pulled it out. *Goldie.* Probably to talk terms and give him all the reasons to say yes.

He didn't need the reminder, thanks. Maggie and her organization sat front and center in his brain most of the time. Thumbing away the call, he heard footsteps behind him.

Turned.

They'd never met, but he recognized Seraphina Grizz right away. A former model, of course, she wore no makeup and appeared tired, her blonde hair mussed. She was trolleying a carry-on, wore an oversized leather-and-sheepskin jacket open, a pink velour workout suit underneath.

Beside her walked their kids—a daughter and son—both carrying backpacks. He put the boy at about sixteen. The girl younger, maybe eight. They looked as tired at their mother.

He walked down the hall to them. "Oaken Fox."

"I know who you are, Oaken," said Seraphina and simply pulled him into a hug, her arms around his neck.

Then she started to cry.

Oh. Um.

He hadn't put down his coffee and now just wrapped the other arm around her as she sobbed.

The boy looked away, lean and bearing the handsome, chiseled features of his father.

The girl was her mother's spitting image.

A beautiful family.

"I'm sorry. I'm . . . just tired." Seraphine stepped back, wiping her eyes. "Is he awake?"

"No." Oaken walked over to a nearby garbage bin and tossed his cup in, coffee and all. Came back to the trio. "But they won't give me much information—I'm not family."

Seraphina nodded, then looked past him toward the ICU. "He's in there?"

"Yes. They'll let you visit for fifteen minutes every hour."

She nodded. "Oh, this is my son, Liam, and my daughter, Jasmine."

Liam turned away. Jasmine gave him a wan smile.

"Listen, I know my way to the cafeteria. How about I get you some coffee? And . . . donuts?"

Jasmine looked over at him, nodded. She also wore her mother's sorrow.

"Skinny vanilla latte," Seraphina said. "Thanks, Oaken."

"Right. I'll be back."

He was climbing into the elevator when he spotted Seraphina talking to the ICU nurse.

Good. Maybe now he could go home.

Except even as the doors opened, he heard Huxley. *"You stick around Alaska for three weeks, maybe a month. You write some music, train with the Air One team, go out on a few calls, and let us inside the life of a training rescue tech. . . ."*

He walked toward the coffee shop, the smell reeling him in.

"Reynolds will get your money."

He ordered Seraphina's latte, a macchiato for himself, and four freshly glazed donuts.

Problem was, he needed the money. Because the lawsuit had cost him. He'd cleaned out his savings and liquidated property.

Felt like he'd given the jerk a piece of his soul.

He got on the elevator and headed back upstairs.

The code's siren blared down the hallway as he got out, and he spotted a doctor pushing into the ICU. A nurse stood with Seraphina and the family, holding them back.

Seraphina pressed her hands over her mouth, maybe stifling a scream. Jasmine had shrunk to the ground, weeping, and Liam stood by the window, his hands deep in his pockets, such a grim look on his face—

"What happened?" He addressed the question to the nurse at the desk.

"Code blue," she said and put down the phone. "You can't be up here."

"I'm with the family," he said and ignored her, heading toward them.

This time he put down the coffee and the bag before Seraphina launched herself at him. He held her, his gaze going to Liam, who turned away.

Please, God, don't let Mike die. Could be a futile prayer, but he didn't care. He had nowhere else to turn.

Seraphina pushed away, crouched down next to Jasmine and pulled her into her arms.

Oaken walked over to Liam.

The kid didn't look at him.

Silence, save for Jasmine, softly crying. Someone had turned off the alarm, and he hoped that meant something good.

The door opened and a nurse walked out. She stopped and crouched in front of Seraphina and Jasmine.

"We got him back."

Seraphina covered her face with her hands.

The nurse patted her arm. "No visitors for a while, though. Get some rest."

She got up and walked away, leaving Seraphina and her daughter in the middle of the hallway.

Oaken walked over. "C'mon. I brought coffee and food." He reached down and helped Jasmine up, then Seraphina. Fetched the coffee and donuts, then led the family to the waiting-room sofa. Set the goodies on the table.

"I have glazed raised, and they're hot."

He got a slim smile from Liam.

Jasmine ate hers, tears still streaming down her face.

Seraphina pulled her legs up on the sofa, cradling the coffee cup. "This is so nice of you, Oaken."

He looked at her. "Listen. I know what it's like to wait and hope and pray that someone you love survives. I'm so sorry I couldn't get help faster."

"Reynolds said you nearly died getting help."

"I wouldn't go that far." He took a sip of coffee. "Mike is the hero—I read his survival book before jumping on that chopper with him. Thought I'd impress him. Turns out it saved us both."

She nodded at his chin wound. "Bear attack?" Then she smiled.

"Yep." He smiled back.

Hers faltered, just a little. "I can't imagine our life without Mike. He's . . . everything." She swallowed. "And now, even if he survives, I'm not sure how we're going to pay for it."

"Reynolds said that finances were tight."

"I'm not sure how, but we're in the red. Mike took a second mortgage out on the house to produce this season, and now . . ." She closed her eyes. Drew in a breath. Opened them. "I keep telling myself not to panic. Mike always has everything under control. But . . . it's hard not to, with him in the ICU. And now he almost died."

He didn't add, *For the third time.*

Instead, "Reynolds wants me to stay around and shoot a reality show with the local rescue team. Train with them, go out on rescues . . ."

"Cool," Liam said.

He looked at the kid, who shrugged. "Jumping out of helicopters, rescuing people from rivers—people love that kind of stuff."

Yeah, they do.

"I think you've done enough, Oaken. Don't put yourself in more danger for Mike. But thank you." Seraphina gave him a small smile.

But his gaze landed on Jasmine, wide-eyed and staring at him like he might be some kind of hero.

And shoot if he didn't want to believe it.

Aw . . . He was standing on the side of a lake again, waiting for a chopper, watching himself dig just a little deeper. But what was he going to do, abandon them?

Besides, he had done an amazing job out there.

"I'm going to go find you a decent hotel." He stood up.

"Reynolds said they booked us at some place nearby."

"Like I said, I'm going to find you a decent hotel. And then I have to call my manager and work out a few details."

She caught his hand. "I never believed anything social media said."

He pursed his lips.

"And Mike didn't either."

Sweet, but . . . it didn't matter what they thought.

Only what was true.

"Thanks." He drew in a breath. "He's going to make it, Seraphina. I know it. And I promise . . . I'm not leaving. Not until Mike is truly out of the woods."

FOUR

MAYBE AN EARLY MORNING RUN WOULD help shake off the nightmares from the last forty-eight hours. Boo had foregone her earbuds this morning in favor of listening to the birds awakening in the trees, the waves rolling against the shoreline of Kincaid Beach. A fog lifted off the water, and in the distance, she could just make out the dark outline of Fire Island. Overhead, the rising sun poured lava along the horizon, burning off the deep teal of night.

Maybe they were just nightmares, the sweaty dreams where Oaken Fox fell to his death, crumpled on the base of some remote mountain. Or drowned, caught in the wild rapids of some Alaskan river.

Just her worst fears playing out.

No, not her worst—those were more private and had to do with seeing herself again the subject of clickbait.

"This is a bad idea, Moose. Really bad. You don't know—producers change footage, make it seem like you said things you never meant."

Never mind the actual demands of being on a SAR team. Physical. Mental. Emotional.

Moose had lost his mind.

She'd spent all of yesterday trying to design a training schedule that wouldn't kill Oaken and would still provide decent footage for the show. Any way she looked at it, her gut said this would be a disaster. For Oaken, for her—and heaven help anyone he actually had to rescue.

Angling onto the trail that led back to Kincaid parking lot, she picked up her speed, pushing to an all-out sprint. Another runner glanced over at her as she passed him, and she lifted a finger to wave. She liked the anonymity of her life in Alaska.

And now . . . yeah, she could just see it: *Boo Hoo Kingston is back in her latest reality-show fiasco.*

And all the old articles would resurface. *Watch Boo Hoo Kingston lash back at Blake Hinton in scathing Instagram rant.*

Bad, bad idea.

Or maybe that's what the producers were hoping for—clickbait, scandal, and sensational press that would only dismantle her life, again.

She should march into Moose's office and resign now, before everything went south. But aw, she really liked it here.

Hitting the pavement, she slowed a bit but kept her pace high, pushing herself as she wound around the coastal trail back to Kincaid Park, leaving the sound behind. Her Rogue unlocked as she drew near it—one of four cars in the lot this early in the morning. Her words to Oaken about the Midnight Sun Killer flitted through her mind. Probably just a rumor, something to scare women into being ultracareful.

Popping the back end, she zipped open her duffel bag, grabbed her water bottle, and sprayed water into her mouth. Wiped the moisture and then put one foot up on the tailgate to stretch.

Then the other.

Hamstrings were tight today.

She pulled off her outer layer, sweating now, and spotted a man emerging from his car.

Wait—"Oaken?"

He wore workout gear. He hadn't shaved, his brown hair was crushed under a wool cap, and he wore a thin pullover, running shoes, and a pair of shorts over leggings, all of it hugging his clearly fit body.

He turned, blinked. "It's Boo, right?"

"Yeah. What are you doing here?"

"I'm at a hotel in the area, and they said this was the best place to get some fresh air." He offered a thin smile.

"All of Alaska is fresh air."

A moment, then, "Right."

Maybe that was a little snippy. It wasn't his fault that—*oh,* she needed to stop comparing him to Blake *right now.* "Oh, sorry. I'm just . . . I haven't slept well over the last couple days."

"I get that. This is the first morning I haven't spent at the hospital."

She reached for a towel and ran it over her face. "How's Mike?"

"As of this morning, no change. His wife and kids got here yesterday. They're staying at a hotel near the hospital."

She hung the towel around her neck, considered him. "Listen—"

"It wasn't my idea—"

Their words ran over each other. He held up his hand. "Sorry. You first."

She shrugged. "I just wanted to say that I'll do my best to keep you safe."

He raised an eyebrow. "Uh, thanks? But I promise, I can take care of myself."

Her mouth made a thin line. *Great. Another tough guy.*

"I was going to say that this wasn't my idea. But Mike and his family need this to work, so . . ." He smiled now, something real, and no wonder he was a star.

So much stun power. Too bad she was immune—*been there, done that, thank you.*

Still. "And Air One has a stake in this. So I'll train you up and maybe get you in on a rescue, and hopefully the show will be a hit."

He had started to stretch, leaning against the car to work his calves. For a country singer, he had decent back muscles.

Oh brother.

"I hope so." He stood up. "Listen. I know what you probably think of me, but I promise, I've had my fair share of survival experiences. And I'm not afraid of hard work. I'll get it done."

His voice held such sincerity. . .

"Okay, then. I'll see you at the Tooth."

"The Tooth?"

She tossed her towel back into the trunk area. "It's what we call the Air One HQ. The Moose's Tooth is a rocky peak just south of Denali." She took another sip of water. "It's a really challenging climb but super worth it—the view is amazing. Sort of like when you actually save someone." She capped her water bottle. "So, yeah, I think it was Axel who first dubbed HQ the Tooth."

"Axel?"

"He was the other guy on the chopper with us. Rescue swimmer."

"Right." He worked his neck, then caught his ankle to stretch his thighs.

"We also have Shep, our team lead, and London, who is our climbing expert. And another pilot north of here, along with a dogsledder and a slew of other volunteers if we need them. It's a small crew, but we're well trained."

He let go of his grip on his other ankle. "Good to know."

Again, the cover-model smile.

She had the sense that she might be babbling. This was why she made great fodder for reality shows. She wanted to thump herself, hard, on the head.

Tossing her bottle in, she shut the trunk. He had started running in place. A real go-getter.

"Don't get too worn out. I have a big day planned."

"As long as it doesn't involve jumping out of a chopper, I'm good." Then he winked and took off for the trail.

Oh boy. But she wasn't cancelling today's agenda.

She got into her Rogue and headed home, only a few miles away.

The sun had baked off more of the snow from the yard, and she spotted London on the wooden deck, on her yoga mat, seated and staring into the sun, her blonde hair long and shimmery.

Sheesh, the woman didn't even have to try. A long drink of water with blue eyes and an easy smile, London was tough, smart, and came with an aura of mystery. All Boo knew was that London knew Shep from ages past and made a mean Scotch egg. And she could beat Boo in Dutch Blitz without breaking a sweat.

Still, they shared music tastes, and London didn't ask too many questions, which Boo appreciated in a housemate.

Although for a second, Moose's weird shutdown of her suggestion that Oaken train with London flitted across Boo's mind.

Whatever.

Boo toed off her shoes at the door and headed into the kitchen, following the smell of fresh-brewed coffee. She poured herself a cup, then headed upstairs to shower.

Twenty minutes later, she found London in the kitchen, cooking scrambled eggs, crispy bacon on a paper towel on a plate, a bowl of berries on the counter.

"Eggs?" London said as she pulled a couple plates from the shelf, then turned off the heat on the stove.

"Please." Boo slid onto the stool at the counter.

London handed her a plate, then set the bacon in front of her. "So, you get all the fun."

Boo looked up at her.

"Oaken Fox. Moose filled me in yesterday." London picked up a piece of bacon. "He's hot."

"He's a celebrity. Hot is a requirement." Boo dished up the berries.

"You have an Oaken Fox album on your playlist."

She looked at London. "I also have Wham!, Elvis, and John Denver."

London held up a hand. "Just sayin', you've been here for two months and never been on a date."

"That's the pot calling the kettle black."

London smiled and picked up her plate. "Yeah, well, I have reasons."

"Like Shep."

London's mouth opened. "No."

"Yes. I see the way you look at him. And him at you."

"We're . . . no. Not ever. He's like a brother to me. And we work together."

"Mm-hmm." Boo finished off her eggs, then went to the fridge and found some plain yogurt. "Well, don't get all dewy-eyed. Oaken Fox is miles out of my league. And even if he wasn't, I'm not on the market."

She brought the yogurt back to the counter, added the berries, and stirred them in. London's gaze was on her when she looked up.

"What?"

"He's not out of your league. And give me one reason why you're not on the market."

About four came to mind—*Blake. Betrayal. Burned.* And not least, getting her heart broken again. Instead, "I don't need a man to make my life better."

"Agreed," London said and lifted her fist.

Boo bumped it.

"So, what's on your training schedule for Oaken today?"

"I'm bringing him to the Shed. I want to see how well he can climb and rappel, and maybe I'll get him up in Harriet."

"Trying to scare him?"

"I don't think Oaken is easily scared, but . . ." She lifted a shoulder. "We're not playing games out there."

"No games. I'll remember that." London winked. "I'm grabbing a shower." She put her dish in the sink, rinsed it, then stuck it in the dishwasher and headed upstairs.

Boo stared out the window as she finished off her yogurt. Thick pine edged the yard but opened to a view of the inlet, the fog now lifted, the sun bright. So maybe this wouldn't be a complete disaster. If she could keep her mouth shut, stay away from the camera, and just do her job.

No stupid sacrifices of the heart.

Her wrist buzzed, picking up a text. She lifted her arm. Read the text.

What? Aw, c'mon.

Blake
_____

Hey Boo. I need to talk to you. Call me.

Blake.

She slammed her hand on the watch, turning it dark. Then she finished off her yogurt, dumped the tub in the trash, cleaned up, picked up her keys, and headed out the door.

So much for escaping her nightmares.

So maybe he was in over his head.

What was his problem that he kept saying yes to all the wrong things? *Three weeks. Smile. Stay alive. Try to pry a tune from his head. Pray Mike wakes up.*

But in all of that, no one had said Oaken would have to dangle fifty feet from a chopper.

It felt like he might be daring God to mess him up.

"So, when I hook you up, you're going to step out onto the skid, and then London will lower you down."

Boo stood on the deck of the fake chopper, the one suspended from a massive hydraulic circular mount that could move the chopper in the air as if it were being buffeted by wind. Although not today. Today they were simply going to hook him up and lower him to the cliffside—also fake—some fifty feet below.

On that cliffside lay a dummy, dressed in orange, wearing a helmet, visor down, sprawled and unmoving, clearly broken from a fall. The cliff overlooked another drop of thirty feet, down into an Olympic-sized pit-slash-pool.

The Shed, as Moose had called it when Oaken arrived at the Tooth earlier this morning, was located off-site, at an area near Elmendorf Air Force Base.

"The Air Force uses the Shed for some of their SAR training," Moose had said as he pulled gear from the back of his pickup.

Honestly, Oaken liked Moose. A big guy, yes, but he had an easy smile and an air of willing camaraderie. He'd even sat for Huxley today as she'd asked him a few questions about Air One—how it got started, what he did before this, why he did what he did.

Navy rescue pilot. Yeah, Oaken could have guessed—the guy had *hero* written all over him. As for why, Moose had lifted a shoulder, smiled at the camera and said, "So others might live."

Okay, then. Although Oaken had a sense there might be more to the story.

The others had arrived as Moose was giving him a tour of the Shed, from the massive climbing wall to the tank that filled for underwater training.

"What's the car for?" Oaken had asked about the very real vehicle attached to a hydraulic skid.

"We can simulate a river rescue—it's not uncommon for drivers to find themselves submerged or caught in overflowing rivers.

"And that's Harriet, our Helicopter Rescue Hoist Trainer." He'd pointed to the massive helicopter shell suspended on tracks and the circular mount from the ceiling. "We can create turbulence and even add wind from the massive turbines." He pointed to the fans on each side of the building. "They can even simulate waves, and if we want, we can add smoke."

"Why smoke?"

"Forest fires. Sometimes we need to rescue the heroes."

Right.

And that's when Oaken turned to the camera, his eyes wide, and mouthed, *What am I doing?*

Huxley loved it and gave him two thumbs up. She wore cargo pants, a thermal shirt, and a vest, her headphones over her ears, listening on Bluetooth as the audio picked up the conversation between him and Moose.

The camera probably also picked up when he spotted Boo entering the Shed. He shouldn't have let his gaze linger on her—Huxley might have a heyday with that. But he couldn't help it. Boo wore leggings, just like today at the park, and a pullover, her hair back in a ponytail, held back with a red headband. No makeup, but she didn't need any, and a sort of fierceness in her expression that intrigued him.

She was a tough nut and not the warmest coat in the closet. But he couldn't stop thinking about their conversation that night she'd saved his life.

Really. Saved it. Because he'd been standing on the highway for maybe an hour, freezing, not sure what to do.

But she had known *exactly* what to do, and that's what mattered. More, her calm demeanor had sort of shut down the roiling inside him. *"We'll find him."*

So, yeah, she might be all business, but he respected that.

Now as he sat on the deck of the chopper and tried not to look down, he met her brown eyes, trying to take in her instructions.

"The key is communication. I'm going to direct the pilot on how to position you, and you are simply going to remain calm and let him do his job."

"Right. And then, what, I'm going to rescue Ronny down there?"

He pointed to the dummy sprawled on the deck, dressed in an orange jumpsuit.

"Ronny?"

"Rescue Ronny?"

"And you write songs?"

He looked at her. She offered a slight smile. *Wait—was that a joke?*

"Just put this harness around his shoulders and under his arms, and this one under his feet. Then we'll hoist you both back up. I'll talk you up the entire way." She tapped her mic with her finger, and he heard it thump in the headphones in his helmet.

"Let's roll!" She looked at the pilot, Moose, who sat in the front, simulating the controls. He flipped on an engine that created the wash of a rotor without the danger.

Someone else added wind.

"I thought this was going to be without the sound effects," he said.

"Where's the fun in that?" Moose said from the cockpit.

Boo shook her head. "I forgot to ask," she said, lifting her voice, although he heard her via his helmet. "Are you afraid of heights?"

"What if I said yes?"

She smiled then, and it did something to her entire face. Sort of like stars against the night. "I'd say get used to fear."

Then she pushed him out of the chopper. He found his footing on the skids.

"Step off and let the hoist lower you."

He looked down.

With the noise and the wind and the height—okay, it felt a little real. His brain went back to the chopper, that moment with Mike—

"Hey. Hey. Look at me."

He met her eyes. "What?"

"You have the look."

"I don't have a look."

"You do. Just breathe. I got you."

Oh brother. But for the camera—he gave her a thumbs-up.

She pointed down. "Eyes on your target."

He didn't know if it was the wind, or maybe the winch, but he started to spin. Around and around.

Oh, this was great fun. His stomach started to lurch—

"Keep your eyes on your target! Don't watch the horizon." Boo's voice in his ear, and it was weirdly centering.

He kept his gaze on the dummy even as he listened to Boo count off the distance, then direct the chopper to place him on the jutting rock where the dummy lay.

He put his foot out, caught the rock, then landed, pulling himself onto the rock.

Bam.

The winch let out slack as he worked his way along the cliff to the dummy. He held on to the ledge above him, barely enough room for both bodies on the cliff.

"Now put the harness on him."

He reached over to put the harness on.

The dummy reached up to grab him.

He jerked back. "What?" He pedaled back and clawed for the rock.

His foot slipped just as Axel flipped up his helmet and reached for him.

"Whoa—" Axel the dummy snagged Oaken's webbed belt just as he lost his balance. Axel yanked him back.

They landed in a heap on the cliff.

Axel looked over at him. "That didn't go quite like I'd planned."

"You think?" Oaken pushed himself up, the cable line slack around his feet.

"Seriously?" Boo shouted through the headphones.

Axel lifted a hand. "Sorry, Boo. We couldn't help it." He looked at Oaken. "Okay, harness me up."

Shep began to tighten the slack.

Oaken leaned over to put the loop around Axel's shoulders—

It was then he felt the pressure, tightening around his leg.

He looked down, and the cable had looped around his ankle, tightening as the winch raised the cable.

"Wait, wait!"

But even as he said it, the cable grabbed him, yanking him off the ledge and flipping him.

He swung out from the edge, upside down, the weight of his body on his ankle.

"Stop!" shouted Axel even as he grabbed for Oaken. Missed.

Oaken bit down on the heat spiking through him, grunted, leaned up, and grabbed the cable above his foot. Hoisted himself up and yanked his ankle free.

He dropped and held out his hand. Axel grabbed it hauled him in.

Breathing hard, he clung to the cliff.

"You okay?" Axel said.

"Mm-hmm." But he closed his eyes, his hands braced on the faux rock, and let out a low growl, deep in his chest.

"Okay, we're coming up. We have an injury here."

Oaken looked at Axel. "I don't think it's broken. Just ... bruised. I'm good." His pride, however—in shards at the bottom of the cliff.

"We'll see." Axel looped the harness over himself, then hooked it to the winch clamp, checked the cable, and grabbed onto Oaken. "Hoist us up!"

They rose, and *oh goody,* they'd gotten it all on film, given Huxley's hard-jawed gaze on him. Oh, that would make for spectacular footage. At least he hadn't let out a scream.

They reached the skid and he grabbed it, then the deck, and stepped onto the skid.

Okay, maybe the ankle was broken. Axel climbed onto the deck and slid out of his loop. Boo hooked him into the chopper's security via his harness.

Then she turned to Oaken.

Now *she* wore the white face.

"I'm fine."

"You could have broken your leg. Or worse, gotten a dislocated hip, or—"

"I'm fine." Sort of. But fine enough until the camera stopped rolling.

Her mouth made a grim line, but she pulled him onto the deck, unhooked him from the winch, then handed him the secure line.

He hooked in as she reached for his leg.

"Wait. They'll want to film this."

She looked up at him.

"Trust me."

"Fine."

Already the chopper was moving on its hydraulics to the deck and stairs. They docked, and of course, Huxley and Beto Gomez, the cameraman, were there. They'd caught the rest of the footage from Oaken's helmet camera along with the chopper camera.

Now he nodded to Boo, who shook her head, then rolled up his pants leg.

The canvas pants had protected his skin from breaking, but a terrible bruise was already forming on his leg, his ankle swelling.

She untied his boot and eased it off.

"Can you move your ankle?"

He did, and managed not to make a sound.

"It probably needs X-rays," Axel said.

Boo nodded as she broke out an ice pack. She put it on his ankle, then reached for a splint. This she affixed with an ACE bandage.

"C'mon, tough guy. Let's get you to the ER." Axel stood up and hooked his hand under Oaken's arm.

Oaken wrangled his way up, then leaned on Axel as he exited the chopper onto the metal deck.

He used both handrails to get down, letting Huxley and Beto go down first. Axel followed him.

Boo did not.

Yeah, well, he'd agreed.

All he heard now were his words from the park earlier today, spoken with way too much hubris. *I promise, I can take care of myself.*

He looked like a fool.

Perfect.

Axel offered him a shoulder, but he shook his head. "You really thought that would be funny?" He limped, aware that the camera caught every expression.

"Sorry."

He looked back just before they pushed through the doors to the outside. Boo sat at the top of the stairs, holding his helmet, just watching him, something dark in her expression.

He climbed into the back of the SUV and managed to keep a grim smile all the way to the hospital, then through the ER exam, and even X-rays.

Not broken, just bruised, and yeah, he was lucky. Or stupid—he couldn't quite decide.

"Sorry, man, this is all my fault," Axel said as they walked out of the ER, Oaken's ankle wrapped. He could walk on it, though, so it wasn't a disaster. "If I hadn't spooked you . . ."

"It'll make for great television," Oaken said. He'd given an interview for Huxley in the ER, and now she and Beto headed for the hotel.

But really, he should book his ticket home right now.

What. An. Idiot.

"I'm going to head upstairs and check on Mike," he said to Axel.

"Dude," Axel said. "Listen. First day. Accidents happen. You'll figure this out."

"I dunno. Boo looks—"

"Naw, that's just Boo. She's just . . . driven. And maybe a little dark. I don't really know her that well—she's only been here a couple months. She's the cousin of one of our pilots in Copper Mountain, and Moose likes to hire family—" He zipped up his jacket, then pointed to himself.

"You're related to Moose?"

"Brother. But I came by the job honestly. I was a rescue swimmer with the Coast Guard." He reached into his pocket and pulled out a stocking hat. "Still, Boo is . . . well, she's like a ghost . . . She's around but appears when she wants to. Disappears. A little chilly around the edges."

A little?

"Listen, we'll be at the Tooth going over today's training if you want to swing by. There's usually pizza. Or takeout from the Skyport."

"Not sure I'm allowed to hang out with you without Huxley around."

"We won't tell anyone." Axel clamped him on the shoulder. "We'll give you an official Air One welcome."

"Now I'm scared." He smiled, sort of.

"Don't be. This isn't *Survival Quest*. No one is going to kick you off the team." He bumped Oaken's shoulder with a fist. "There might be a real rescuer in you somewhere. We'll find it." Then he walked out the door.

Oaken turned and headed toward the elevator. Took it upstairs
to ICU. The place was quiet, but he spotted Seraphina sitting in
the waiting room. Alone.

She was on her phone. He walked over to her.

"How is he?"

She put her phone down. Clearly she'd had some sleep, her face
less blotchy, her eyes clearer. She wore a pair of leggings and an
oversized sweatshirt. "The same. But no code blues today, so . . ."

He sat next to her. "Where are the kids?"

"They're with my parents. They flew in. We got an Airbnb this
morning. Sorry to abandon you at the hotel."

"Reynolds is supposed to be getting me an Airbnb too. I'm
starting to run out of clean clothes."

She nodded. "The coffee there could kill a person."

He smiled, and she sighed and drew up one knee. "I'm waiting
for the next fifteen minutes, then I'll go back." Her eyes filled. "I'm
not even sure he knows I'm here."

He couldn't help the urge to take her hand. Squeeze it. "He
knows."

She shrugged, nodded. Then, "Why are you doing this, Oaken?"

"What?"

"Sticking around. Doing the show with Air One."

He looked down the hall, then back to her. Stared at her a long
time. *Good question, really.*

And then for some reason, Mike walked into his head, that
moment before they jumped out of the chopper. *"There's nothing
like jumping out of a plane to figure out what you're made of!"*

Huh. "Because I want to . . . I don't know . . . maybe figure out
if I have what it takes . . ."

"To do what? Survive?"

He frowned at her. "Maybe." But right behind his answer was
the echo of Axel's words— *"This isn't* Survival Quest. *No one is
going to kick you off the team."*

Wait . . . "Call me if you need me," he said even as Seraphina frowned.

"Where are you going?"

"I think . . . to find something." He lifted his hand to her and headed to the elevator.

And maybe it started with Boo Kingston.

FIVE

D ID NO ONE BESIDES HER SEE THE LOOM-
ing disaster? Screams, tragedy, death— "Moose, c'mon, you
can't actually think this is a good idea. Not after today."

Boo planted herself in Moose's office, the door partially open to
the radio playing in the lounge area of the Tooth, the tangy smell
of lasagna lingering in the air from the small but decent kitchen.

The rest of the team lounged in the main area on the two big
sofas, a flat screen playing an old *Magnum, P.I.* episode. Pictures
of Denali and other Alaska-scapes hung on canvas on the walls,
along with a giant map of all of Alaska, with pins in the locations
of past rescues. A whiteboard also listed off the training schedule,
various announcements, and upcoming events.

Beyond the main room, down one wing, were the showers and a
gear area, with ropes and climbing gear and extra litters and back-
boards, along with a parachute drying tower and a weight room.

Past Moose's office off the main area was the dispatch office,
and farther, two bunkrooms.

A real home away from home, and Moose practically lived here, although apparently he had a beautiful timber-framed home on the Knik River.

Now he stood at the window looking out into the room, arms folded, jaw tight, as if mulling over words.

"You agree, right?"

He looked at her, blinking. Then, "Yeah. No . . . what?"

"Were you even paying attention?"

He drew in a breath. "Yes. Of course. You're freaking out about today's near accident."

"Accident, boss. Oaken Fox could have broken his ankle. Or worse. I mean, depending on what weight was on that line—I can't even think it. And Axel—seriously?"

"It was just a prank."

"For what—the show? Since when do we play pranks in training? Please tell me you didn't give the okay—"

He held up his hand.

She clamped her mouth shut, folding her arms against the roiling in her stomach.

She just couldn't replay today's events without shuddering. Good thing she'd been wearing her helmet visor down, or the camera would have replayed her near scream as stupid Oaken Fox flipped on the line.

"No one anticipated Oaken's reaction—"

"Of course not. That's how accidents happen—"

"But it was good training. He'll never make that mistake again."

She just stared at Moose. "You've got to be kidding me. That's the takeaway? That we all learned a valuable lesson for when Oaken Fox *joins the Air One Rescue team*? You can't think that we'd actually take him on a callout, can you?"

He cocked his head at her. "I think that's the point, right?"

"Oh. My—no. No, that is not the point. The point is to do a few stunts, offer a show to viewers, and hopefully, please God, no one actually gets hurt."

Moose raised an eyebrow.

"It's not real! None of it is supposed to be real." She drew in a breath, blew it out, shook her head. "I . . . I can't do this."

"Boo."

"You do know that if anything happens to Oaken on our watch, we're done, right? No one will trust us. We won't be called out to rescue a cat in a tree. Let alone missing hikers or a climber on a cliff or an overturned car in a river—people might actually die, Moose, because—"

"Okay, okay." He took a step toward her, put his hands on her shoulders. "It'll be okay. We'll be more careful."

"And no callouts."

He drew in a breath. "Maybe just as an observer."

She narrowed her eyes. "Observers get in the way. They get hurt too."

"Seems to me that Oaken has his wits about him. He scrambled back onto that ledge pretty quickly. If the slack hadn't been pulled up—"

"So now you're blaming me?"

His eyes widened, and okay, maybe that came out too bright, too harsh. "Sorry."

"Is that what this is about, Boo? You getting blamed for something?"

Her mouth tightened, and her eyes burned. She looked away.

Out in the main area, Axel was setting the table, London pulling lasagna from the oven. Shep had turned on the radio to country music. Brett Young played "In Case You Didn't Know."

She loved this stupid song.

"I just . . . you know . . . I've been burned by the media before and . . ." She shook her head, then turned and looked at Moose. "I just never thought all of this would follow me to Alaska."

He just stared at her. Frowned.

He didn't know. "Never mind."

"No, Boo—what are you talking about?"

She swallowed, sighed. "You really don't know?"

She liked Moose. Wasn't sure where he'd gotten his nickname, but he was anything but a big oaf that might be associated with that name. Tough, yes, and capable, but he had a soft side, evidenced by the fact that he'd taken her on without any questions.

And there was midnight chicken.

"When I was on *Survivor Quest,* I teamed up with a guy named Blake Hinton. He was . . . well, I thought we had something. He teamed up with me right away, and we worked together through all the first eight legs. And then he got food poisoning out on the trail. Part of the show was making it to our destination by the deadline. But he spiked a fever, and I suggested that we stay. So we did. We were in the lead until that night. And by the time we arrived the next day, we were dead last."

"You were disqualified?"

"No. We made the deadline. But . . ." She closed her eyes, looked away. "He voted me off the race and partnered up with the only other woman in the race."

A beat, and she couldn't look at him.

"Sounds like a real piece of work."

She lifted a shoulder. "It wasn't until I saw the show that I realized he'd betrayed me. And you know, it's just a stupid show. In the end, he didn't even win. Misty Buchannan, his now fiancée won."

"Oh."

"And whatever, right? But . . ." She blew out a breath. "He said some pretty . . . he said . . ." *Aw,* she couldn't get it out.

"It's okay, Boo. I get the picture." She looked at him, and he crossed his arms, took a breath. "I'm sorry. You shouldn't have been treated like that."

And now she really couldn't tell him the rest. So she simply nodded.

"But Air One Rescue is your home now, and these are your people, and you're never going to be voted off our crew."

She couldn't breathe, the words finding all her soft places. Her mouth opened, closed, and then she simply closed her eyes, nodded. "Thanks." Her voice barely emerged.

"And no one is going to blame you if something goes south. So . . . look at me."

She opened her eyes, met his gaze. Gritted her jaw to keep anything from leaking out.

"Just do your job. That's all we can ask. I'll take care of Huxley and Reynolds, and even Oaken if you need me to step in, okay?"

"I can handle myself."

"I know you can. But . . ." He smiled. "You don't always have to."

He hadn't lived her life, but she nodded anyway.

Movement at the door made her glance toward the main area. Oaken Fox walked in carrying a couple two-liter sodas and nodded at the team.

They waved him over and he grinned, and already he was their bestie.

"Go get something to eat, Boo."

She looked at Moose, who gestured with his head.

"I think I'll head home."

"Boo—"

But she was already leaving his office.

"Hey, Boo!" said Axel from where he was taking the soda from Oaken, bringing it to the refrigerator. "London made lasagna—"

"It's from Costco and it was frozen about four hours ago, so I'm not sure that qualifies as *made lasagna*," said London. She sat, dressed in her uniform, her blonde hair pulled back, utterly perfect for the role of reality-television trainer in Boo's opinion. *Whatever.*

Boo lifted a hand. "I'm headed home."

"Aw, c'mon and join us," Shep said. He was retrieving garlic bread from the oven, wearing a couple of hot pads. Axel brought over cups.

Her gaze went to Oaken.

Oh, he was a handsome man. With his sandy brown hair curling out from under a ball cap, and bottomless blue eyes. Country music practically oozed from him, with the faded jeans, boots, red flannel shirt. Looked like he'd showered maybe, but he hadn't shaved. He limped a little, but he was clearly on the mend.

"We did our debrief. Fill Oaken in. I'll see you guys tomorrow." She picked up her backpack with her water bottle and training manual—she'd look through it for tomorrow's fun—and grabbed her jacket.

"Boo, wait," said Oaken, but she flashed him a smile.

"We're good, Oaken. See you tomorrow."

Then she headed outside.

The sun was still up but falling into the backside of Mt. Talachulitna, gold shining upon the whitened peaks, bronzing the waters of Cook Inlet. She unlocked the Rogue and it beeped.

"Boo, wait up!"

What is with this guy? She opened the back door, threw her pack in, and turned.

He jogged up to her. Stopped. Met her eyes, hands on his hips, and took a breath.

"What?"

"I know."

She just blinked at him. Swallowed. "What?" Her voice emerged high and silly.

"Boo Hoo."

Her jaw tightened and she looked away. Back. "Wow."

He hadn't moved his gaze from her. A beat, and something in his expression softened. "And I get it," he said gently.

She had to reach out and brace her hand on the top of her car. "What?"

"I know how it feels to be judged, wrongly, by the media. By the world. To have words you didn't mean—"

"Oh, I meant them."

He cocked his head, narrowed his eyes. "I'll bet you did. At the time. But . . . my guess is that there was a whole lot of hurt behind that post that people never got."

And now she couldn't swallow.

"I came out here to say two things."

She just stood there, her mouth tight.

"Thank you."

Her mouth opened. Closed.

"You didn't have to agree to the show. But you did, and I don't know why, but I can't imagine that the idea of getting in front of the camera again was easy for you."

She shook her head, her arms crossed now. And he wore such a stupid, sweet, kind expression she just shrugged. "Air One can use the money."

"Yep," he said. "I get that too."

She exhaled. "Okay, and two?"

"I won't let it happen again."

She couldn't move.

"I won't let Huxley edit something in, or out, that you didn't mean to say. Or . . . if you even want to stay completely off-screen, I've got your back. I will not let them use . . . well, your past to promote the show, let them drag you back through social media or even in any way betray you."

Oh. Wow.

And again, she had nothing.

"That's all. Just . . . we're in this together, and . . . you promised to do your best to keep me safe . . . and I'm making you the same promise."

She shoved her hands into her pockets and for the first time found a response. "If I remember right, you said you could take care of yourself."

He just let a small smile ride up his face. "I did say that."

Another beat, and maybe she was the most foolish girl on the planet but, "I want to trust you, Oaken. I do. But the fact is, I have a good thing going here, and . . . this is my last shot. This gig goes south, I don't know where I'll end up."

He frowned. Then nodded. "I get that. I really do. But you're already signed up for the fun and games. It can be torture, or you can give me a chance and trust me a little. Or a lot." He held out his hand. Raised a stupidly handsome eyebrow. Looked at her with those hypnotic blue eyes.

She could probably claim temporary insanity, but what choice did she have? This could be three weeks of torture or . . . "Okay, Oaken Fox. It's a deal. I watch your back, you watch mine."

She took his hand and let it close around hers, warm and solid and real. And tried not to listen to the person shouting in the back of her head.

Oaken didn't want to make any proclamations, but really, he was nailing this gig. Starting with his ability to rappel and anchor onto the ledge and "rescue" Axel, still playing the victim.

And maybe success included the thawing work relationship with Boo, who had told him a rare "Good job" today as he'd tied his own bowline on a bight, the clove hitch, an overhand knot, and a mule hitch. Of course, this was said quietly as she stood out of the camera's view, but it counted. He'd gotten a lesson from London yesterday on the climbing knots and spent most of the evening practicing, but to have Boo notice and then assign him to rappel down the cliff felt like a victory.

An actual callout might be another story, something that Huxley had been arguing with Moose about earlier today when he arrived at the Tooth. He wanted to raise his hand and say that, hello, he wasn't a real rescuer and he certainly didn't want to put anyone's life at risk.

Been there, done that.

"How you doin', Axe?" he said now as he landed on the ledge.

Axel gave him a thumbs-up, his gaze on Oaken now working his rope through the carabiner below his descender, then twisting to tie a mule hitch. Oaken then pulled out a foot of rope and tied an overhand knot to the rope above the descender.

"Good job," Axel said. His gaze travelled past Oaken to where Beto hung on another rope, capturing the rescue. "We have self-locking descenders, but this teaches you how to tie a brake in case you don't have one."

Oaken gave him a thumbs-up, ignoring the camera. "I'm supposed to assess your wounds."

"I have an ankle injury," Axel said. "But the priority is to get me off the cliff. In this case, I don't need a litter. The best scenario here is for you to clip my harness to your rig, then continue with the descent."

Oaken pulled out his walkie and relayed the information to Shep, who stood on top with Moose and London. They had him on belay, but only as a secondary safety. The rest was all him.

They'd worked out the scenario at the Tooth, in the gear room, with Boo showing him how to affix Axel's harness to the carabiner on his descender, transferring the weight onto the rope.

Despite the cool air in the massive shed, a thin line of sweat dripped down his spine. But he ticked off the steps in his head.

Connect Axel's harness to the descending rig with a carabiner. He knelt and clipped a carabiner to his rig, then bent and connected that to the carabiner on Axel's harness.

"Now, while you're still off load, take off the brake and ease me onto the rope load."

He untied his braking system, then put the rope around Axel, drawing him closer, and looked down.

Thirty feet to the ground, so not a huge fall, especially with the padding, but—

"You got this," Axel said quietly.

Oaken nodded, then pushed away from the cliff, easing Axel with him. The descender immediately released, and adrenaline rushed through his veins.

But he braked and held, pushing out with his legs, Axel's body almost seated in his lap.

"It helps if you grab my harness, right around my leg strap, just to steady me as we descend," Axel said. Oaken grabbed the thigh strap and worked his hand into it, the other controlling the rope.

"Now you see why we made you wear gloves," Axel said as the rope fed through Oaken's grip.

Sweat lined his helmet and he said nothing, focused on his foot placement, the rate of descent, walking down the side of the rock wall.

"We also have a rescue harness we can send with you, or even a folding litter that you wear on your back like a pack," Axel said.

"Save it for your interview," Oaken said and glanced at him. "You seem to be a hit with Huxley."

"Not as much as Shep is. Sheesh, the camera loves him."

They were almost at the bottom.

Oaken had waged a face-off with Huxley about interviewing Boo, and she'd reluctantly agreed to keep her off camera. In trade, he'd agreed to let them film him off-hours. Like during his morning run, working out in the weight room, and even grabbing a bite with the team.

Something about the Air One lifestyle—minus the cameras—felt weirdly relaxing. Freeing even, despite the danger, the responsibility.

Although, with Shep belaying him from the top and the massive padding at the bottom . . .

Oaken reached the padding and then lowered them all the way to the ground. He unhooked Axel, who lifted his hand in a high five.

Huxley stood at the bottom. "Cut. That's a wrap for today." She walked over to Oaken. "That was fantastic. If you want, you can stop by later and check out the dailies."

He was unhooking himself from his belay rope. "I wanted to ask you about that—I'm a little tired of living out of a hotel, despite being in the executive suite. And on my own dime. I have a load of laundry that I need washed. I was hoping for that Airbnb you promised?"

She made a face. "Right. I'll talk to Reynolds."

Yeah, that didn't sound hopeful.

Shep's voice came through the radio. "We're hauling up the ropes. Meet us up top with your gear."

Axel had gotten up, headed for the stairs that led out of the pit, and Oaken followed him. The air in the Shed smelled metallic, the massive fans off, the view through the expansive windows of a clear blue day, snowcapped mountains to the west, piney forest to the east, and Elmendorf Air Force Base to the north. So different than his condo in Nashville, although not a great leap from King Studios in Mercy Falls, Montana, where he did much of his recording. In fact, it was his producer, Ben King, who had suggested this adventure with Mike Grizz to Goldie.

Not sure why, really, but a week ago today he'd been standing on the edge of a river, questioning his motives, and wondering if he'd survive.

Still didn't have an answer to either, but the roiling in his chest had died.

Shucking off his gear, he spotted Boo heading his direction carrying a massive gear bag over her shoulder. She wore her dark hair back and a red jumpsuit with the Air One badge on the chest and carried her helmet. And she didn't appear angry.

Even offered him a smile.

"Good job," she said as she walked by him. She lifted a hand. He clapped it.

She kept going, toward the doors.

"Wow. You two besties now?"

He looked at Axel, who was also unclipping his rig.

"That was a real smile. Someone is on the thaw." Axel winked.

"We have a truce," Oaken said. "That's all."

"Right."

Oaken shook his head, then added his harness and helmet into the open gear bag. Moose had joined them, dropping another heavy bag onto the ground. "It's going to be a beautiful weekend," he said. "I'll be throwing some steaks on the grill tonight, if anyone wants to come over. There's a Polar Bear game on."

"Polar Bear?" Oaken said.

"Hockey," said Axel. "He's crazy about the Anchorage P-Bears. Had a dream of playing, once upon a time."

"So did you, little bro," said Moose as he zipped up the gear bag.

"Half of the population in Alaska wants to play hockey," said Axel. "It's bred into us as youth. Pond hockey in every town." He pulled on a ball cap, backwards, to cover up his helmet head. His dark blond hair stuck out under it.

They seemed from two different mothers, the Mulligan brothers. Moose with his big stature, serious demeanor, dark brown hair, gray-green eyes. Axel, just a little smaller but still built, with blue eyes and an easy smile.

"Sorry," Oaken said. "I know this is lame—but I need to find a laundromat. My hotel only does dress shirts."

Moose picked up one of the bags. "Forget the hotel. Stay with me. I have four bedrooms, and Axel is only using two."

"Funny." Axel picked up the other gear bag. "But true."

"I think Reynolds is getting me an Airbnb."

Moose stopped, glanced back. "C'mon, Oak. You're one of the team now."

He didn't know why Moose's words hit a soft spot, sank in.

"Besides, I can think of a much better way to spend a Friday night than doing laundry." Axel followed his brother out.

Yeah, he could too. Oaken joined them outside and Moose was standing at his truck, his phone out. "I'm texting you my address." He then pocketed his phone. "Bring chips."

He got into the truck, Axel on the passenger side.

The sun still labored over the mountains, lengthening the day, and the last thing Oaken wanted to do was go back to the hotel or drive around Anchorage looking for a laundromat.

He wanted to ask if Boo might be there, but he'd already picked up her vibe—she worked hard but usually disappeared right after training. Which had him asking all sorts of questions, but maybe it was none of his business.

Still, the fact that she hadn't looked like she wanted to strangle him since their showdown four days ago seemed like enough.

On his way to the hotel, he called Seraphina. Still sedated, Mike's heart rate had steadied, his stats rising. She sounded less tired today.

So maybe this wasn't a disaster. No lives lost because of him, no reason to believe he was going to screw this all up.

He pulled into the Summit Hotel, so Alaskan with its A-frame entrance and three-story atrium, and took the elevator to the top floor. Housekeeping had already swept his room, and he dug out a tip for them, left it on the bed, then packed his bag, trying not to argue with himself too much.

He didn't know why the impulse to take Moose up on his offer drove him, but the idea of hanging out with the Mulligan brothers felt better than a dry pizza and channel surfing.

Maybe he just missed his band. He probably owed his band

leader, Mills, a call, although Mills had needed a break too, what with his wife having a baby.

None of the guys deserved what he'd put them through, but he was fixing that.

He hauled his duffel bag over his shoulder, grabbed his guitar, then checked out and popped the bag beside his dirty laundry in the trunk. He opened Moose's text message, pulled up the GPS, popped on the radio, and headed out of town.

Thirty minutes later, he turned onto Old Glenn Highway, the sun casting deep amber rays through the piney forest. The road ran along a ridge that dropped to the river below some thirty feet, maybe more. But between the trees glistened the beautiful blue of the Knik Arm. As the road veered away from the river, a few houses sat on the ridge, mostly log cabins, all at the end of long dirt driveways.

He turned onto one of these and trekked in toward the river. The drive opened up to a massive lawn, a beautiful two-story timber lodge with a garage wing and a stunning view. He parked in the gravel drive and got out, opening his back seat for his guitar, then the trunk to grab his gear.

The front door opened, and Moose walked out onto the long covered porch. "I just fired up the grill." He came down the steps and grabbed the duffel bag. "No chips?"

"Aw. Sorry." Oaken grabbed his laundry.

"We'll live." He led him up the steps and into the beautiful home.

Inside, double doors led to a home office, and the hallway opened to an expansive great room, but Moose stopped in the entry, shook off his Crocs, then carried Oaken's duffel up the stairs to the second floor.

Oaken undid his boots, left them on the mat, took off his jacket and hung it on the wrought-iron hooks, then followed Moose up with his laundry and his guitar.

The winding stairs led to a bridge that overlooked the grand A-frame lookout with the wall of picture windows. On one side of the bridge, a set of closed double doors. He found Moose on the other, in a smaller bedroom with a view of the river.

"Axel is in the basement rooms." Moose had set the duffel on a king-sized bed. An en suite led off the room.

"This is five stars."

"You should check out the in-house restaurant." Moose grinned. "Steaks going on in five. Laundry is in the basement, unfortunately."

"Thanks," Oaken said and dropped the bag. Stepped to the window.

Yeah, he could like this view. Like this life. He couldn't remember the last time he'd looked at his phone other than to get a text or for the maps.

He hadn't thought about Maggie or the fight or even his empty song notebook for a week.

Maybe he should quit and simply stick around. Become a real rescuer.

He picked up his laundry and carried it downstairs. Moose cut up bread in the kitchen and pointed to a doorway. Oaken found the stairs and headed to the basement.

Not your typical basement with the walk-out entry. A pool table sat in the middle of one side of the room, and on the other, a leather U-shaped sofa faced a hundred-inch theater screen. A glass door led to a tiled room, and he peeked in and spotted a hot tub and a sauna.

Wow, the rescue business paid well.

A hallway led off the main room, and he passed a couple rooms, the doors closed, music emerging from one of them, and found the laundry room at the end of the hallway.

He dumped in half his clothing, found the soap, and turned on the water.

When he emerged, one of the doors was open.

Upstairs, he found Axel seated at one of the high-top chairs at the black granite countertop. "Hey, Oak."

Moose was peeling garlic.

"Nice place," Oaken said, sliding onto a stool. Massive center island, stainless steel hood and appliances, double oven, subzero fridge. And behind him, a towering stone fireplace that rose two stories. Three leather sofas framed it, in front of a stone center table.

A long walnut table stretched out in front of the window, benches on each side.

The place was made for a crowd.

Or a family.

"What can I do?"

"Grab the garlic bread," Moose said, picking up the garlic and a bowl of melted butter. He gestured to the board, where cut pieces of French bread lay. Then he let himself out of the side door onto the porch, where smoke billowed from the grill.

Oaken grabbed the bread and headed outside. The smell of the grilling meat could turn him into a bear. He nearly growled.

Moose lifted the hood of the grill and added the bread to the top shelf. The steaks sizzled. Then he spread butter on the bread, added garlic, and lowered the top.

"You do this a lot?" Oaken asked.

"Every Friday night. Shep should be here soon."

"London?"

"Maybe."

"Boo?"

"Probably not." Moose glanced over at him. "Although she might change her mind if she knew you were here."

Oaken raised an eyebrow. "What?"

"She seems to like you."

"Hardly. She barely talks to me."

"But she watches you. And today when she hooked you up on belay, she gave you a smile. And a 'good job.'" Moose glanced at Oaken. "She's just guarded."

"I know." Oaken stared out at the river. "Such a great place here."

"Yep." A beat. "I inherited it."

Oaken turned back to Moose. "Really?"

"Yep. A guy I rescued, early days. Before Air One was started. He and I got to be friends. He gave me the money for the start-up and then gave me the place when he moved to the lower forty-eight. Died a year ago, and I got the title."

"You always want to do this—run a rescue op?"

"Nope. I wanted to play hockey." He checked the steaks. "Just sort of fell into it." He lowered the lid. "You always want to play music?"

Oaken laughed. "Nope. Sort of fell into it." He drew in a breath. "But I like it here. Maybe I should ditch the music, join the team for real."

Quiet beside him. He finally looked at Moose. "What?"

Moose's expression was serious. "Is that what God is telling you to do?"

Oaken's eyes widened. "Uh ... I'm ... I don't—God and I aren't actually talking."

"You mean you're not talking to God. Because God never stops talking to us."

He gave a harsh chuckle. "Yeah, that's true." He shook his head. "I can't seem to get out of his sights."

Moose raised an eyebrow.

"It's just ... aw. Nothing."

Silence.

"I just feel sometimes that maybe God is stalking me."

"You've heard of the Good Shepherd, running after his lost sheep, right?"

"Yeah, except ... well, I'm not sure he's interested in rescuing me as much as . . ." And suddenly he couldn't even say it, his throat tight. He lifted a shoulder, looked back out at the river.

"You think God is against you."

He looked away. "He has his reasons."

"Or you have your reasons for not believing he could be on your side."

Oaken's mouth tightened.

"Sometimes when we're trying to rescue someone, they get so panicked they do stupid things. Like jump on us, or even grab the litter before it's ready for them. And it only makes the situation worse. And then we have to untangle them, or even get rough with them—especially if it's a water rescue—so we can actually rescue them."

"I'm not sure God needs to get rough with me to rescue me."

Moose made a sound. "He did with me. It got really rough before I figured out that I didn't have to fight so hard to rescue myself."

Oaken looked at him.

"Listen, I get it. You look at your trouble and think . . . God is against me. But what if he's trying to rescue you?"

"Tell that to Mike Grizz."

"You don't know what God is doing in Mike's story. But he did use it to get you to stick around." Moose checked on the steaks again, then flipped them. Smoke luffed out into the twilight. He turned the bread, then closed the lid again. "Could be he's trying to get you back into the real story he has for your life."

"Real story?"

"There's the story we create and the story we're created for. Maybe that's what this adventure is all about."

"All I see is me trying to fix the mess that God made."

Moose let out a sound something like a chuckle, although Oaken had the sense that he wasn't laughing. "What you have, Oaken, is a vision problem. You see things through the lens of your own perspective, your own goals and hopes and fears. But when you open your eyes to God's view, you might see that the story is a lot different than you think."

Moose grabbed the bread platter, opened the lid, and picked off the bread. Handed the platter to Oaken. "Whatever is going on, you're here now. And from my view, I think it's not by accident." He plated the steaks. "I hope you like them rare."

Oaken smiled and followed Moose inside.

Shep had arrived, with chips. Behind him, London was peeling off her shoes, her jacket.

And behind her, holding a box of Oreos stood . . . Boo.

Well, well. She wore her hair down, a fleece jacket, jeans, and running shoes, and the memory of the woman he'd met in the car a week ago, who had kept him calm and made him believe that everything would be okay, simply snapshotted into his head and stayed there.

Moose set down the steak and leaned over to him. "Bet you like the view now."

He looked at him, and Moose grinned.

Whatever. Oaken turned back and watched Boo hand the Oreos to London, take off her jacket, then her boots.

And he was still looking when she turned to enter, saw him, and smiled.

Yes, interestingly enough, he did like the view.

SIX

BOO DIDN'T DO PARTIES OR GET-TOGETH-ers or even hangouts, and the moment the door had opened to the smell of steaks and garlic bread, to country music playing on the speakers, to laughter from London and Shep, she'd wanted to pivot and run.

Because probably they'd want conversation from her, and maybe even a joke or something, and eventually the conversation might turn serious and . . .

Yeah. Really. What had she been thinking?

And then she'd seen Oaken. Looking at her with something of a smile on his face, and oh boy, the man had a nice smile.

Too nice. And he looked good, too, wearing a pair of jeans and a blue thermal shirt that matched his eyes, and he hadn't shaved, and for a second all she could think about was the way he'd met her gaze right before he went over the cliff in the Shed. Like she might be his lifeline.

Which of course sounded crazy, no matter how she said it in her head, and really, it was simply the conversation in the parking lot four nights ago that had her a little woozy.

Like he might, maybe, care about her and her nightmares.

But seriously, the man had charisma oozing out of his pores. No wonder the world loved him. As they ate dinner at Moose's beautiful table, Oaken told jokes and complimented London on her teaching him how to tie knots—which she deserved—and told stories of being on tour and some of the crazy moments with his band and the fans, and she'd said it before . . . The man was miles out of her league.

So, really, what had she been thinking?

"I'll clean up," she said as soon as the plates were empty. She got up, reaching for London's plate.

"I'll help," said Oaken and also rose, gathering up the plates of Moose, Axel, and Shep.

Oh, perfect.

"I think I need to challenge Shep to a little eight ball," Moose said, carrying over the empty steak plate.

"Let's put fifty on it and I'll really make it hurt." Shep followed with some glasses.

"I don't mind doing the dishes," said Axel.

"You wash, I'll dry," said London.

"No, I'm good." Boo took the glasses from Shep. Set them on the counter. Then she turned on the water in the sink and opened the dishwasher.

Only Oaken stayed to help her, bringing more dishes from the table. She loaded the dishwasher, then ran water to do the platters.

He arrived, towel in hand. "Hit me."

She looked over at him and couldn't stop a smile.

"Two in one day. What's going on?"

She rolled her eyes. "What are you talking about?"

"You know what I'm talking about. We might be becoming friends."

"Don't get excited. I'm not a great friend." She handed him the salad bowl.

"What makes a great friend?"

She grabbed the steak platter. "Someone who, you know, cries with you?"

"I'm not a big crier."

"Someone who goes to your events."

"That's a big ask for a guy like me."

"Maybe. Someone who always has your back."

"I'm starting to think we're besties."

She handed him the bread plate. "Thanks for . . . you know."

"Respecting your privacy. Yeah, that's a big sacrifice. You owe me."

She pulled her hand from the soapy water and shot bubbles at him. He dodged.

"Really? Don't start. You do not want to tangle with me. I did dishes for a year in the college kitchen after I lost my scholarship."

She considered him, then grabbed the steak platter. "What kind of scholarship?"

"Baseball. I was a pitcher."

"What happened?"

"Dislocated my shoulder working at my dad's ranch one summer. Never healed right."

"What, were you bull riding?"

"Nope. Broncs."

She looked at him. He didn't appear to be kidding. "Really."

"Yep." He took the steak platter from her. "My dad works on our family ranch in South Dakota."

"Huh." She pulled the plug on the water, debating another splash. "No wonder you have that cowboy thing going."

"Cowboy thing?"

"All this." She moved her hand in front of him. "Very Yellowstone."

"That's in Wyoming."

"You get what I mean."

He set down the platter. Met her eyes. "I think that might be the nicest thing anyone has ever said to me."

She laughed. "Hardly, Mr. CMT. I know you've won awards." She ran her sponge over the counter. "You have fans all over the world."

He stacked the dry dishes. "Yeah. But no one knows about South Dakota. They all think I grew up in Nashville."

She drained the sink. "Why's that?"

"My mom moved us to Nashvegas when I was eight so my sister could pursue her singing career." He folded the towel and set it on the counter.

"Hollie Montgomery."

He touched his nose. "Good memory."

"I remember hearing about an accident on the news. I was at a school in San Antonio. Something about her going off the road in a blizzard?"

"Yep. They didn't find her until two days later. She froze to death."

Oh. "I'm sorry."

He lifted a shoulder. Crossed his arms over himself.

And the silence between them was why she didn't do conversations or small talk or even—

"I'm glad you came out tonight. Put on pants and everything."

"Pants?"

"My dad is an introvert. He likes long rides with no conversation. I got used to it. But he always says that he needs a mighty good reason to put on pants and leave the house."

She smiled at that. "Yeah. I guess. I get all worked up in my head and worry that I'm going to say something stupid—and usually I do. And then I regret it for weeks. Years. My entire life."

"Aw, c'mon. If you're talking about the Blake thing—it's not that bad."

She stared at him. "It is *that bad*. Always. In my head. In real life. Google *Boo Hoo* and I'll pop up first in images, with a thousand crazy memes. Someone made a meme of my face, crossed out 'drama queen' and wrote my name, and it trended. Boo Hoo became a gif response for anything no one actually cares about. There's a Bored Panda quiz about what crazy person you are, and I'm listed as an option. Believe me, it's that bad."

He raised his eyebrows.

"This is why I should never leave the house." She looked away. "The fact is, I came to Alaska to put all that behind me, and I thought I had until—"

"Until I invaded your life."

"No. Yes. But . . . that's not . . . well, Blake has been texting me." She didn't know why she said that, and now couldn't even look at him.

"Really?"

"Yeah. Three times. Asking to talk." She pulled out her phone, pulled up the text, and showed Oaken.

He took the phone. Read the texts. Handed it back. "Wow. Listen. I have people. We can fix this."

She looked up at him. He wore such a serious face she couldn't stop herself from laughing. "Thanks. You're my hero. But no, you'd have to get in line behind at least two of my brothers. And my sister. And maybe my parents, although I don't know."

"What do you mean, you don't know?"

"I just . . ." *Aw,* how had she gotten *here?* "They're pretty conservative, and when the show came out and Blake said things that made it sound like . . . you know, we . . ."

"Oh."

"And my mom was upset and I got defensive, and then my family sort of took sides, and suddenly . . . Not a great moment. I left shortly after that and haven't been back."

He drew in his breath. "Families . . . are . . . well, my parents aren't divorced, but my mom lives in Florida. My dad in South Dakota.

And I haven't seen either of them for a long time. Not since my dad
told me to get my act together after . . . well, the state fair fiasco.
And Mom said that I'd disgraced Hollie's legacy. So that was fun."

"Sorry."

"Gotta love social media."

"I deleted everything. I'd be happy to be completely off-grid."

"Hard to order pizza that way."

Okay, she liked him. Maybe too much.

Definitely too much. She slid onto a stool.

"You mentioned that you were a Marine, so maybe you don't
need anyone's help. You said you could hurt me."

"I can."

"I have no doubt. Is that where you learned search and rescue?"

"No, but yes. I actually wasn't a Marine. I was in the Navy—
corpsman. But I deployed with a Marine combat unit and had to
learn to survive with them. In training they shot a pig, then went
out on field maneuvers, and I not only had to keep up, but I had
to keep the pig alive."

"Did you?"

"Yep."

"Of course you did."

Oh, he had the charm nailed, didn't he?

He threw his towel over his shoulder, crossed his arms, and
leaned a hip against the counter. "So how did you join *Survivor
Quest*?"

"A dare. From my brother Jack. He's my oldest brother. I told
him how I could keep a pig alive and he said I couldn't keep myself
alive, and I sort of snapped and it went south from there. I made
a video on my phone and sent it off before I could stop myself,
and . . . the rest is history. Disastrous history."

"Listen. If you want to compare disastrous internet stories, I'll
get out my checkbook and show you how much I had to pay in
so-called damages to the jerk who threw a beer at me onstage."

"I googled that. There's a lot of footage."

"Unfortunately."

"He shouldn't have done that. One minute you're singing, the next, beer."

"I know. He said it was because I sang to his girlfriend—but the fact is, I sing to everyone's girlfriend. It's just a song. Just an act. His issues with me had nothing to do with me."

"And yet you jumped off the stage."

"I remember, thank you."

"I'm not blaming you. Listen, I understand—"

He leaned away, held up a hand. "No. Actually. What I did was wrong. I know that. I landed on the guy, got a couple good hits in, and the crowd pulled me back." He sighed. "But it wasn't about the beer for me, either." He hung the towel on the oven handle. The sun had set, and Oaken walked over and opened the door. "It's gorgeous out here."

"And cold."

He reached over, picked up a blanket off the sofa, and tossed it to her.

She caught it and appreciated that he didn't do something cheesy like try to wrap it around her shoulders.

Friends. She could probably do that.

She stepped outside, wrapped in the blanket. He turned off the kitchen light and closed the door behind her.

Moose had set Adirondack chairs around a fire table on the deck. The stars glinted off the surface of the lake, adding more ambiance, and of course she sank down on one of the chairs, Oaken in the other one.

"So, what was it really about?" she asked.

He looked at her, then back at the stars.

"The fight."

"I know what you mean. And . . . let's just say that you're not the only one who has a past that haunts you."

Silence then, and maybe a friend didn't pry. So she stared at the stars, so bright, so close she could reach out and grab one.

"I love Alaska," he said finally. "I can see why you'd like to get lost up here."

"I actually don't want to be *lost*. Just not found."

He nodded and let her have that without prying. Although maybe she wouldn't have minded.

Oh brother. Still, the sway of the wind and lure of the stars and the cozy blanket suggested they'd found a good place. So, "Hey. I remember you telling me that you were having a hard time writing. How's that going?"

More quiet, and then a small hum from the man next to her. She looked over at him. "What is this—inspiration?"

"I think maybe it is." He grinned. "Maybe you're more than a rescuer, Boo. Maybe you're my muse."

"And I think maybe you've had too much to drink."

"Moose is a teetotaler. That was lemonade."

"The altitude had gone to your head."

"We're at sea level."

"Then I'm going to blame the stars."

"Yeah," he said softly. "Blame the stars."

He looked over at her, his eyes fixed on hers, and she simply couldn't look away. And weirdly, it didn't hurt. As if he saw her. Understood her, maybe.

No, that was just crazy.

But that moment held her, a pocket of time, of breath, a space in the universe where the past, the future, even the voices in her head stilled, dropped around her.

Just the deep sounds of the night and Oaken Fox, looking at her with those devastating blue eyes.

Her breath caught.

"Oaken—"

The sliding door behind them opened. Oaken's gaze broke away even as Moose's voice shattered the moment. "Hey, guys—we need to go. We have a callout. Hiker, fell over a cliff."

Boo got up, Oaken right behind her.

She looked at him. "What are you doing?"

"Going with you?"

She drew in a breath, looked at Moose, who stood at the door. "Fine. Yes. But no cameras. You do this right and maybe we film a real rescue."

He smiled, and it did a crazy thing to her insides.

Oh boy. See, this was why she should never put on pants.

Watching the Air One team deploy, gear up, rig the anchoring systems, then descend down to the twenty-some-year-old woman who lay some thirty feet down in the darkness, Oaken almost regretted not calling Huxley.

Then again, Boo had relegated him to holding lights and relaying information to Shep, working the Maestro semi-static downward rescue system.

Boo had explained it to him on the way over—two anchor points, with semi-static ropes that held two climbers—in this case London and Axel. They'd descend, a litter strapped between them, then load it up, and using pulleys, the team would pull them back up top.

"According to the dispatch from the state troopers on the scene, she's fallen on the Thunderbird Falls trail, below the falls. It's too dense to get a chopper in there. There's a canyon trail that runs along the river, on top, and then an overlook over the falls." Boo had pulled out her tablet and zoomed in. "She's not far from the falls. It's about a mile in, and usually there are no vehicles allowed, but we'll go in on our ATVs so we can transfer her out quickly."

Boo had changed into her red rescue jumpsuit at HQ and

checked the medical kit, while Moose and Shep hooked up the ATVs on trailers and London packed the climbing gear. He'd helped Boo check her medical supplies, then loaded them into the rescue vehicle.

Shep drove the rescue vehicle with London in the passenger seat, Boo and Oaken strapped into the side seats, and space in the back for a litter. Moose and Axel towed the ATVs.

When they arrived at the trail head, Shep and London piled onto the ATV while the rest climbed into the four-passenger Polaris, and they took off down the trail, headlights cutting through the forest.

State troopers had set up a perimeter of lights, and it wasn't hard to spot the panicked boyfriend, who met them with explanations and details.

Oaken got then why Boo wasn't keen on Huxley and Beto filming. Too much actual horror. And in the darkness, someone could easily get hurt.

"I need two long-tail interlocking bowlines," London said, handing him two ropes. "We'll hook them onto the bridle on the litter."

He looked at her. "Me?"

"I'll check your work, but yes, you. I need to set up the anchors. Make sure you leave a long tail on both, as they'll be our secondary safety lines."

He nodded and knelt, picking up the lines.

In the distance, the falls shushed the air, and conversation from the team belied swift work. Shep and Moose tied the anchors onto nearby trees, affixing the pulleys and adding the ropes.

Meanwhile, London and Axel stepped into their harnesses and Boo checked them. She, too, wore a harness, probably in case she needed to go down. London checked the work of Shep and Moose while they geared up and then connected to a top safety line.

She checked Oaken's bowline knots, smiled at him, and then

walked over to the litter, now open and rigged with webbing attached together in an X with a carabiner. She connected the bowlines to the central carabiner, then added a short pulley rig with yet another line.

"That's an AZTEK rig," Boo said, startling him. "It keeps the litter at the right distance, allows Axel to move it around. I'll be there in case she needs any immediate care."

He stilled. "I thought London was going."

"After talking to the boyfriend and checking over the edge, we think she's nonverbal, which doesn't bode well. I'm going to go down to assess."

An unexpected fist formed in his chest. He shook it away—she knew what she was doing.

"Put on a harness so you can rope in and watch." She handed him a harness, and he just stared at her.

"Really?"

"You want to deploy on a real rescue someday? You need to watch and learn." Then she winked.

What?

She walked away then, grabbing a walkie and clipping into the semi-static line.

"Let's get the rollercoaster on the edge here for the ropes," London said, and as Oaken donned his harness, Moose set down a metal roller at the edge.

London then walked over, checked his harness, and snapped him into a static line. "It's separate and attached to a different anchor point, but we need you to shine this down the cliff face as they descend." She handed him a massive Maglite.

"I'm on it."

She patted his shoulder. "I knew you'd come in handy."

He looked over and Boo's gaze was on him. She looked away, however, and he watched as she and Axel backed up, the litter in front of them, and stepped over the edge.

He walked right up to the edge, too, and shone the light down near them, just enough to illuminate the cliff.

At the bottom, A woman dressed in a puffy white jacket lay prone, her leg bent at a painful angle. He caught himself holding his breath as they walked down the side, the wall falling another hundred feet beyond the cliff. Mist from the water rose around them, dampening the air.

Her boyfriend stood not far away, such pain on his face that Oaken had to look away.

But he got it. Especially when the team—okay, Boo—landed safely and his chest released.

Calm down. He barely knew the woman.

Except somehow, tonight, she'd started to trust him. And her laughter—even better than her smile. And those eyes—when she'd looked at him under the stars . . .

It was just Alaska and the sense that, up here, he might leave everything behind.

Moose decided then to whisper in his head. *There's the story we create, and the story we're created for. Maybe that's what this adventure is all about.*

"Moose! Slack!" The falls nearly ate her words, but he relayed Boo's shout. Maybe London had picked it up on the radio too, because Moose and Shep eased up on the line.

Boo and Axel had unclipped from the litter, relying on their secondary, and Boo had affixed a C collar onto the woman. They rolled her onto a backboard, eased her onto the litter, then strapped her in.

"How's that pulley reset coming?" London asked. She was on the radio with Axel.

"Almost reset," Moose said.

Below, Boo and Axel reclipped into the AZTEK rigs.

"Okay, pulley is set."

"Let's get them up."

Moose and Shep stood up, each on a line, gloved and belayed in, and began to pull. Axel and Boo held the litter steady and walked up the cliff.

Textbook.

And he was a part of it. Okay, he was holding a flashlight, but he was learning. *"Whatever is going on, you're here now. And from my view, I think it's not by accident."*

And then there was the music. The smallest trickle of a melody inside. He hadn't been kidding when he looked at Boo and called her his muse. And yes, it was meant to be funny, but maybe not.

Boo and Axel reached the top, and London helped pull them in. He stepped back as Boo got to work, taking the woman's vitals—

"Her name is Amber," the man kept saying.

Boo flashed her penlight into Amber's eyes. "We have good pupil reaction. And her blood pressure is stable. Let's get her on the ATV."

A sound came from Amber then, and her boyfriend stepped in, grabbed her hand. "I want to go with her."

"Sure thing," Moose said and clamped him on the shoulder.

It wasn't until after they moved her to the ATV that Oaken did the math.

"I guess we're walking out," said Axel.

"Naw, you guys wait here. I'll come back for you," Moose said.

Oaken watched as Boo climbed into the four-person Polaris, her hands on the litter. She looked up and met his gaze a moment before they pulled out.

He lifted his hand, then gave her a thumbs-up.

And got a nod, along with another smile.

Yeah, he'd count this as a win in his book.

The next morning, not so much.

"You're kidding me, right? You went on a callout and didn't tell us?" Huxley stood in the main area of Air One Rescue, holding a cup of coffee, her hair back in a handkerchief, her green eyes on fire. Behind her, Beto tried to make himself invisible.

Outside, a light rain had started to fall, the sky dour despite the morning hour.

"Listen, Huxley, it was nearly midnight before we got to the site, and it took three-plus hours to haul her out. You would have hated the lighting, and the fact is, with so many state troopers on scene, you wouldn't have gotten a good shot. Besides, all I did was hold a flashlight."

Huxley narrowed her eyes at him, her jaw tight. She took a sip of her coffee. Looked past him to where Moose sat in his office, typing on his computer. The rest of the crew, except Boo, hadn't arrived yet. But Oaken had been buzzing with adrenaline and hitched a ride with Moose this morning.

It had nothing at all to do with seeing Boo. Nothing.

"I'm going to talk to Moose. This is almost breach of contract. You do this again and the show is over. You'll owe the production company the cost of filming to date. And believe me, we'll collect. And forget about the 50K for Maggie's Miracle."

He stared at her as she marched past him and headed into Moose's office. Shut the door.

"She's like Tinker Bell—small but fierce."

He turned. Boo had come out of the workout room, a towel around her neck, holding a water bottle.

He pinched his mouth and nodded, trying to hide a crazy smile.

So, she couldn't sleep either apparently.

He picked up his bag of clean workout clothes and headed into the locker room. Changed and then emerged. Huxley was still in with Moose. Beto had helped himself to a cup of coffee, now sat at the table staring at his phone.

Oaken headed back to the weight room.

Boo was on the bike, pedaling hard, her earbuds in. She took one out and set it on the tray in front of her. "You good?"

He walked over to the treadmill, climbed aboard and turned it on.

A line of mirrors along one wall near the weight set reflected back a vision of his tired self. But weirdly, despite only three hours of sleep, a buzz of energy sluiced his veins.

"How's the woman we rescued?"

"She roused on the way to the hospital. Once we got there, she gave a statement to the police. Apparently, she was ahead of her boyfriend on the trail and spotted a bear. It was eating what she thought looked like a body."

He looked over at her, his pace in warm-up. "An animal?"

"A person. A woman. I think the state troopers went back to check it out. But that sort of thing happens here sometimes. Someone goes missing during the winter, is never found, and then in the spring, during the thaw . . ." She made a face.

He popped up his speed, settled into a jog.

"Huxley is pretty steamed."

"Yep." A flatscreen played the morning news, the sound off, closed captions on. They were reporting on the weather—a few days of thaw with a snow front coming in.

"They'd really fine you for not doing the show?"

"It's in the contract—so maybe."

"Who's Maggie, and what's her miracle?"

He glanced at her through the mirror.

She had her head down, pedaling hard.

He popped up his speed and let the sound of his slapping feet fill the room.

When he reached the two-mile mark, he lowered the speed to a walk, then finally stepped off the treadmill, his pulse thundering. He checked it and then grabbed a towel and wiped the sweat from his face.

She'd slowed her pedaling too.

"Maggie Bloom and her mother were in the car that my sister

hit on the highway. They spun off onto the other side of the road. Maggie was eight and suffered a spinal-cord injury. Because it took so long for anyone to find them, by the time they did, she had so much swelling—the injury paralyzed her."

He said it all without looking at her. But she'd gotten off her bike and now came to stand in front of him, holding her water bottle.

"Maggie's mom was a single mom, so their church and community really came around them, and because of it, Maggie got great care. She's been in rehabilitation for eight years and now has full use of her upper body. She got some kind of stimulation implant a while back, and that's helping. Because of all of it, Maggie's mom started a charitable organization to help others with similar injuries."

"You were doing *Go Wild with Grizz* to donate to that."

"Fifty thousand, if I could finish the fifty hours. Which I didn't. And apparently they aren't into charity. Funds are tight over at Grizz Productions. But they'll honor their commitment if . . ."

"If you and Moose let them film their show—which means coming on a real rescue."

"Yeah."

She took a drink, then wiped her mouth, her gaze on him. "Well then, I think we need to give them a show."

Then she smiled, and despite the fatigue and the dour day, the sunshine came out and filled his soul.

SEVEN

NO ONE HAD TO KNOW.

Okay, the team knew. And Oaken knew.

And of course her cousin Larke and her husband, Riley, knew, but so far they'd kept the operation details on the DL from Huxley and Beto.

Maybe they'd even pull it off.

"I see him!" Boo held on to the winch at the top of the open door of the chopper, the cold air buffeting her jumpsuit as she searched the river gorge for their "victim," a.k.a. her cousin-in-law, Riley McCord. But his security clearance as an active-duty SEAL meant he had a steel vault for secrets.

And the Air One team was diving full-on into her brilliant plan to put on a show using her cousins from the north.

Please, let it be brilliant.

Below, the raucous rush of the Copper River dropped some thirty feet from a rocky waterfall to a pool below, where rocky islands jutted to the surface like so many stepping stones. A frothy pool of foam and whitewater jettied around them, dangerous whirlpools.

Just downriver some sixty feet from the spray of a waterfall, just beyond the protection of a granite boulder, an ATV sat half submerged and upside down, all-terrain wheels up.

And on its undercarriage, stranded, their victim balanced out of the water.

The ATV had gone over long ago, but Air One used the abandoned vehicle for training every year. Now Riley poised on it like a hapless adventurer, dressed in a helmet, orange hunting coat, canvas pants, and boots. He looked dry, but her guess was that he'd gotten wet during his trip via kayak to the ATV, having been deposited there by her cousin Dodge, who'd finished paddling downstream and gone ashore at a tall bridge.

No doubt her cousin watched via binoculars.

Now Riley sat, helpless, alone, scared, waiting like a gift for Air One to pluck out of danger.

It would look fantastic on camera.

Most importantly, they'd squeeze in serious training with a so-called live rescue, and everyone could go home happy.

Or that's at least how she'd pitched it to Moose, who seemed on the grizzly side after his showdown with Huxley.

So, yeah, no one from the production team needed to know better.

And as for Air One, Riley was all too happy to get in on the gig before heading back to Pensacola. Besides, as a SEAL, he was better equipped than anyone to self-rescue should things actually go south. And being former military, Dodge refused to be left out of the action.

The camera on the chopper caught the victim below, and Oaken's helmet cam would capture his descent. But just for extra footage, Moose allowed them to attach a camera to the hoist.

Beto and Huxley, safely on the cliffside above the river, would film the high-angle rescue from afar.

SUSAN MAY WARREN

But they'd miked up Oaken, and Boo had no doubt that his mic also caught her voice as she shouted directions at Moose.

"Bring us around over the rock!" Boo shouted. "I see him below. He seems to be uninjured."

Indeed, Riley played his part, waving almost frantically for help. She'd had to practically accept bribes from Dodge and Riley as to who would get the privilege of going into the water.

Although, with the glacial run still icy cold, she'd promised Riley no dunking. Now she turned to Oaken and ran down the particulars for the camera while she double-checked his rig.

"He managed to climb out of the car, but as you can see, any longer down there and he'll be hypothermic. I'm going to lower you down just like we trained. You get him into the basket, and then we'll pull you back up."

Oaken gave her a thumbs-up.

She wore her visor down but caught his smile even as he put his down.

Okay, she might have had too much fun planning the entire thing with him. In fact, hanging around Oaken had felt almost easy after that night at Moose's.

Or maybe after he'd told her about Maggie and the way he had invested in her healing. That didn't sound like a guy out for his own fame.

"Step out onto the skids."

He did so, and she leaned out, her safety line attached to the chopper, and helped maneuver the egg basket, named for its shape, out with him. His harness attached to the basket, and the entire rig attached to a cable. Next to her, Shep worked the winch.

"Try to keep my feet dry, will you, Moose?" Oaken said through the radio.

She had to give him kudos—he'd come far from that first day in the Shed. Despite the training scenario, any number of disasters could send the chopper, or the line, into the nearby cliffside.

"Okay, easy forward, easy left," she said, watching as Oaken descended. "We're still quite a ways up—easy . . . Hold there. He's about sixty feet up."

Overhead, the sky cast blue, but dark clouds tumbled out of the Alaska Range to the north, sending before it a brisk wind forecast. So far, it hadn't messed with the chopper, but she didn't want to take chances. "Oaken, how are you doing?"

"Good."

"Okay, Moose, easy back now. Hold . . ."

Moose was a needle threader with the chopper, and although they hadn't had many rescues that had necessitated the chopper since she'd arrived, she appreciated his skills. No wonder he had that small rack of medals on his desk.

"I'm nearly there." Oaken.

"Ten feet. Easy right, Moose. Hold there."

Oaken reached out a foot and touched the rock.

"Stop, Shep."

"I'm on the rock," Oaken said.

"Careful, Oaken. You're pretty precarious there. A wrong step could put you both in the water."

What the cameras probably couldn't pick up was the wetsuit under Riley's clothing. Just in case he went in, she wanted some protection from the frigid water.

Oaken, however, wore a dry suit, a nonnegotiable. Now he braced himself on the rock and steadied the egg for Riley to climb into. It had a flat bottom, but the shape cocooned him in for extraction. Safe and efficient, it was used when the victim showed limited or no injuries.

"Give him a little slack," Boo said to Shep, seeing the egg twist. Shep let it down, and it settled onto the ATV carriage.

Riley slipped inside.

"All right, let's get some tension on the line," Boo said, watching as Oaken snapped him into the egg. He looked up and gave her a thumbs-up.

"Going up in three, two, one. Power and controllability look good, Moose. Let's bring it up and then over."

Shep winched up the cable as Moose lifted the chopper.

"We've cleared the cliff. Bring the basket up easy, and forward. Now left."

The wind caught the basket as the chopper drew it out of the gorge, and it swung.

"Not too fast, Moose."

He eased the chopper over toward the cliffside.

Huxley, Beto, and the rest of the Air One crew, all dressed in bright red jumpsuits and helmets, waited, on the ready for their "patient." They'd driven in on ATVs and would transport him to the rescue truck, then up to the hospital in Copper Mountain, which was closer than Anchorage.

And away from the scrutiny of the camera.

In truth, Dodge and Larke waited in Dodge's truck on the other side of the river. Boo probably owed Riley a pizza, despite his begging to be the patsy.

"Almost there, Moose. Easy left—"

The forecasted gust hit. Just swept down the canyon through the trees, and in a second, it slammed against the chopper, took the egg, and swept them askew.

Moose fought the controls, rising up, then righting the chopper, but below, the cable swung in a crazy, wide loop.

And then the egg began to spin.

Boo had been leaning out, and the sudden jerk had pushed her off the deck. She fell, slammed against the skid, her harness catching her but her helmet thwacking against the struts.

Heat exploded up her arm, and the wind burst out of her. She gasped, the world spinning.

"Boo!"

Shep's voice. It cleared out the clutter, and she blinked away the gray.

She was flopping against the struts, her feet missing the skids as the chopper pitched, spun. Looking up, she found the deck, and Shep's hand.

Grabbed it.

He hauled her back inside as Moose righted the chopper, evened it out.

She rolled inside, lay for a moment, breathing hard, the juice still hot in her veins.

Then she scrambled around, still prone, and looked out.

The cable still spun, but somehow Oaken had gotten his knees into the basket, his arms around the edge of the egg, cocooning it and its cargo in his embrace.

Now he and Riley rode the carnival ride around and around.

It was too dangerous to put down. But the longer they stayed up here, the more likely they'd be hit again.

"Axel, can you grab the egg as it comes down? Without getting swept off the cliff?"

She spotted Axel and London on the cliffside, backing away from the spinning egg.

London came on the line. "Tell Oaken to drop his secondary line. We can steady him as he comes down."

"Oaken?"

"Yep, I got it." He was already digging into the pouch at his hip, the one that held the coiled rope attached to his harness. As she watched, he dropped it down, then unclipped the rope from himself and reclipped it onto the egg.

Smart. Because the last thing they wanted was for him to get wrapped up in the rope.

Axel grabbed the rope's end.

London had affixed a piece of webbing to the ATV hitch, attached a carabiner to it, and now ran the rope through it. Not tied down, they could let the rope go and the chopper would be free. Now Axel simply held it taut as Moose lowered them to the ground.

"Easy."

The basket stopped spinning.

Oaken eased off it and stepped back, unhooked Riley, who tumbled out.

London helped their victim over to the ATV and began to assess him.

Axel unclipped the rope, and Oaken wound it up even as Shep brought him up. He'd tucked the length into his pouch by the time he reached the skids. Boo grabbed the cable and brought him in, onto the deck. Clipped him into the safety line and off the cable.

"All clear, Moose," she said.

Below, Huxley and Beto filmed London and Axel helping Riley into the Polaris.

Moose angled them away from the river and she closed the door. Sat back.

"Let me look at that arm," said Shep into the mic, but she held up her hand.

"I'm fine."

"You hit the strut pretty hard."

"I'm okay." She lifted her visor. Smiled at Oaken.

He wasn't smiling. "How hurt are you?"

She shook her head. Because yes, she hurt, but the last thing she wanted was Huxley hearing their discourse.

They rode in silence back to Anchorage, some thirty minutes away. She watched the storm clouds pour over the mountains, turn the sky dark.

Okay, so it hadn't gone quite as swimmingly . . .

Oh, who was she kidding? She could have gotten Oaken killed. So much for her bright ideas.

He nudged her with his foot, and she looked over at him. He frowned.

She looked away.

She wasn't sure what it was—why whenever she tried to do something, well, *good,* it went south.

They landed on the Air One square at Merrill Field, and she got out, holding on to her helmet, her emergency medical kit.

"I'll get that," said Oaken, coming up beside her. He held his helmet in one hand, a ropes bag over his shoulder, and now grabbed her kit.

"I got—okay. Knock yourself out."

He said nothing until they got inside the Tooth.

She had her jumpsuit off, dressed in only her thermals when he returned from dropping the bags off in the gear room.

"Let me see your arm."

She looked over at him. He had stripped off the dry suit down to a pair of long johns, workout shorts, and a thermal shirt. And of course, it showed off all those rescue muscles. Not to mention the skim of whiskers on his chin—probably designed for today's on-camera interview, but it didn't hurt his stun factor.

Now he sat on the bench next to her and leveled those blue eyes on her.

"It's nothing." But she didn't recognize the look he gave her.

Or maybe she did. The same look he'd worn when they'd found Mike tucked under a cave, wounded and maybe dead.

She couldn't remember ever being under that much scrutiny—or rather, the caring kind of scrutiny. Staff Sergeant Hecktor, her Marine squad leader, had given her plenty of scrutiny during her early days.

At the end, of course, he'd given her his life.

"Of course it's something," Oaken said, his tone a little terse. "You hit that strut pretty hard—I saw it. Show me. I know you have a tank under your thermal—so . . ." He raised an eyebrow.

"Fine." She pulled off her outer layer. She did wear a tank underneath, and okay, as she moved her arm down, she grunted.

"Yowza," he said, gripping her elbow. "That's a serious bruise."

She angled her head, tried to see the darkened, raised hematoma.

"I'm getting you some ice. It's probably too late, but maybe we can stop some of the deep bruising."

He got up and headed out of the room.

She angled toward the mirror. Yeah, that did look mean. She'd hit her bicep, and a fist-sized bump rose from the side of her arm, blackened, deep purple, and red.

"Here we go." Oaken carried an ice pack wrapped in a cloth sleeve and now wrapped it around her arm, pulling it taut and velcroing tight. "Now, some ibuprofen."

Opening his locker, he took out his backpack and dug in the outer pocket. Found a container and slapped out a couple pills. Handed them to her, then cracked open a bottle of water.

"You're quite the medic." She downed the meds. "And you did great out there today. Hopping onto the egg like that—almost like you were the real thing."

She knew, as soon as the words emerged, that they hit wrong. He drew in his breath, forced a smile, nodded.

"Oh, Oak—I ... I'm sorry. I—"

"I know what you meant."

"No, actually, you're becoming a fantastic rescue tech. I have to admit, when Moose suggested this whole gig, I just thought ... you know ... someone was going to get hurt."

He made a face.

"No—I wasn't thinking of me. I mean, maybe a little, but really, I meant ... you. I worried *you* would get hurt."

"I'm not sure if that's sweet or incredibly emasculating."

A beat, and then, "Oh, yeah. I guess ... it does sound that way. I just ... you're not what I thought, is all."

"I hope that's a good thing."

She sighed. "Yeah. I'm sorry about today. It could have really gone south."

He sat down again. "Agreed. It's a good thing Riley is cool-headed." He looked at her. "It wasn't a bad idea. I think Huxley and Beto really got a lot of great footage." He held up his fist.

She hesitated a moment, then bumped it. Weird how he made all the knots inside her loosen, helped her breathe.

"You hungry?" He reached for a towel and slung it over his shoulder.

"I could eat," she said, standing up.

"Moose keeps talking about this place called the Tenderfoot. Good food?"

"I dunno. Never been there."

He looked at her.

"I told you—I don't do hanging out." Except, now the idea didn't seem so suffocating. Not with Oaken and the stupid handsome way that he smiled at her.

Aw, this could be Blake all over again. "Maybe—"

"I'm going to take a shower. Then we have a date." He winked. *Oh. Oh no.*

She watched him walk away to the private showers, not sure if she should run. Probably, yes.

Changing into a pair of jeans and a pullover, she refitted the ice pack on her arm, let her hair down and brushed it, and then headed out into the main room.

Moose had come in and was seated at the table, working on his laptop, nursing a cup of coffee.

"What are you doing?"

"Incident report. Just . . . dotting the i's for our board." He looked up at her. "You did a great job staying calm out there. How's the arm?"

"It'll mend." She sighed.

He put down his pen. "What's going on?"

Oops. "Oh, I . . ." She shook her head. "Just thinking about how my best intentions go south. I just can't seem to get it right."

He stared at her. "Boo. Today's wind shear wasn't your fault."

"I heard the weather forecast—"

"You can't predict wind. We can look out for it and take care to stay safe, but . . . wind happens."

"Right. I just . . ." She looked past him toward the closed door to the locker room.

"You're afraid Oaken will get hurt."

In more ways than one. She nodded.

"Because he likes you. And you like him."

She looked at Moose.

"Now *you* have the look."

"I don't—I . . . we're co-workers."

"Yep. Like my favorite waitress."

She smiled. "You going to ask her out?"

"Dunno yet. Maybe. But . . ." He leaned back in his chair. "Oaken has been good for you. It's nice to hear you laugh. You keep too much bottled up."

"Trust me, you want all this bottled up."

He didn't laugh at her poor attempt at humor.

"There's nothing wrong with letting someone into your life, Boo. Trusting them. You don't always have to hold your emotions so tight to your chest."

She considered him a moment, the words working through her. "I don't even know what that looks like," she said, and couldn't believe that whispered out.

"Maybe you give it a try," he said, equally soft.

The door opened, and Mr. Country Music walked out of the locker room, his hair still a little wet, wearing a denim shirt over his thermal undershirt, a pair of jeans, hiking boots, and a leather jacket.

And no Huxley in sight.

"Ready?" he asked.

Moose looked at him. "Where are you going?"

"Tenderfoot," Boo said, but her voice sounded strange.

Probably because no, she wasn't ready at all.

Moose smiled. "Oh. It's karaoke night. Have fun."

She and Oaken frowned at him, but he just leaned forward and starting typing.

"I worried you would get hurt."

Somehow Oaken couldn't get those words out of his head the entire drive over to the Tenderfoot. Mostly because that's exactly what he'd thought when he saw her slam against the chopper. And then again when he got a good look at that bruise.

It bothered him more than he wanted to admit. Another person getting hurt because of him? Or at least while they were with him?

But in truth, if he took a look at the reasons why he'd stuck with this crazy project, probably yes, this was all his fault. Because he was selfish. And maybe a coward. And weak. And probably stubborn. And most of all, worried too much about disappointing the wrong people. At least, that was his current list, based on the comments of too many followers.

And yet, still, here he sat, hoping to make her laugh, ignoring the fact that he should walk away from her, and probably from the whole show.

Because the last person he wanted hurt was Boo Kingston.

Still, he pulled up to the Tenderfoot, glancing over at her with a grin as he heard country music pouring out from under the door. "This sounds like my kind of place."

"Apparently," she said and got out.

"I can't believe you've never been here before." He closed his door, locked it.

Vehicles packed the parking lot, tall lights casting down over more pickup trucks than all of South Dakota, and that was saying something. A long front porch flanked the front of the building, where a couple Alaskan cowboys lounged, the red eyes of their cigarettes glowing against the twilight.

As he approached the long log building, he recognized the song as one by Chris Stapleton, "Fire Away," and something just sort of tugged at his soul.

He held the door open, and Boo walked inside ahead of him.

Bigger on the inside, the place hosted a stage at one end of the building, with a man at the mic crooning out Stapleton's cover. Men and women in flannel and jeans crowded the long bar, every round high-top chair occupied. A few more high-top tables crowded the center, with booths affixed around the room. At the other end, more patrons crowded the two pool tables, some of them laughing at the apparent smack talk.

The smell of fries and cheese curds and everything deep fried hung in the air. And above the bar, a row of flatscreens played all manner of sports—hockey, baseball, soccer, and even a fishing show from the lower forty-eight. Made his mind go to his father and his annual fishing trip to northern Minnesota.

Maybe he could consider . . .

He shook the thought away and followed Boo. A couple slid out of their booth and Boo claimed it. He slid in opposite her. "Good nab."

A female server walked up, cleared the glasses, and wiped the table. Threw down a couple coasters. "What do you want to drink?"

"Do you have chocolate milk?" Oaken said.

The woman considered him. "I'll check."

"I'll take a Coke," said Boo. "And maybe something really fattening, like a pile of those fries." She pointed to another server walking with glistening fries and O-rings.

"And the rings," Oaken said. He leaned in when the waitress left. "I like how you order."

She laughed. "Moose says I eat like a two-year-old. But I like junk food after a rescue."

"So how did you go from being a medic with the Marines to this rescue gig?"

Another song came on—"H.O.L.Y." by Florida Georgia Line. He hummed along.

"After the survival show and the fiasco with my parents, I just needed to get away. I hadn't really considered the SAR option, although I had met a private SAR team the summer a tornado came through our town. They were from Montana and helped rescue some local high school kids who'd been trapped. I was on leave from the military at the time and thought I'd be a lifer. So it wasn't on my radar at all. But then suddenly I was back in Minnesota, not sure what to do with my life. My cousin Ranger and his wife, Noemi, had moved to Minneapolis, and my brother Steinbeck was hanging out with him, so I went along. And pretty soon Ranger was calling up Dodge, and a few days later, I was moving in with London and training in the snow."

"Steinbeck? After the author?"

"All my siblings are named after literary giants. My sister is Austen, I have a brother Jack—"

"After Jack London?"

"Yep. And Doyle."

"Sherlock."

"Yep. And Conrad, after Joseph Conrad."

"*The Heart of Darkness*. Wow."

"Apparently Mom read it in college. It really impacted her. Said that no person should be alone in the wilderness. I agree."

"Says the rescuer." He smiled at her, leaned back as the waitress brought their drinks.

"One chocolate milk." The waitress set down a frothy cup in front of him. She put a Coke in front of Boo and dropped a couple of straws.

Boo unpeeled her straw. "Yeah, well, it's not just that. When I was eight, I was lost for two days in the wilderness."

"Seriously?"

"Yeah. We were on a family canoe trip, and we'd set off on a two-mile portage. My dad and my brothers were carrying the canoes, and he told me, my sister, and my mother to go ahead. I was first and maybe a little stubborn—"

"You?"

He got a smile. And a twinkle in her eyes.

"And being the youngest, I had something to prove, so I kept walking. Except, I took a wrong turn somewhere, and suddenly I was lost. Really lost. I couldn't find my way back, and I got turned around and . . . anyway, they had to call the Forest Service, and it became a massive search in the woods."

"Wow. That's terrifying."

"Yeah. But see"—she leaned forward—"I was carrying the sleeping-bags pack. So I just got into all the sleeping bags and stayed put, and eventually they found me."

"Smart."

"Scared."

He could imagine her then, eight years old, just her face sticking out of a sleeping bag, listening to the night sounds.

"I did learn that I was pretty resourceful, however. And—not to panic. If I'd kept moving around in the woods, they might have never found me. So . . . lesson learned—when you're lost, get to a trail or someplace where people can find you, and stay there."

"Thanks, Ranger Rick."

"Hey, I used to get that magazine."

He took a drink. Got a mustache and wiped it off.

She laughed at that. It felt so easy, like it had always been this way between them.

"So, who is Boo the famous author?"

She considered him. Then shook her head.

"Aw, really?"

"Maybe someday." She sipped her Coke but kept a smile. "What's with the milk?"

"It's better than whiskey."

She raised an eyebrow and he smiled, also keeping the rest to himself.

She rolled her eyes. "When are those fries getting here? I'm starved."

"I'm still full from last night. Moose is a great cook. Last night we had grilled chicken and Caesar salad." He leaned back. "I may never leave."

She folded her arms. "What? And give up your life in music?"

Her words, however, had pinged inside him. *Yeah, maybe.* He drew in a breath and glanced at the next singer. Of course, a Brett Young cover of "In Case You Didn't Know." The guy had a rabid following.

"Oh boy."

He looked at Boo. "What?"

"That face—is your creativity still blocked?"

Actually, no. "I got some music down last night. Toying with lyrics."

"Really? That's great."

She probably didn't know how pretty she was, without even trying.

"Yeah. My manager, Goldie, sent me an email a few days ago, and for the first time in a long time I answered her. I might actually figure this out."

Except her question stuck inside him. *"Give up your life in music?"* Dangerous how much he suddenly liked the idea.

"So, have you been playing music since you were two or something?"

He laughed. "No. That was my sister, Hollie. She picked up a guitar when she was about four years old, mostly because my dad played, just for fun, and she was daddy's girl. He taught her how to play, and then she started singing and getting really good, and then she won a talent contest in Aberdeen. My mom got really excited and decided that she needed to move to Nashville to help Hollie get started."

"That's a bold move."

"My dad didn't agree. He played music, but he wasn't the guy to get onstage, and he especially didn't like the idea of leaving the ranch . . . So my mom packed up me and Hollie and left him."

And he hadn't realized how brutal those words sounded until they came out and he saw them reflected in Boo's eyes.

"Wow."

"Yeah. They never got divorced, but my dad . . . he never got over it. I think my mom thought he'd someday move to her, and he thought she'd come home and . . . She lives in Florida now. He still works the ranch."

"And they're still married."

"Yep."

"That's . . . really sad."

"It is. We'd spend Christmases with him, and I spent most of my summers with him on the ranch. I loved it—always thought I'd be a cowboy. We'd ride fence for days, camp out under the stars. It was . . . peaceful."

"So how did you start singing?"

He took a drink, and for a second considered something stronger. But after the state fair fiasco . . . *Yeah, no.* He didn't need to be that out of control ever again. "I mentioned that I tore out my shoulder, lost my baseball scholarship, right? Instead of going to the ranch, I went back to Nashville and started playing the guitar. My dad taught me too, on all those camping trips."

She had leaned forward, her chin on her hand, listening, her dark hair draping around her face. He had the strangest urge to push it back, tuck it behind her ear.

Take a step back there, cowboy.

"After Hollie died, some people in Nashville were putting on a memorial concert for her, and her manager, Goldie, called me up and . . . apparently Hollie had told her that I could sing. So she asked if I'd play one of Hollie's songs. I don't know why I said yes. I think . . . maybe for my mom. She was so wrecked. So I played one of Hollie's favorites, and the next day Goldie offered me a contract for representation."

"That easy."

"Yeah, well, the first year all I did were Hollie's covers, so that wasn't fun."

Boo made a face. "Nope."

"Yeah. But I wrote my own songs, got out of purgatory, and then Goldie signed me with Wild Mountain Records, which happened to be run by Ben King, Hollie's old partner, and he sorted me out. He's a good guy. Was still touring at the time, and I opened for him a few times, then went out with a couple big names—and suddenly I had my own gigs."

"And your own number-one songs." She nodded toward the stage, and sure enough, someone had requested "She's My Girl."

"Oh no." He ducked his head.

She got up and walked around to his side. "Scoot in. I want to see if he butchers it."

Oaken glanced at her and slid in.

Right about then, the waitress appeared with their fries, the O-rings. Plunked ketchup on the table. "Anything else?"

Boo looked up at her. "You know who sings this song?"

The woman sighed. "Uh, yeah. Oaken Fox, I think. It's a favorite."

"Yeah, it is," Boo said as the waitress walked away. She looked at him, grinning.

He sat in the semi-darkness as a younger guy got up, took the stage, bobbed his head a few times, then leaned into the mic and dove into the song.

Out on a dusty road, my heart was alone.
Life's twists and turns had left me on my own.
Then she walked into my world, like a shining pearl.
With every step, my broken heart she unfurled.

His gaze was on the crooner, maybe early twenties, grinning at someone in a nearby booth. *Aw,* this song was for her.

"He's not bad." Boo reached for a fry. Dunked it into the ketchup.

"This was one of my first songs. It's a little corny." The kid hit the chorus, and Oaken hummed a little.

She's my girl, my guiding light.
In her arms, everything feels right.
With her love, I've found my place,
Blessed each day by her sweet embrace.

"I think it's romantic. And sweet. Who is it about?"
He drew in a breath. Looked at her. *Oh . . . um . . .*
"Oaken?"
"Nobody. It was just . . . you know. A young man's fantasy."

Her laughter's like a song, a melody so pure.
In her eyes, I see a love that will endure.
Through stormy nights and sunny days,

She's the anchor that keeps me from drifting away.

Boo looked over at him. "Oaken Fox, the romantic."

"Oaken Fox, the man who knows how to make money."

She laughed, and there it was.

The song he wanted. It hit him like the sunshine, a burst of heat inside him. He almost gasped. Swallowed.

She *was* his muse. He could almost hear the entire song, the words rich in his mind even as he stared at her.

"Wow, you're pretty."

She blinked at him. Turned and looked at the singer onstage, breathing. Wide-eyed.

Aw.

And the singer didn't make it easier.

I thank the stars above for this love so true.
Grateful for every moment, every "I love you."
Hand in hand, we'll face this world as one.
With her by my side, our journey's just begun.

Okay, now he'd made it weird. So he reached for the ketchup, made a pocket in the fries, and poured it in.

It squirted out everywhere, across the table, splattering him. And her.

"Oh!"

"Sorry!" He set down the container. "Aw—"

She picked up the ketchup. Put it over her shoulder and aimed it at him.

And just like that, he got doused.

"What—hey!"

She started laughing.

Oh, wow, he didn't stand a chance.

"Seriously?" He reached around her, wrestling for the ketchup, but she held it away, jamming her elbow into his ribs, trying to spray him again. He grabbed ahold of her wrist, shooting it away from him—

"What are you two—wow. Just wow."

He froze. Looked over. Huxley stepped back to dodge more ketchup.

She wasn't laughing.

He let go of Boo. "Hey, Hux."

She stared at both of them, and he couldn't help the strangest feeling of being actually in trouble.

"Want a fry?"

"What I'd like is the truth."

He froze.

Boo picked up a napkin and started to wipe ketchup from her shirt.

"You guys must think I'm stupid. That I wouldn't do my due diligence and figure out that today's victim was actually Boo's cousin."

"Not technically. He's *married* to my cousin."

Oh, Boo. Stop. Talking.

Huxley could take her apart with a look.

To his surprise, Boo stared back. "Listen. You wanted a real rescue. You got one."

"He wasn't in danger."

"He absolutely was in danger. And if you missed it, the chopper could have gone down. You got great footage and even a signed waiver from Riley. So I'm not sure what the problem is here."

"The problem is that we want real reactions, from real people, telling real stories—"

"That could get people real hurt." The words came from Oaken. He thought.

Boo turned and looked at him.

Yep, he'd said that and now picked up a napkin to wipe the ketchup from his cheek, staring at Huxley. "The fact is, I'm not a rescue tech. Yeah, I figured out how to get the basket down safely, but that's the furthest extent of my skills. You want a real rescue story—you should follow the real heroes."

Huxley looked at Boo. "What do you think of that?"

"I think you leave her out of it," Oaken said. He pushed Boo a little, and she scooted out of the booth. Yeah, she was pretty soaked.

He pulled out his wallet, found a couple twenties, and put them on the table. Turned to Huxley. "One more week of footage. If you get a real rescue in by then, great. If not, my contract is done—and we're done. But you should know, I'm not risking anyone's life. And I'm happy to get on camera to tell that to the world. C'mon, Boo."

He grabbed her hand then, just to make sure she followed him, and led them out of the Tenderfoot, into the cool air. It had started to drizzle, the temperatures frigid.

He walked them to his car.

"That was epic," she said.

He glanced at her. "The ketchup?"

She smiled. "Yeah. The ketchup."

He unlocked his car and slid inside. She got in the passenger side. Stayed quiet as he pulled out onto the highway, back toward the Tooth. Ahead, the Eagle River ran under the bridge, glinting black under the lethal drizzle. He drove under the speed limit.

A van passed him, too fast in his opinion. But maybe he just wanted to figure out what had happened back there before they got back.

How, again, he'd screwed up. "You okay?" he finally asked.

"You meant it."

He looked at her. "Meant what?"

She drew in a breath, and if he wasn't mistaken, her eyes glistened.

What?

"You meant it when you said you'd watch my back."

He blinked at her. "Of course I—"

"Oaken!" She slammed her hand on the front of the dash. He turned—the van had started to slide in front of him, and he hit his brakes.

Black ice.

The rental slid and he eased up on the gas, righted it, touched the brakes again.

Ahead of them, the van kept careening, crashing against the guard rail, bouncing off—

"Oaken, look out!"

He steered out of the way, barely missing the van as it crossed the median.

His car came to a stop.

The van hit the far railing, blew it apart, and flew out over the edge . . . and into the frigid waters of the Eagle River.

"Chocolate shake or coffee?"

Moose looked up from his phone to see Tillie standing at his table. When he'd come in, she'd been serving a group of bush pilots laughing loudly about some recent exploit. Reminded him of the after-mission cooldowns with his Navy buddies.

Now he just kept rewinding today's training through his brain. The team handled it well—even with today's wind shear.

He'd been easy, no problem, in front of Boo, but the entire thing could have gone south—"Chocolate shake, I think."

Tillie narrowed her eyes at him. "Really?"

"I don't know." He leaned back. "Maybe . . . a mocha shake?"

She laughed. "Right. We have fresh apple pie tonight."

"You're singing my song."

"Fries, midnight chicken?"

"Let's change it up." He pointed to the stack of onion rings set in front of the bush pilots.

"Really?" She wore her hair back in a messy bun tonight, no makeup, her dark eyes twinkling. "Living on the wild side."

He thought of his conversation with Boo, about her eating like a toddler. Well, sometimes he just wanted to throw caution to the wind.

"Yeah. And maybe . . . I dunno. You want to share them with me?"

Her eyes widened. "Um."

Oh, he was an idiot. But his answer to Boo about asking Tillie out sort of stuck inside him, a gut response that clearly he shouldn't have acted on.

"Sorry—"

"I have a break coming up. I'll sit with you for five."

He smiled.

She smiled back. "I'll get that shake."

He leaned back, setting his phone down. Maybe this was a stupid idea, this reality show. What if they did have a rescue that went south? The world would know—and frankly, it was bound to happen, right?

Yeah, this show could be his demise.

She returned with the shake. "O-rings will be out in a minute. Let me just check on my other table . . ."

He watched her walk away, his heart rate maybe a little too fast at the idea of her sitting down, actually having a conversation with him.

And then what? He'd ask her out? *Just take a breath here, pal.*

But then she came over, setting the onion rings in front of him. Taking off her apron, she wadded it into a ball and slid into the booth.

He shoved the plate toward her, then handed her the ketchup.

"Oh, I'm a mayonnaise girl," she said and grabbed the white

container. Squirted it into a pile at one side of the plate. Grinned at him as she picked up a ring.

"I'll bite," he said and reached for his own ring. Dipped it into the mayo. "That'll eat."

"Right?" She laughed. "Learned it in Europe. Delicious."

"Europe, huh? Did you go to school there?"

"Something like that." She got up and grabbed a glass, filled it with water, then returned. "How'd you get into the rescue business?" She picked up another ring, dipped it.

"Navy. Then sort of got entangled in it by accident when I got home. But it's been in my bones my whole life." He watched her take another ring and sort of wanted to give her the entire plate. "Had a cousin who died after getting lost, and always sort of wondered if we could have found her before . . . well, before she died."

She sat back. "That's rough."

"Yep. Are you from Alaska?"

A huff, a smile. "Nope. Actually, I grew up in Florida."

"That's a hike."

She lifted a shoulder. "I like Alaska. The summer is great—so much sun. And the winter can be . . . quiet."

"You like quiet?"

"I like safe." She met his gaze, fixed on it. Seemed to be asking a question.

He answered it with silence, and a nod.

Another beat went by, and then she got up. "Break is up. I'll get your pie." Tying on her apron, she walked away.

He reached for his shake and took a sip, his gaze on Tillie.

Yes. He very much was going to ask her out.

EIGHT

OAKEN WAS NO HERO, BUT SOMEONE WAS going to die if they didn't get to that van.

"Do not go in there, Oaken. Wait for the state troopers. Wait for Moose!" Boo scrambled after Oaken down the embankment, and he turned to catch her before she slid into the icy waters.

She caught up to him, wrapped her arms around him. They stood halfway down the rocky embankment, the rain sheeting down over them, and all he could think was . . .

Hollie.

Hollie had died because no one stopped—or even saw her, maybe—but no one had taken even a moment to check out the car buried under a tree on the side of the road.

And maybe that wasn't fair, but the last thing Oaken was going to do was wait while someone drowned. Or froze to death.

The van had landed wheels down in the water, but already the current had dragged it twenty feet, and it bobbed, jostled by the tumult of rapids and rain.

"It could go over, Boo. And maybe the people inside are unconscious."

Boo had already called Moose while Oaken dialed 911. But help couldn't be sooner than ten minutes away, so he'd gotten out of the car, slid across the road, and spotted the vehicle in peril in the water.

He hadn't even thought about it as he'd run to the edge of the bridge and thrown his leg over the guardrail. Started down the embankment.

Now he wished he'd at least grabbed a flashlight. Darkness hid the tumble of rocks. "Careful," he said as he continued down, Boo's hand now captured in his.

The hiss of the water rose over the thunder of rain, but he didn't hear any panicked yelling from the van.

An older-model Caravan, maybe mid-nineties. Probably had airbags.

He slipped on a boulder, let go of her hand, and stopped his foot from sliding into a crevasse, bracing himself on the slippery rock.

They needed light—

Behind him, a light flashed on. Boo's phone. *Smart.*

See, that's what she did—she stayed calm, didn't let her emotions lead.

He didn't have time right now to think about her words in the car— *"You meant it when you said you'd watch my back."* But he was going to get to the bottom of that.

Later.

Now he picked his way under the light down to the river, the rocks black, icy, the rain soaking him through. The river swelled, frothed, roared, the headlights of the vehicle winking out as the van rocked in the water.

Boo grabbed his arm to steady herself as she reached the shoreline and flashed her light over the water.

The Caravan now sat at an angle, dipping toward the driver's side, away from them.

"I think there's someone in the passenger seat!" The roar of the rain and river nearly ate his words. He shucked off his jacket.

"What are you doing?"

"The river is going to take that van any second. I need to get them out."

"Oak! You'll get swept away—*don't*—"

"Keep the light on the van!" He stepped out into the river.

Icy, brutal, the water gushed into his boots and sucked away his breath. Even more as he took another step.

"Oaken! Don't!"

Sirens moaned in the distance.

The water jostled the van. He took another step, the water up to his knees, rising fast. The next step had him catching his balance, gritting his teeth.

"Okay, fine—take this!"

He turned and saw her half in the water, holding a rock.

"For the window!"

Good idea. He took the rock, then eased his way deeper, fighting the pull of the current. He'd entered some ten feet above the vehicle, the river pushing him downstream as he ventured closer. The water reached his hips, and the pull nearly knocked him over.

Another step and suddenly the river swept out his feet. He swam hard for the van as the river grabbed him and flushed him downstream.

He hit a rock with his feet and pushed off it, nearly got his hands on the sliding door. The river yanked him away. *No!* He fought, kicking hard, and his hands grasped the door handle, then—yes, the mirror. Fingertips frozen, he still managed to hold on, then pull himself against the current.

Boo's light illuminated a woman trapped inside, banging against the passenger window.

He tried the door, but it wouldn't budge. Shoving one foot into the wheel well, the other grasping the sliding-door latch, he lifted the rock. "Get back!"

Maybe she heard him, because she leaned away and buried her head in her arms.

He slammed the rock against the window. It cracked and he hit it again.

It shattered, jagged edges around the frame.

"Hey!" he said, and the woman looked up.

Early twenties, so much fear in her eyes. His resolve hardened. "Get back! I'm going to clean out the window."

She turned again, and he banged at the shards of glass around the rim, clearing it as best he could.

A glance past her to the driver revealed a man stuck to his seat by the airbag, unconscious.

Hers hadn't deployed. Maybe a good thing.

The woman was already unbuckled. "Get me out of here!"

"Trying!"

He looked over, and lights beamed from the bridge overhead. State troopers. Maybe he should wait—

The van rocked, and the back end started to move. Only then did he realize that the van's undercarriage balanced on a submerged rock.

"Can you climb out?"

She dove out the window, launching for him. He held on to his perch as she clamped her arms around his neck, nearly dislodging him. As it was, the force of her loosed his grip on the sliding-door latch, swung him around. He fought for his hold on the mirror.

"Don't let me go. Don't let me go!" She wrapped her legs around his waist, clinging to him.

He steeled an arm around her, his hand still viced to the mirror, the river an icy cauldron, fighting to wrench her from his grip. From the wedge in the wheel well, his foot loosened.

He gritted his teeth, his legs nearly numb, and found a submerged rock to brace his other foot against.

If the van pitched, loosened, or rolled, he'd be swept downriver.

A couple state troopers had worked their way down the cliffside. Boo ran to meet them—*no, wait*. She ran to meet the Air One team, all dressed in their red jumpsuits, London carrying a rope, Shep and Axel, an extension ladder. Moose came down with a massive floodlight.

"Just hang on to me. It'll be okay."

Okay, so maybe this had been stupid, because—

The van rocked, started to edge off its balance.

"We're coming, Oak!" This from Moose, flashing his light on the river while Shep and Axel extended the ladder.

London was setting up some anchors in the tumble of rocks, working with the state troopers who'd come with the team.

"Get us out of here. Please, please," said the woman.

"Hang on. My team is coming for us." He scrambled for ideas. If the van cast off the rock, he'd have to let go, but then what? Maybe he should hold on to the van like a buoy?

The vehicle rocked again, the weight of it pitching to the driver's side.

The movement tore his grip away.

The woman screamed as the river grabbed them.

His hand found the bumper. "Get on my back! I need both hands!"

For a second, she didn't move.

"Listen, lady—"

"It's Ashley. My name's Ashley—"

"Ashley, you can do this! Get on my back!"

She unlatched her hands, then quickly moved one under his arm, then released her legs and ducked her head.

In a second, she'd transferred to his back, nearly choking off his breath, but at least now he had use of both hands.

"Hurry up!" he shouted.

Moose had passed off his light and now helped Shep hold the ladder as London and the troopers secured the far end to the rocks. Axel stood onshore, dressed in a dry suit, clipping rescue and belay ropes to his harness.

The team angled the ladder toward the van, across the water. It fell into the foam, the light glinting off the metal.

Axel stepped onto it, checked the balance and weight. Then, "I'm coming for you!" His voice barely lifted above the rapids.

Straddling the ladder and attached to a belay line, Axel inched out along the ladder, toward the van.

The van wobbled, nudged by the current, and any minute—

"Hurry up!"

Axel held a length of rope, a buoy on the end, and now flung it at Oaken.

It swept downstream, caught against the van, and Oaken grabbed the line just as the van released.

He wrapped his arms around the donut, Ashley like a backpack, as the van ripped away, caught in the whitewater. The vehicle bumped down the river into the darkness.

Oaken had his own problems. The water took him, yanked him downstream. Ashley's weight pushed him under, and he fought to leverage himself against the riverbed, find air.

But he hung on to the ring. Axel had hunkered down on the ladder, braced his feet, pulling against the current. More state troopers had arrived and now braced the ladder as London set up a belay for Shep. He followed Axel out onto the ladder, then sat behind him, his legs around him, braced also against the rungs, and grabbed the rope.

Four hands pulling against the rapids, and even then Oaken barely moved. But he found footing underwater, shoved against it, fought for air. "Don't let go!" he shouted, but Ashley clamped on to him with an iron grip. Even when he lost his footing again and twisted in the lethal waters. His lungs seared before he finally found purchase again on an underwater boulder and surfaced, hard and fast.

Shep and Axel reeled him in.

He reached the ladder and grabbed hold. Axel held him tight as Shep scrambled up and over to Ashley. He hauled her out of the water, onto the ladder, then held her as she shivered, trembling and crying, trying to work a harness around her body. He got it clipped around her waist, then lifted her up and helped her work her way to shore.

Oaken just gripped the ladder, his strength wasted.

"Not a great night for a swim, buddy," Axel said, still sitting, just a few feet from him. "Just sayin'."

Oaken looked up at him. "Yeah. Well, weather took a turn."

"Alaska."

He nodded. Shep returned, harness in hand. "Let's get this around you." He slid into the water next to Oaken and strapped the harness around his waist.

Then he pushed Oaken up onto the ladder, in front of Axel.

Out of the water and into the air, Oaken started to shake.

"You're probably hypothermic," said Shep. "Can you walk?"

"I'm not sure I have legs."

Shep nodded. "They're there. But you're pretty banged up. You have some blood in your boots."

"I hit some rocks."

"No duh," said Axel. "I can't wait for the debrief with you and Moose. I'm ordering pizza. Gonna sit in the corner and watch the action."

"Not now, Axe," said Shep. "We need a stretcher!"

"No—I can walk. Or crawl. No stretcher."

Oaken gripped the sides of the ladder even as Shep hauled himself out of the water.

"Grab on to me," Axel said, and Oaken grabbed the back of

Axel's harness. Axel stood and Shep got behind Oaken, his hands on his harness.

Oaken couldn't feel his feet.

But they *were* there, and in a moment, he balanced on the edge of the ladder, secured between his teammates, and worked his way to shore.

Ashley sat, wrapped in a blanket, shivering hard, Boo attending to a wound above her eye. Oaken walked over to Ashley and collapsed on the shore.

"There's . . . a . . . man . . . in the van," he said, even as Moose brought over a blanket. Oaken shook so hard he thought his teeth might crack.

"Let's get some spotlights, and we'll see how far the van's gone downriver," Axel said. "I'll go in after him."

"No!"

Ashley's outburst had even Oaken staring at her. "No—he *kidnapped* me. And assaulted me! I was walking to my car after work, and he grabbed me and shoved me into the van. He—he . . ." Her breaths came fast.

"Okay," Boo said softly. "It's okay."

But Ashley shook her head. "I was in the back, my hands taped, but I got free and tried to get out, and that's when we started sliding. I got into the front seat—I was so scared. I buckled in right before we went over."

"Smart," said Boo.

"Brave," said Axel.

She looked at Oaken. "You saved my life."

He had nothing.

Then she threw her arms around him, her face in his neck. "Thank you. Thank you."

He patted her back, but his gaze was on Boo. And the terrible expression she wore. Horror, fear, pain.

She swallowed, looked away.

And that's when, of all people, Huxley came down the embankment, Beto in tow.

"Right here. Set up here, Beto, and let's get this shot."

Ashley let him go and looked over at Huxley. "Are you the news? Because he's a hero. And everyone should know it."

Huxley smiled. "Yes, they should."

"Not until we get to the hospital and get them both treated for hypothermia," Boo snapped. "And if you haven't noticed, Oaken is bleeding, so there's that."

Then she got up and stalked away.

And as Oaken watched, in the dim shadows, she turned, her hands over her face.

Then his entire body went from numb to a deep, bone-searching ache as he watched her quietly, privately, fall apart.

Boo was fine. Just. *Fine.*

So what that she'd nearly seen super country star Oaken Fox be swept away into the lethal black waters of the Eagle River.

So what that only an hour earlier, she'd been laughing with the man, thinking, *What if?*

Yeah, what if he dove into a river like a fool and nearly died trying to be a hero?

"Can I get you anything?"

Boo looked over from where she stared out the window of the ER lobby, watching the rain on the slick parking lot. London stood, still dressed in her jumpsuit, having come right from the scene, holding a cup of coffee. "You should really change out of those wet clothes."

"It's just my jacket." Okay, and her boots, but the heat of the hospital had warmed her feet to simply soggy instead of soggy and frozen. And her wool socks wicked away a lot of the moisture.

And she wasn't going anywhere while Oaken still sat in the ER getting his leg stitched up. He'd sliced it pretty good on the rocks but hadn't even seemed to notice it.

Hopefully he hadn't noticed her falling apart either.

She blew out a breath and found a smile for London. "I'm fine."

"You look exhausted." London touched her arm. "And at the scene—"

"I don't want to talk about it," Boo said, holding up her hand. "I'm fine. Everything's fine."

London raised an eyebrow, then nodded. "I'll get you some hot cocoa."

She smiled then, something thin. "Okay, yes. That might help." Put a chocolate Band-Aid over the gaping hole in her chest, ease the pain a little. Maybe forget that she'd unraveled with relief when Oaken came to shore.

This was why she didn't date teammates.

Or even date at all.

She shook her head and turned back to the window. It was just trauma. And emotion. It didn't mean she was repeating the past.

"Hey, there you are."

She looked over, and Moose came out of the ER hallway. "Oaken is nearly stitched up. I'm headed back to the Tooth with the rig. Ashley is being admitted for trauma and sexual assault, but she's talking to the police. You talk with the cops?"

"Yep. Gave my statement. Where are Axel and Shep?" She'd followed the ambulance in Oaken's car, leaving Moose and the team to deal with the second victim, the possible kidnapper.

"We came back together. They're in the truck. No-go on the driver. We found the van, but it was empty."

She nodded, not sure how to feel.

"You sure you're okay to drive?"

"I'm fine."

He frowned. "What about—"

"Nope. Just . . . adrenaline, okay? I'm fine."

His mouth made a tight, grim line, but he nodded. "Okay, then. We'll talk about it later."

"Or never."

He narrowed his eyes. "In case you're confused, I don't want to see you in the office tomorrow."

She cocked her head at him.

"Really. It's Saturday. Take a walk. Decompress." He glanced back at the ER. "Maybe take Oaken with you."

"You're not helping."

He grinned. "Or am I?"

She shook her head, inhaling.

"Okay, don't get your jumpsuit in a knot. Just . . . good job out there."

"Oaken was nearly killed."

"But he wasn't killed. And people were saved. I think there's a place on this team for Oaken, if he wants it."

"He has a life. And a career. And none of it includes Alaska."

He raised an eyebrow. "You keep telling yourself that and you might miss something happening right in front of your eyes."

Aw, this she couldn't leave alone. "Moose. Listen. I . . . I've been there, and this doesn't end well. Not with me."

"What doesn't end well?"

She looked over, and of course there was Oaken, disheveled, his pants ripped, a bandage over his calf where they'd stitched up his wound. He wore such a fierceness in his eyes that probably Oaken already knew the answer to the question.

"I'll leave you two," Moose said. "See you Monday." He turned, pointed at Oaken. "Good job not dying tonight, but next time, wait for the team." He lifted his hand, then headed out the front door.

Oaken limped over to her. "What doesn't end well?" he asked again.

She glanced around the waiting room. Just one other person, but she'd seen Huxley and Beto around earlier, so she gestured with her head down the hallway, then turned and headed away from the lobby.

She found a small unoccupied alcove and rounded on him, keeping her voice low. "I think you know."

He stood there, probably a half-foot taller than her, no jacket, his shirt mostly dry, no ketchup remaining, smelling of the river and antiseptic and bravery, and she just . . . "I can't do this again."

"Do what again?"

"Fall for . . . for a Blake."

He flinched, and she hated herself for it, but—"It's the truth, Oaken. You're . . . famous. And handsome. And crowds of women love you. And the minute someone like Misty Buchannan shows up—"

"Stop." His deep timbre found her bones. "I'm not Blake."

She swallowed. "But you could be."

He frowned.

"I could fall for you. Hard. And even . . . even . . ." She looked away.

"Oh, Boo, what happened?"

She closed her eyes. Shook her head. Opened them. Sighed. "I made a choice, back with Blake, that night. We . . . were together. Which I almost immediately regretted."

His mouth tightened.

And now she just wanted to run. Her eyes burned.

"That jerk."

She looked at him. "It wasn't just Blake—"

"Oh, yes it was. Maybe not all Blake, but . . . I'm a guy. Trust me on this. Blake is a jerk."

She looked away.

"Boo," he said softly and nudged her attention back to him. "I understand. And it doesn't matter to me—not what happened between you and Blake. What matters is that he hurt you. And because of him, you can't trust . . . well, what might be going on between us."

She swallowed, her chest hollow. "What is going on . . . between us?"

"I think you know," he said, his gaze on hers.

Her heart thundered hard in her chest. A beat. And then his gaze lowered to her mouth.

Oh.

Run.

But of course, she didn't listen to herself. In fact, she took a step toward him. He hadn't moved and still possessed a sort of hypnotic pull, his eyes drawing her in.

Yes, she knew exactly what was going on between them.

"I'm not Blake."

No, no, he wasn't.

He might actually be the opposite of Blake. Kind, self-deprecating, humble . . .

She touched his shirt. "The thing is, I do trust you." Her breath quickened. "And that's . . . that's a problem."

"Is it?"

She nodded. "I don't have a lot of room in here for . . ."

"Trust?"

"Or relationships."

"I don't need company." He lowered his head, his breath near hers.

"Don't hurt me." She lifted her face to his.

"Not in a million—"

She kissed him. Just rose up on her tiptoes and pressed her mouth to his. A sudden, desperate impulse of desire that would slip away if she didn't take it.

So yeah, she kissed him. Hard, and for a second—no, not even a second—he froze.

And then he ran his hand behind her neck and crushed her against him.

She grabbed his shirt, held on as he braced his hand against the wall and moved her into the pocket of his embrace. The wall at her back, she wrapped her arms around his torso and let herself relax.

Just like that, the knots inside loosened, fell away, and her mouth opened, and she let him deepen his kiss, drinking him in.

Maybe she'd never felt so safe.

Maybe she'd never felt so seen.

Maybe this wasn't the worst mistake of her life.

Especially when he made a little noise, like a sigh, then lifted himself away and met her eyes. Smiled. "Through stormy nights and sunny days, she's the anchor that keeps me from drifting away."

She blinked at him. "What?"

"Oaken?"

Under her hands, she felt his body still as a female voice cast over them. He looked over his shoulder, then stepped away from her.

It felt like a punch to her sternum.

A cover-model-gorgeous woman dressed in an oversized sweat-shirt, leggings, and Uggs stood at the end of the hallway carrying a coffee. She wore her long hair down and looked every inch like someone Oaken should be with.

Of course.

"Seraphina. What are you doing here?"

Oh no, no, this couldn't be—

"Mike's awake."

Boo nearly felt Oaken's caught breath. "What? When?"

"Not long ago. He's still in ICU, but he woke up for a little bit and . . . he was asking for you."

Mike. Grizz?

Oaken turned to her. "I need to go talk to Mike."

Boo stepped back. "Absolutely. No problem." She lifted her hand to the woman. "Hi. I'm Boo."

"Hi," the woman said as she walked up to Oaken. She put an arm around his neck, and he pulled her into a hug. "Mike will be so glad to see you." Casting another look at Boo, she offered a thin-lipped smile. Then she turned back to Oaken. "I'll meet you up there."

He nodded and turned back to Boo as she left.

"That's Mike's wife."

Oh. *Oh.* "She gave me a funny look."

He frowned. "No. She's just . . . you know. Stressed out, maybe."

Mm-hmm.

"There you are!" London appeared, holding a cup of cocoa. "I was looking for you." She came up to them, and as she did, Oaken moved away from Boo. Again. London eyed him, then looked at Boo.

"I'll catch up with you later," he said.

"Wait," Boo said and reached into her pocket. "Your keys."

He drew in a breath, and for a second, she stupidly, foolishly hoped he'd say "Wait for me."

Instead, he held out his hand. "Thanks." Then he walked away from her.

Aw, see? Already this had gotten away from her. She wanted to rewind time and heed her own instincts. *Run.*

London handed her the cocoa. "So . . . what did I walk into?"

Boo took a sip of the hot chocolate, suddenly wrung out. "I'm not sure, really." They walked out into the hallway. "I think I need to go home. Can you give me a ride to the Tooth?"

"Yeah. I have keys to the rescue truck." London pulled them out, then glanced toward the elevator banks, where Oaken was just disappearing. "You two . . . okay?"

Five minutes ago . . . yes. But something had dropped in her gut, and she couldn't explain it. Still. "We're fine. Just . . . talking about the rescue."

"Yep. That's it." London smiled.

Maybe Boo was just . . . overreacting. Letting her fears lie to her.

He *had* quoted her his own song.

They pushed outside, and London unlocked the rescue truck. Boo slid into the passenger side, fatigue sweeping over her. Every muscle ached.

Clearly, exhaustion had her brain playing games with her. Oaken *wasn't* Blake. He wasn't going to break her heart, smear her through social media, and make her feel like she was the villain in the story.

She leaned her head back, closed her eyes.

Her phone vibrated in her pocket as London got in. She pulled it out.

A text from Austen. She opened it.

Austen
———————————————
Did you see this? I'm so sorry, Boo.

Boo clicked on the link.

And then everything inside her turned to stone.

"Boo? You're breathing funny."

Yeah, she was. "Blake broke up with his fiancée, and according to the Instagram post Misty put up, she's blaming me." She flashed the post toward London, who had put the truck in Park and now took the phone. "She says it's because he's still in love with me. She's calling me a marriage wrecker."

"It has over ten thousand likes," London said quietly. She scrolled down the comments and froze. "Uh-oh."

It was the way she said it that made Boo go cold. "What?"

London turned the phone around. "Apparently, you and Oaken had a little food fight at the Tenderfoot tonight." A grainy picture captured Boo in Oaken's embrace, him trying to grab the ketchup bottle, her head back and laughing.

London clicked on the picture and then flinched.

"What?"

"The picture has gone viral. And someone has figured out that you're with Oaken Fox." She turned the phone around again. "'Boo Hoo haunts Blake Hinton while hooking up with another victim.'"

Perfect, just perfect.

"I'm sorry, Boo."

Outside, the rain spat down on the car, the night gloomy and wretched. "Yeah, well, it was only a matter of time. Let's just go."

"Boo—"

"At least now I know why I got the dark eye from Grizz's wife." She took the phone and shoved it into her pocket. "The good news is that Huxley has finally gotten her rescue. And now, hopefully, Oaken can go back to his life."

And maybe, somehow, she could disappear into hers.

NINE

H E SHOULD HAVE ASKED BOO TO WAIT FOR him.

Oaken stood in the ICU waiting room, nursing a cup of coffee as Seraphina went into the ICU with the nurse.

Boo's expression as she'd handed over the keys haunted him. He'd said something wrong. Or maybe done something wrong. And maybe yes, Seraphina had surprised him, but only because suddenly her presence jerked him back into the world where his celebrity status mattered. Where, because of him, people got hurt.

Where he had responsibilities beyond himself.

And even as Seraphina told him the good news, all he could hear was Boo's voice, soft, a little fragile. *"Don't hurt me."*

He couldn't escape the idea that somehow, he already had.

Seraphina emerged from the ICU, took off her hospital mask, then motioned him over.

"They said you can say hello to him for a minute or two, but he's weak, so . . ."

He nodded and took the fresh mask she offered him. Set his coffee on a nearby table.

Then he followed her into the ICU. A room with curtains pulled between beds, so much equipment beeping and hissing it felt like a laboratory. The pungent smell of antiseptic tightened his gut.

A nurse stood at the end of Mike's bed. He lay, eyes closed, his body painfully stripped of girth after over a week in the hospital. An oxygen cannula fed air into his nose, and a pulse oximeter attached to his finger, along with an IV in his arm. A sling elevated his casted leg, and his wrist also wore a cast.

Seraphina kept her voice low. "He's not really awake, more in a semi-sleep status. But if you talk to him, he can hear you."

Oaken wanted to turn and walk out. He barely knew Mike, really. But he'd seen the look Seraphina gave him when she hugged him—she needed someone to be here to celebrate this. To share this miracle with her. So he walked up to Mike and bent down.

"Hey, Mike. This is Oaken Fox. You might not remember me, but we had a couple days together out there in the bush. Thank you for not dying on me."

Mike's eyelids flickered.

Oaken looked at Seraphina. She nodded, as if he should keep talking.

"I'm doing a new reality show with the people that rescued you. I think you'd like it. I rescued a girl from a river tonight."

Mike's eyes fought to open.

"Keep fighting, bro. Your wife and kids need you."

Mike's eyes opened. Wide-eyed, almost zombielike, he stared straight ahead. Oaken froze.

Then Mike's attention turned to him. He just blinked at Oaken.

"Hey," Oaken said. "I might not look familiar to you, but I promise, we're friends."

Mike seemed to focus on him now. Took a breath.

Then he tried to speak. It came out whispered and garbled.

"Babe, do you need a drink?" Seraphina turned to the nurse and asked for water.

The nurse left, and Seraphina stepped close and moved her head down to his mouth. "Say again?"

He seemed to try again, and even as he spoke, Seraphina stiffened. She looked at Oaken, then back at Mike. "Are you sure?"

The nurse returned with water in a cup, with a straw. "Don't let him drink too much, or too fast."

Seraphina took the water and fed the straw into his mouth. He took a drink, and she pulled it away before he had too much.

He sighed, lay back, and closed his eyes.

"What did he say?"

She squeezed Mike's hand, then motioned for Oaken to leave. "I'll take care of it, honey."

They stepped outside the door and she pulled off her mask.

Oaken did the same. Seraphina walked to the windows, stared out.

Now she was freaking him out. "What's going on?"

She took a breath. "He said that someone tried to kill him."

"What?"

She turned to him. "Actually, he said, 'He tried to kill me.'" Her eyes had turned cold.

Oaken just stared at her as her words crested over him. "Wait. You think I tried to kill Mike? After dragging him through the woods for two days and nearly dying myself?"

Her eyes filled, and the coldness vanished. "I'm sorry. You're right. That's stupid. Mike's clearly confused. But . . ." She wrapped her arms around herself. "It doesn't sound like him—to accuse someone of that. He's such a personal-responsibility guy. He'd never blame someone for an accident if he didn't think, or know, that something wasn't right."

Yes, that sounded like Mike. "I'll talk to the police."

She shook her head. "I'll talk to them. Maybe you need to, well, distance yourself from this. And us. And . . . maybe you need to go home, Oaken. Back to your real life."

Her words landed like a blow to his chest. "What?"

"I just think maybe . . ." She turned to him, then pulled her phone from her back pocket. "I don't want you getting hurt. Socially or emotionally. And I don't want the show to get hurt financially."

"What are you talking about?"

And that's when she opened up her Instagram account and turned her phone around.

A picture of him and Boo. Tonight. During their food fight. And the caption wasn't flattering about Boo.

But most damaging were the comments.

ZAG5058
Oaken Fox, showing off his fighting skills, again.

DRQUIB2020
Will Oaken never learn? Stay away from crazy fans.

JDIDDY1987
Alaska, where country music stars go to die.

There were more, but she turned off her phone and pocketed it. "I'm sorry, Oaken, but . . . they're right. If you want to resurrect your career, you need to get back to wooing girls onstage and writing love songs and stop hiding in Alaska."

"I'm not hiding."

"I know. But . . . I talked with Huxley. She said something about a fake rescue?"

His mouth opened. "No . . . I mean . . . okay, yes, there was a staged rescue. But tonight was the real thing. I nearly died trying to help a woman from a car."

Her eyes widened. "I didn't know that. Are you okay?"

He certainly wasn't freezing anymore. "Yes. Fine. And that woman in the picture is a fellow rescue tech named Boo—"

"I know who she is, Oaken. She was on *Survivor Quest*. She was

Blake Hinton's partner, the one who slept with him to try to get him to lose the race. Diabolical. And then she went online after he outed her and told the world that he'd faked his illness to play her. That he was a predator and didn't deserve to finish in second place."

Oaken's throat tightened. "I know."

"And yet you're kissing her? Hello—do you know what kind of fool that makes you out to be? I'm not sure we can even air this show—"

"She hasn't been on camera. At least, not officially."

Seraphina's mouth tightened. "It'll come out. And we'll be sunk." Her eyes turned glossy. "I'm sorry, Oaken. I'm not trying to make this about money. I really do care what happens to you. You're a good guy. An honest guy. A real hero—and a real talent. I just don't want you to give up everything for . . . well, whatever is going on, because you're feeling sad about your career."

Feeling sad . . . oh, the social media fiasco. The lawsuit. He'd, well, forgotten, at least for a while.

"I've never felt more alive than the last week with Air One. It might be the best thing that's happened to me since . . ." He shook his head. "I don't know how long."

Seraphina nodded, wiped her cheek. "Well, that's good. Really good. And maybe it's helped you get on your feet. And we can probably spin this—"

"I don't want to spin this!"

"Well, I do." The voice came from a few feet away.

He turned, and Huxley stood there, dressed in wet clothing, a soggy wool hat. "Spinning this is *exactly* what we need to do. And by the way, keep your voices down. I heard you all the way down the hall."

He stared at her. "What are you talking about?"

"I'm talking about the fact that the reason *Survivor Quest* got such high ratings was because of the romance between Blake and Boo. Everyone saw it on-screen, and maybe you don't read the comments on the episodes, but it's my job, and I'm telling you, after the episode where he voted her off the show, there were plenty of women on Boo's side, who saw right through Blake. The media wanted to make her into Boo Hoo, but for many, she was the victim."

Seraphina's mouth tightened. "Maybe if she hadn't come out and said terrible things about him."

"Did you expect her not to defend herself?" Oaken said.

Seraphina looked away, out the window.

"Some women found that to be exactly the right thing to say," Huxley said.

"What are you suggesting?" Oaken asked Huxley.

"I'm saying . . . maybe we go the other way. Maybe you give us a romance, on-screen. Show us the charismatic Oaken, the one women swoon for, and why their boyfriends throw beer at you. Be a hero, not just as a rescuer but as a guy who woos women with your music."

"I do not woo women with my music. You make me sound like the Pied Piper."

"I've seen your concerts. Love your songs. *'She's my girl, my guiding light. In her arms, everything feels right.'*" She even added a little singsong to her voice. "Please. You can't think that every woman doesn't wish you were singing to them."

He felt his body, his face, heating.

"So, play to the fantasy. Woo Boo, and let the audience see her smile, see her fall for you."

He wanted that too. Except *off* camera. "She doesn't want to be on camera."

"Maybe I can convince her. Her shot at redemption. After all, she's a hero too. Maybe this show redeems her, too, on social media."

"I don't think she cares about redemption."

Huxley raised an eyebrow.

"I don't know, Hux. Maybe Seraphina's right. Maybe we end this thing . . ." He ran a hand behind his neck.

"You're tired and hungry. C'mon—there's a diner near here that makes late-night chicken. Let me buy you something to eat." She looked at Seraphina. "Join us."

Seraphina shook her head. "It's late and I'm exhausted. Besides, I need to get back to the Airbnb and see the kids."

"Okay. Reynolds said that Mike woke up. That's good news."

Seraphina looked at Oaken. "Yes."

"Reynolds wanted me to stop by and see how coherent he was."

"In and out," Seraphina said. "He's still foggy."

"Okay." Huxley turned to Oaken. "Beto and I will get a booth. Meet you there. Skyport Diner."

He nodded as she left. Then he turned to Seraphina. "Maybe you should alert the police about Mike's accusation?"

She considered him a moment. "I think I want to wait until he's more awake and can give us details. Right now, they might dismiss it as medically induced or something."

"Are you dismissing it as that?"

"I don't know. Who would want to hurt Mike? He's . . ." She gave him a wry smile. "He's Mike. Live big, live wild. He loves everyone, and everyone loves him."

"Yes, they do." He touched her arm. "In the meantime, I'm going to talk to Air One and see if they still have his chute and supplies."

She nodded. "I'm sorry about what I said about Boo. I can see that you care about her. I just hope that she's not playing you too."

"I do care about her. And she's not playing me. And as usual, social media doesn't have the entire story." He gave her arm a squeeze and let go.

"Agreed. Just . . . be careful, Oaken. You've worked too hard to have it all crumble." She lifted herself up on her toes and kissed his cheek. Patted his chest.

"Thanks," he said.

He found his car in the dark, forlorn parking lot, then set his phone's GPS for the diner. When he pulled up a few minutes later, he spotted Beto and Huxley sitting in a booth by a window.

The smells of coffee, fried chicken, and juicy hamburgers met him, and his stomach woke with ferocity as he stepped inside.

He slid into the booth beside Beto.

They were sharing a plate of fries, a couple of malts. A woman walked up, the name Tillie on her badge, and set water down in front of him. "They ordered chicken. You want the same?"

Huxley nodded for him.

"And a chocolate milk," he said.

She wrote it down and left, and Huxley pushed the plate of fries toward him. "So, Beto and I have been talking. And yes, I guess we have enough footage for the pilot and a short run of shows. Especially after tonight's rescue." She leaned back. "But I still like the romance option. It adds to the story. And I think you can sell it, Oaken."

"I don't want to sell anything."

"Please. That's what this business is—giving people what they want. Selling them on the fantasy. In this case, it's country music hero turned real hero. And maybe finding love along the way. Maybe I'm misreading what I saw tonight at the restaurant. So if you're not into her, you don't have to kiss her. Just . . . you know. Dance with her once. Get her to smile at you. Leave a little to the imagination, but give them enough to speculate."

He leaned back. Fact was, he very much wanted to dance with Boo. Get her to smile at him. And especially, kiss Boo again. But he didn't want it on-screen.

And most of all, he wasn't about selling a lie to the public. Or to himself.

He was shaking his head when the bell above the door dinged, and he looked up to see Moose and Axel and Shep walk in.

"Look what the storm dragged in," Moose said and walked over to him as Axel and Shep took the booth behind them. Moose held out his hand.

Oaken shook it. "So you're the source behind the late-night chicken?"

"Guilty. You guys having a production meeting?"

"Nope," said Huxley. "We're talking about scope and direction." She put her arm over the back of the booth.

"Well, our man Oaken here is killing it," Moose said. "Suddenly we looked up and there he was, a real member of Air One." He clamped Oaken on the shoulder. "When you're done here, join us for the after party." He gestured with his head to Shep and Axel.

"Maybe," Oaken said.

Moose sat down, his back to Huxley.

She leaned forward. Considered Oaken.

"You heard him. I'm part of the team."

She nodded. "I heard him."

"Still want to shut this down?"

She leaned back. "Ready to play the game?"

And that's when Boo popped into his head, her words right before the accident. *You meant it when you said you'd watch my back.*

His mouth tightened. "No. I'm not playing games."

"Then we're done shooting, Oaken. We'll do our final interviews and call it a wrap."

Oh. He hadn't thought her words would cut off his wind.

"Or you could talk to Boo and see if she's up for some on-camera time. In light of the current viral post, maybe she'd like to do some damage control too."

His mouth tightened. "No."

Tillie arrived with their chicken. Set it in front of them and looked at Oaken. "Yours is on the way."

He slid out of the booth. "Deliver it here," he said and walked over to Moose's booth.

Moose looked up, smiled, and slid over.

The waitress followed him.

"Hey, Till," Moose said, his eyes warm.

She smiled at him. "Hey. Chicken?"

"Of course." He kept smiling at her. "And a mocha shake."

Now, this was the drama that Huxley should be shooting.

Especially since Axel and Shep seemed to be onto him too, both wearing silly grins.

Tillie walked away, and Moose swallowed and turned back to Merry and Pippin grinning at their fearless leader.

"What?"

"Just ask her out already," Axel said.

Moose sighed. "Speaking of . . ." He turned to Oaken. "Officially, we have a no-dating policy on the team. But maybe we can make an exception."

Oaken stared at him. He didn't have the heart to tell him it might be over. Or maybe he didn't have the heart to tell himself.

Axel clearly took his silence as argument. "Please. We see the way you look at Boo."

"But," Moose said, "don't hurt her." He raised an eyebrow.

Good grief. "First, I'm not going to hurt her. But second . . . I think taping is over."

Moose stilled, turned, and looked at Huxley. "Really?"

Huxley shrugged. "Ask the star."

Moose turned back. Cocked his head.

But no, the last thing Oaken wanted was for Moose to know about Huxley's proposal. He took a breath, suddenly unable to speak, his chest so tight it was cutting off his breathing.

Instead, Oaken took a drink of his milk. Probably he didn't need anything stronger. Finally found his voice. "Is Boo back at the Tooth?"

"I saw her leave with London," Shep said. "She looked upset."

Yeah, well, he didn't want to suggest why, but that social media post sat in his chest, burning. "I should go talk to her."

"It'll keep until morning," Moose said, leaning back as their chicken arrived. "Everything looks better with the light on it."

Oaken wasn't sure that was true. Because even as he dug into his chicken, Seraphina's words found him. *"You've worked too hard to have it all crumble."* And as if on cue, a song came over the radio.

Oh, great.

Shep looked up, then at him, grinned. So did Axel.

But oh well. Because even as he listened to his own lyrics, eating the chicken, the words sank in, found home. *"Through stormy nights and sunny days, she's the anchor that keeps me from drifting away."*

Huxley picked then to get up and walk past him, slinging him a look.

He ignored her, preferring Moose's words instead. Yes, everything was going to be just fine.

For Pete's sake, he had turned into a stalker.

Moose sat in his truck, gut churning, lights off, watching the rain turn to snow and cast down in the glow of a streetlamp.

Just go back inside and ask Tillie out.

He didn't know why he had the sense that tonight possessed some magic to it, but the urge simply burned in him. So much that after he'd returned to the Tooth and dropped off Shep and Axel, he'd rounded back to the Skyport.

And sat like a creep in the parking lot.

Go in. Go in.

Maybe it was the mocha shake tonight, the mixed sense of victory amidst tragedy. The fact that Axel had found the car but not the victim.

But if Ashley's story was true . . . that she *had* been kidnapped . . .

So many thoughts, not a few that settled on anger. He struggled with the idea of risking his team for someone like the man Ashley had described. But it wasn't his place to pick and choose, to judge who lived or died.

Still, the idea of anyone, ever, hurting a woman . . .

For a moment, Aren crept into his head. He closed his eyes, gritted his jaw, the old ache in his chest.

Breathe.

He opened his eyes and startled at the sight of Tillie leaving the diner, her jacket on, her purse over her shoulder. *Oops.* Now he *was* really a stalker.

And stuck. He'd have to wait until she left.

She bent her head against the wind, the snow, then flipped up her hood. She wore mittens and reached into her purse, fumbling with her keys as she trekked out to an old-model Ford Focus. Even from here, the car looked like it had seen better days—dirty, the bumper a little skewed.

The dome light flickered on as Tillie got in. Shut the door. Flicked on her headlights.

So much for—

She got back out, carrying something, went around the front and wedged herself in between her hood and the chain link fence that surrounded the lot.

Then she stuck her gloved hands under the hood and wrestled it open.

What?

A phone light flicked on and passed over the dark tangle of her engine.

She reached in with the stick—looked like a tire iron—and tapped on something, then went around and got in the car.

Got back out.

Aw.

The light shone on the engine again, and by the time she repeated the action, then the attempt to start it, he was out of his truck and walking over, trying to figure out a reasonable explanation as to why he might have been sitting in the lot.

Maybe she wouldn't ask.

She had just gotten out of the car, closed the door, her phone pocketed, when he came up behind her.

Not great timing, and maybe he should have called out, but she must have heard him because she whirled around.

He barely dodged the shot to his chin with the tire iron. As it was, it skimmed off his chin even as he stumbled back, tripped, and fell—*bam*—onto the pavement.

She took a step toward him, knelt, and pulled back the iron as if to swing again, then gasped. "Moose?"

His chin burned and he opened his jaw and moved it even as he backed away, sitting up. "That'll leave a mark."

"Oh, wow. I'm sorry. I—what are you doing creeping up on me?"

She seemed fierce in the darkness, her eyes blazing as she stepped back. She had the tire iron still raised, a fighter's stance, and for a second she reminded him of an action hero—maybe Wonder Woman—ready to take him out.

Oh no. "I'm not—I'm not stalking you. I was ... okay, I was ..." His mouth closed as she eyed him. "I came for pie." *Oh, lame.* But the fact that he hadn't gotten pie tonight saved his hide, because she lowered the tire iron. "And I saw you out here, and I thought maybe I could help."

She took a breath. Then sighed and shook her head and offered him a hand. "I did think it was weird that you didn't take any home. Cherry tonight."

"I know. I was ... I ... What's going on with your car?"

Pulling out her phone, she flashed it on the engine as he stepped up to it. "The starter is getting stuck. Usually if I tap on it a few times it'll start. Sometimes I need someone to start it while I tap it."

Snowflakes landed on her dark hair, like glitter.

"Get in," Moose said. He held out his hand for the tire iron, and she handed it over. "You're a little dangerous with this thing."

She smiled. "Don't sneak up on me."

"Noted, Gal Gadot."

Laughing, she got into the driver's seat. He tapped on the solenoid on the side of her engine, and in a moment the car's engine turned over.

He dropped the hood as she got out, standing in her open door.

"Thanks." She took the tire iron from him. "Should I go get you that pie?"

"Naw." He shoved his hands into his pockets.

Now. Ask her now.

"Then I gotta go."

She looked up to the sky, snowflakes landing on her face, her nose. She stuck out her tongue and caught one. Grinned at him. "Don't have those in Florida."

"Nope." Oh, she was pretty. He drew in a breath—

"Next piece of pie is on me. Thanks, Moose." Then she got back in the car and pulled out.

He watched as her brake lights flashed red, then she turned onto the wet, shiny street and disappeared.

TEN

SO MUCH FOR THE BRIGHT LIGHT OF TO-
morrow. Oaken sat on the floor in the guest room of Moose's
beautiful home, his back against an overstuffed chair, his
guitar over his knee, trying to pick out a tune, maybe squeeze some
lyrics from his brain.

Hard to do when he kept looking out the window at the snow
and ice that had descended two nights ago and now pelleted his
window. Over two days, spring in Alaska had morphed back into
January, with howling winds and white as far as the eye could see.

Which, honestly, wasn't very far.

His room looked out over the river, barely visible in the snow
and gloom. Wan light bled through the clouds, and really, maybe
he should just go back to bed, pull the covers up, and forget the
email from Goldie.

*"Oaken. Checking in on your songs. Wild Mountain Records is still
waiting on your first pass. And venues are asking about confirmation
of dates and deposits. It's time to come out of the woods. Call me!"*

Maybe he should be thankful cell service to Moose's place had cut out. It meant he couldn't rabbit trail down social media. It also meant, however, he couldn't call Boo.

Every bone in his body ached for her, and he would have gotten in his car yesterday morning, but the driveway out of Moose's house had turned to ice, the snow like cement.

Outside, Moose's truck growled as he ground through the heavy snow.

Focus.

He picked out the tune he'd been toying with, a simple minor key chord progression—Am-Em-F-C.

He heard music, felt words, and maybe he should be grateful for that at least.

He hummed, trying out the lyrics.

"In a dusty old town, where the sun set low,
Lived a man named Coop with a heart of gold.
He'd ride the plains, a lone cowboy through,
With a past so dark, he couldn't undo."

To his ears, it just sounded sappy. But maybe that's what they wanted.

"You going for something dark there?" said Axel from the doorway. Oaken looked up and saw the man with his arms folded, leaning on the frame.

"I think it's supposed to be. It's for a movie—a Western. When I talked with the producer months ago, he told me—Western song, reluctant hero, true love, and sacrifice."

"Yeah, that sounds like a Western. You got more?"

"Not much." He sang the pre-chorus.

"But when he laid eyes on sweet Blossom,
A beauty that could save him, he began to understand,
He must rise up, though his soul's weighed down.

For the woman he loves, he'll wear the hero's crown."

"Yeah, that's heavy," Axel said.

Oaken nodded.

"So, why is his soul weighed down?"

Oaken looked up at him. "I think because he . . . feels guilt about something. Or shame."

"Which one is it? Because guilt is real and it makes us run to forgiveness. But shame is what the devil uses to get us to hide from God."

Oaken stared at him.

Axel shrugged. "Moose. You live here for a while, he'll rub off on you."

"Yeah, well, I've never heard that before. But I don't know. Maybe shame?"

"How do you know?"

He'd read the script, so, "I think because maybe he thinks he shouldn't get the girl. That he doesn't deserve her."

Axel cocked his head. "Really."

"Yeah. Maybe . . . maybe he's been living a lie all these years of being this amazing gunslinger when, in fact, it was a fluke."

"Interesting," Axel said.

Oaken set down his guitar.

"You got a chorus for this song?"

He picked up his notebook. "Words."

"Hit me."

Oaken made a face, then read out his notes. "He's a reluctant hero, a cowboy with no choice, caught between his demons and the love he can't ignore. With every step he takes, the stakes get higher . . . For the woman he loves, he'll face the burning fire."

"Sort of on the nose, but again, it's a Western, so maybe that's what the audience wants."

"I've been staring at the same blank notebook for about three months. This is the best I've got." He dropped it onto the carpet. Leaned back. "I sort of thought coming out here might clear my head, help me feel the song, the words. And . . . at least now I have a tune. And a start. But . . ."

Axel came into the room. "But?"

"Both Goldie—my manager—and Seraphina said something to me. They told me to stop hiding."

"From what?"

He looked at Axel, and the word just bubbled out. "Shame, I think."

"So, God, then."

Oaken narrowed his eyes. Drew in a breath. Picked up his guitar. "Maybe."

Silence passed between them.

"Ever feel like you don't deserve the life you have?" He didn't know where the question came from, and he picked out a tune, his gaze on the paper.

"All the time, dude. I should be dead, at the bottom of the Bering Sea, fish food."

He looked up at Axel. "What?"

"Long story, but yeah, I cheated death, and there are some nightmares. But I try to make it right every day. Sometimes, however, I don't." He folded his arms across his chest. "Like losing that driver a couple days ago. Haunts me."

Oaken nodded. "Yeah. I'm sorry I couldn't get him out."

"You saved Ashley, armed with nothing but your bare hands, so I think maybe you need to let that go."

"Back at ya."

"Right. So, what's the life you don't deserve?"

Oaken put his hand over the strings to silence them. "This life. This career. I sort of fell into it . . . and I feel ungrateful for not being grateful for it."

"You're not—"

"Okay, yes, I'm grateful. But I'm also . . . I feel trapped, I guess. And that burns through me, because everything I have is because of what Hollie built. And I inherited it."

"Hollie?"

"My sister. Hollie Montgomery."

"She was your sister? I loved her albums. So tragic."

He nodded. "Yeah. But if she hadn't died, I wouldn't be where I am today, so that's fantastic."

"You don't know that."

He frowned at Axel.

"That's just how God got you into the place where you are today."

"I never thought of it that way."

"That's because you think this whole thing"—Axel moved his hand over the guitar, the notepad—"is because of your efforts. And in large part, yes, it is. But if you're exhausted, it's probably because you feel like you're rowing the boat."

"Rowing the boat?"

"When you row a boat, you're in charge of everything—the work, the direction, going against the waves . . . You gotta learn to sail, bud. The sailor rigs the sails and puts them up, has to know how to use them, but he depends on God for the wind. You show up for your part, but God is in charge of the power, and the direction of the wind."

"Moose again?"

"You can thank my coast guard instructor for that one." He leaned up from the doorframe. "But this one is all me: Who is the king of your kingdom, Oaken? God or you? The answer to that question is everything. I'm going to make a sandwich. Want one?"

"Sure."

Axel left and Oaken pushed himself off the floor, put his guitar away, took another look at the lyrics he'd jotted down just before Axel came in.

Haunted by shadows, his heart starts to race.
The past won't let go; he can't find his place.
But Blossom's smile, like a beacon in the night,
Guides him through the darkness, towards the light.

Still sappy, but maybe closer. He set the notebook on the bed and headed downstairs.

Axel had bread out, buttering it, the griddle on the stove behind him heating.

The front door opened, closed, and Moose came in, snow and ice littering his snowmobile suit. "I think the blizzard is dying. The weather report says it's going to clear up by tonight."

Axel turned and slapped the bread, butter side down, onto the griddle. "But there's another one right behind it."

Moose peeled off his gloves, his hat. His dark hair stood up on end. Then he pulled off his boots, set them on the mat. "I almost have the driveway clear. But who knows about the roads. Any cell service yet?"

"No," said Oaken, who pulled his phone from his pocket, just in case. "This happen a lot?"

"That's why we have the ham radio," Moose said. "I can connect with Dodge with Air One over at Sky King Ranch. And the local state troopers, if we're needed."

He had worked off his one-piece snowmobile suit and now hung it on a hook to dry. Came into the kitchen in his stocking feet and thermals. "Whatchya cooking, Axe?"

"Toasted cheezers," he said. "I know it's not healthy, but it's comfort-food time."

"Amen to that. I'm going to build a fire." Moose walked over to the hearth.

Oaken followed him, handing him kindling from the copper

wood bin. Outside, the wind seemed to be dying, despite the occasional rattle of the windows.

"I probably should start packing up. I really appreciate you letting me stay here."

Moose looked at him. "You're leaving?"

"Now that the show's over . . . right? At least, that's what Huxley said a couple days ago."

Moose's mouth tightened. "Yeah. Huxley emailed me this morning, asking for some wrap-up interviews."

"Which means maybe I should stick around for a few more days, at least. Oh, by the way, does the team have the parachute from Mike's fall?"

"I think it might still be in our gear. Why?"

"Mike woke up, and he said someone tried to kill him."

"Seriously?"

"Seraphina isn't sure—he was still pretty out of it—but I told her I'd look into getting the parachute."

"I have a buddy who is a detective at the Anchorage police department who we could ask for help."

"Seraphina wanted to wait until he's awake and get a better picture of the truth, so I'll let you know."

"Will do." He gave Oaken a look. Then, "You could stick around and be a real part of the team."

Oaken handed a piece of firewood to Moose. "Oh, I don't . . . I mean . . ."

"God has you up here for a reason, Oak." Moose stood up and took a long match from a container on the mantel. Struck it and put it to the crumpled newspaper and curled birchbark.

"Yeah, to clear my head, make some money, maybe write some new music."

Moose stood, shook out the match. "Those are your reasons. What's God's reason?"

Oaken tightened his lips. Looked at Axel in the kitchen. "Sorry,"

Axel said. "Snow day spiritual conversations. I'd offer you whiskey, but this is a dry house."

"Your liver can thank me," Moose said to Axel. Then he turned to Oaken. "Listen. I believe that nothing happens by chance. There is a purpose behind everything—whether we've orchestrated it or it's out of our control. The answer isn't to seek the purpose but to ride the waves, respond to what God is teaching you."

"I've never considered the things that happen to me as God trying to teach me something. I've always thought . . ." Oaken looked out the window. "Maybe he was punishing me."

"For what?"

He looked at Moose. "For hating my sister." And he didn't know why he'd let that out. He'd blame it on the crackle of the fire, the smell of grilling food, and the way Moose seemed to consider him without judgment.

"So you let anger get a root inside you and tell you lies," Moose said.

Oaken stilled. "I wasn't angry—"

"Where do you think hatred comes from? We feel like someone got something we should have had, or that we were treated unfairly, or they hurt us and didn't care—any number of things. So we get angry, and it roots inside us. And with that root, the devil gets a foothold in your life." Moose closed the grate. "And then he seeds all sorts of chaos." He slapped the debris from his hands. "So why were you angry at your sister?"

Clearly Moose had no idea that he'd sent claws through Oaken's chest, turning everything raw and bleeding. "She wrecked our home. Our life. She didn't care about our dreams—just her own."

Moose walked back over to the counter. "Yeah, I'd be angry about that too—" Oaken followed him, sat on a stool. "—if I didn't know that God could put me exactly where I'm supposed to be, if I trust him."

Axel set a grilled cheese sandwich in front of him. "Made with good old American cheese singles."

"Yuck," Moose said.

"You're such a purist." Axel plated his own sandwich.

"But how can I trust God when—" Oaken started.

"When bad things happen to you?"

Oaken made a face. "Maybe when I cause bad things to happen."

"Like punching out a guy at your concert?" Axel said and sat on a stool next to him.

"Wow. This is a rough crowd."

Axel grinned. "Nice to be the one dishing it out." He glanced at Moose.

"Yeah, well, maybe that," Oaken said. "But also maybe . . ." He exhaled. "It's my fault my sister died." And maybe he did need that whiskey. "You guys have any chocolate milk?"

"Milk's in the fridge, hot cocoa mix in the pantry. Knock yourself out," Moose said.

Oaken got up and found the milk.

"Why is it your fault? Did you make the storm? Cause her to go into the ditch?" Axel said. Clearly the man knew the details.

Oaken shut the refrigerator door. "No." He turned to them. "But I did tell her that I hated her. That she was selfish and that she should leave. Oh, and this was on Christmas day—that's a fun memory."

"Oaken. We all say things we don't mean," Moose said.

Oaken reached for the cocoa.

"But based on your earlier words, you meant it."

He scooped in chocolate and stirred, not looking at Moose.

"And now you think God is punishing you."

"I would."

"Good thing you're not God."

Oaken looked up.

"First, God doesn't punish other people for something *we've* done. He's not going to take Hollie's life because you let anger have its way."

Oh.

"Second, the world is broken. Storms happen. Accidents happen. And people die. We can't escape that. So the question is—how are we to respond to that?"

He leaned a hip against the counter. Took a sip of milk.

"You can blame God," Moose said as Axel ate his sandwich, "and go it alone. Or you can trust that God loves you and that he'll carry you through the storm."

"It's been a long time since I've considered that God loves me." Oaken walked over to his own sandwich.

"You're here, aren't you? With us?" Moose slapped him on the shoulder. "God is not content leaving us in our lies. He wants to set us free, and he'll keep running after us, in every storm, trying to get our attention."

Oaken looked at him. Then, "Okay, fine. He has it."

Moose gave him a small grin. "I think he's had it for a long time. He started something in you, Oaken, when you jumped out of that plane. And I don't think he's done yet."

From the counter, a buzzer sounded, and Moose got up and headed to the source.

"You still use a pager?"

He picked it up. "Alaska." Then he headed into his office.

"I probably should have warned you before you moved in," Axel said. "Moose loves these get-in-your-face conversations." Axel sopped up the last of his ketchup with his bread. "Just glad I'm not the only target."

Moose came out of the room. "That was Deke Starr, up in Copper Mountain. The ski resort has lost a group of skiers and needs our help."

Axel slid off the stool, carried his plate to the sink.

Oaken didn't move.

Moose walked by him. "What do you think you're doing? Get moving. We have lives to save."

Boo was tired and crabby and unshowered and had spent too many hours over the past two days on social media, reading comments and rabbit trailing into past adventures and . . .

She'd even watched the episode where Blake threw her under the bus, like some kind of glutton for misery.

"You look terrible." The words came from London, emerging from her upstairs bedroom into the small family room of their tiny home. A fire flickered in the fireplace, Boo's one nod to trying to cheer herself up.

"Did you sleep on the sofa again?"

Boo sat curled up in a comforter, her pillow from her bed upstairs crammed against the arm of the couch. "Sleep? What's sleep?"

London wore a pair of leggings and a white knitted pullover, her hair back in a ponytail. "It's something we do from six to eight hours every night. And we usually do it with our phones off." She came over and picked up Boo's phone. "Ten percent battery left. I feel like it's time to tuck this baby in a drawer with a charger, and for you to do the same. Aw, look at the deck."

Indeed, the rain from Friday night had turned into a full-on blizzard, with icy snow and sleet pinging the deck and metal roof, loud and obnoxious and obliterating any hope of sleep. Hence, the sofa. Last night the snow had turned heavy, the wind adding menace, and she'd already made a nest here, so she'd stayed.

Now Boo looked out the window and saw that the snow had completely covered the deck, the yard, the trees, the shore and turned everything a stark white. A meager sun cast over the sound, but the trees didn't seem quite so tousled. "I think the wind is dying."

"I don't know. It's still looking wicked outside," London said, glancing out the sliding door. "There are darker skies to the north. Brr. Good day for a movie fest." She handed Boo back her phone. "You also have a couple missed calls."

"I know. I turned my ringer off. Couldn't take it anymore."

"Oaken?"

She glanced at London, shook her head. Although it did sort of bother her that he hadn't called.

Then again, maybe he never wanted to talk to her again. He couldn't have missed the crazy viral posts, right? Although, maybe he wasn't glued to his phone like the rest of the population of the planet. *Please.*

"Blake."

London had walked over to the kitchen area and picked up the pot of freshly brewed coffee. Now she paused and looked at Boo. "The guy from *Survivor Quest*?"

"Yes. Blake Hinton. The guy from *Survivor Quest* who betrayed me and is now dismantling my life."

London reached for a mug. "He's not dismantling your life." She set the mug on the counter. "As I see it, your life is fine. You have a job, friends, a hot man who was kissing you when I walked in."

She looked askance at Boo, smiling. Raised an eyebrow.

Boo drew in a breath. Made a face. "Okay, yes, we kissed."

London nodded, pouring her coffee. "Funny, I would have thought you might have sounded happier about that, given your food fight at the Tenderfoot."

"Not a food fight—okay, a little food fight. And I was—I think. I mean, I am. I think. I don't know."

London came over and sat on an armchair opposite her. "Please, don't stop there." She took a sip of coffee.

"I don't want to be stupid and have a repeat of Blake."

London cradled the coffee mug in both hands. "First, Boo, you can't let Blake and your anger for him get inside your heart. It'll do all sorts of destructive things, like make you afraid and controlling and bitter . . . Anger is the root of so much tyranny in our lives. You gotta figure out a way to forgive the man."

Yeah. No. Never.

"And second, Oaken is not Blake. He's not going to turn on you."

This she had an answer for. "You should have seen the way he walked away from me when Mike Grizz's wife showed up."

London took another sip.

"Like I was some sort of disease."

"You mean Seraphina Grizz? Former supermodel?"

"She is? Or was?"

"She's a social-media influencer, and very much about making Mike look good. They have two perfect children and a perfect house and a perfect life . . ." London finger quoted the last words. "But what people don't know is that once upon a time, she got picked up for drunk driving back in her small hometown in Iowa."

"What?"

London smiled. "I don't know that. Maybe she doesn't have a DUI history—let's hope not. But everybody has a past, Boo. Something they don't want people to know."

"I don't have a past. I have a present. And it keeps following me."

"But no one who knows you cares. *Your* people couldn't care less what MysticWinds382 thinks about you or Blake or anything that went down between you. Don't let random, anonymous people tell you who you are or what you're worth."

Boo just stared at her. "I . . ."

"And now, let's apply some truth to it. God's truth to it. What does God say about you and who you are?"

She had nothing. "I don't know."

London drew up one knee. "I can tell you. Jesus says that God sent him to bind up the brokenhearted, to proclaim freedom for the captives and release from darkness for the prisoners, to comfort all who mourn. God very much cares about your soul, your heart, and even how the world looks at you."

"I'm not sure you're helping," Boo said softly. "Because if he looked at my soul—"

"He'd see a woman he loves. And whom he wants to set free. And already has paid the price for her freedom, if she'll believe and accept that."

Boo swallowed. "You sound like my father. Or my sister Austen."

London smiled. "I'll take it." She took another sip of coffee. "How about this? God told his people that he would strengthen them and help them, and that those who raged against them would surely be ashamed and disgraced. So we're not supposed to be afraid. Or try to fix everything. Because we're not in control anyway. By the way, that's straight out of Isaiah 41. I can keep going if you want."

"When did you become a Bible scholar?"

London's smile fell and she took a breath. "Actually, I was a missionary—"

A knock sounded at the door.

London put down her coffee. "Did you invite anyone over?"

Boo pulled her hair back, found a fastener. "No."

London got up and headed to the door. Opened it.

Not Oaken, but Shep stood at the door, stamping his feet. "Hey, London. I came by to check on you guys and see if you needed a ride to the Tooth."

"Check on us?"

"Moose called both of you, twice. No answer."

Boo picked up her phone. *Oops.* Yes, two calls had come in while she'd been talking with London. And she guessed that London's phone was upstairs.

"Sorry. We didn't get them."

"Some skiers went missing last night up at the Copper Mountain ski area. Air One has been called out—both us and Dodge."

Boo had gotten off the sofa. "Does Oaken know?"

Shep had come in, closed the door. He wore a stocking cap and hadn't shaved. "I don't know. But it doesn't matter—they're not shooting anymore. According to Oaken, the show is done."

She was gathering her duvet into her arms, about to head upstairs to change. Now she just looked at him. "What?"

"Apparently Huxley has called a wrap. So I dunno. Is that coffee?"

"Have at it," London said, heading upstairs.

Boo followed her, not sure how to react to the stone in her heart.

But by the time she'd changed clothes, gotten into the back seat of Shep's warm truck for the ride through the slickened streets of Anchorage to the Tooth, she'd decided that, wow, she was an idiot.

See, this was why she shouldn't ever put on pants—

Oaken was standing outside the Tooth, dressed in a parka, snow pants, wool hat, and gloves as they pulled up.

He walked up to the truck as Shep put it in Park and they got out.

Boo looked up at him. "What are you doing here?"

Oh, that hadn't come out at all like she'd hoped. Or maybe he'd hoped either, because his mouth opened. "I . . . uh, I knew I should have called Friday night. Or come over."

"It's fine." She headed inside to the locker room.

But he grabbed her arm and pulled her down the hall into the gear room. Shut the door and rounded on her. "I'm sorry, Boo. I saw the meme."

Everything emptied out of her. She looked away, her eyes burning. *No. Not here. Not now*—"It doesn't matter—"

"It does. I should have called and checked on you. It was late, and I was out for chicken with Moose and—" He actually looked pained. "And that's no excuse."

She wanted to push past him, but he was standing in her space, blocking the door.

And she'd forgotten how to breathe.

"It's not fair, and it's not right, and social media is all lies, and I'm sorry that being with me has dragged this all up again."

She looked up at him. "This isn't your fault."

"Really?" He pulled off the hood, shoved his gloves into his pocket. "Because if you weren't with me, then none of this would matter." He swallowed. "But . . . you need to know that . . . I meant what I said."

She wasn't sure—

"There's something between us. Something good. And something . . . well, I lied when I said I didn't write that song 'She's My Girl' for anyone. Because, Boo, I think I wrote it for you."

Her mouth opened. What? "I thought . . . but . . . what's happening here?"

He touched her face, his thumb caressing her cheek. "What's happening is that maybe this isn't over. Maybe it's just starting."

Then he bent and kissed her. Just a whisper on her lips, and maybe it would have been more, but in that moment, the door slammed against Oaken, which pushed him into Boo, and it was all she could do to hang on to him, let him pick her up and hold her to keep her from falling.

Then he turned her around, and Moose came in. "Sorry. Oops. But this is not the time, guys."

And now she wanted to slink away into some dark hole and hide.

But not Oaken. "Moose. This is *your* fault. So give us two moments here."

His fault?

And then Moose held up his hands and walked out.

Walked. Out.

Wait, what just happened here?

Oaken turned to her, his blue eyes on hers. "Listen. We have things to sort out. And talk about. And maybe even decide. But for now, I'm going on this callout with you. So don't die on me, and . . . we'll continue this little chat when we get back." Then he smiled, leaned down again, and kissed her, shoving his foot against the door.

Oh boy. But London was in her head with, *"He's not going to turn on you."* So Boo held on to Oaken's jacket and let him kiss her, hard and fast, and when he leaned back he smiled, those blue eyes sweet and twinkling.

And maybe today wasn't a disaster. "Okay," she said quietly. "But you don't die on me out there, either."

"Me?" he said, holding the door open for her. "Have you met me?"

"Oh boy," she said as she pushed into the locker room. "Let's make sure we have extra batteries for our PLBs."

"What's a PLB?"

"Personal Locator Beacon. We wear them on our packs." She pushed past him to the locker room.

He followed her in. "That would have been nice to have when I was out with Mike."

"He probably had one. You just didn't activate it in your panic to save him."

His mouth opened. "That hurt."

She grabbed her gear from her locker. "First rule of rescue— don't panic. Use your resources."

He laughed. "Sorry, honey, but the show is over. You can stop giving me lessons."

She pointed past him to where Huxley had come in with Beto. "Tell that to them." She walked past the camera and gave it a thumbs-up.

ELEVEN

VEN FROM A LAYMAN'S PERSPECTIVE, THE odds didn't look good.

But Oaken was also starting to think like a rescuer. Which meant he considered the weather, the low ceiling for the rescue choppers, the falling temperatures, and the blizzard forming on the horizon.

They needed to get moving.

Which Moose must have agreed with, because he held a hasty meeting with Deke Starr, the sheriff from Copper Mountain, and the Air One pilot from Sky King Ranch, a man named Dodge Kingston. He recognized him as the pilot who flew the chopper they'd jumped from.

They huddled over a map of the Copper Mountain ski resort in a conference room that overlooked the wide ski runs and silent gondolas, buried in snow and ice.

"I give us about three hours of decent searching time before the ceiling crashes. Maybe four, if it holds, before darkness sets in," Moose said.

Dodge, tall, dark haired, embodied a sort of calm, the kind

that came before a storm, maybe. He leaned over the map. "There are five girls missing. They're here for a girls' bachelor weekend, although the guys are also here." He looked up at Moose. "And making noise. A few already went out looking, came back nearly frozen. I wouldn't be surprised if we have casualties. The groom is nearly frantic, and the bride's father is here too, so that's even better."

"They're all in the resort restaurant, in the catering room," Deke said. "A few are drunk, which doesn't help. But it was the best place to put them for now."

"What were the women doing out there?" Axel asked. He wore his insulated jumpsuit like a wetskin, unzipped to his waist, the shoulders and arms of the garment hanging around his hips. Shep did the same, but Moose had simply unzipped his, leaving it gaping around his chest.

Oaken took a note from Axel and kept his unzipped too. He stood in the room, listening, thinking, one of the team.

Huxley stood with Beto in the corner, capturing the conversation.

Boo and London were packing med kits outside near the choppers.

"There's a hot spring down a shoveled trail on the backside of the resort," said Dodge, running his finger along a trail. "It descends about four hundred feet to a river. The resort has created a sort of rocky pool there. Apparently, the women were headed there, but when they didn't return hours later, the groom went down to check on them. No one there had seen them. And by then, the blizzard really hit."

"How long have they been out there?"

"Since last night." Dodge stood up. "Apparently they were tired of being cooped up."

Silence. And Oaken could guess what Moose might be thinking. Moose took a breath, then studied the map. "Okay, let's sort this out. Any bear activity in the area?"

"Of course," Dodge said. "Some of the mamas are already venturing out of their dens. And wolves are in the area."

"So let's say they saw something. Maybe they'd run down here, to the river. It's probably still passable, most of it frozen. If I were running from something, I'd want to get back to the lodge. So . . ." He traced his finger down the river route. "I'd head south, toward the road."

"Or north—you can see the upper chalet from there," said Deke, leaning over now to point at the building marked on the map.

"Yeah," Moose said. "Okay, Dodge, you take the northern part of the river with Shep and London. Axel, you and Oaken are with me. We'll take Boo too." He looked at Deke. "Stay here. We'll keep you posted."

"A local pilot took a plane up with some of the volunteers from Copper Mountain," Deke said. "She's doing low sweeps of the area."

"Let's get some eyes on the riverbed," Moose said. "Axel, Oaken, be ready to hoof it."

Moose had lent Oaken some pack boots, thick and sturdy, along with a wool face mask, mittens, and a radio.

He barely recognized himself, just his eyes poking through like he might be an axe murderer.

Huxley, however, caught him leaving the room, behind Axel, and followed him outside.

"Oaken! A word for the camera before you leave."

He'd pushed through the double doors of the lodge and now stood outside, backdropped by the parking lot, where the two choppers sat. Moose had followed him out, eyed him as he hurried past. "Hurry up."

Oaken pulled off the mask. Huxley held up three fingers. Two. One. Pointed. "We're headed out to look for the lost women.

They've been out overnight, and with another storm coming, we need to work fast." He turned.

"Wait—Oaken. How do you feel about being included in the rescue?"

He looked at the camera. "I can't imagine being anywhere else right now." The words shook through him, settled. *Yes.* Then he raised his hand to wave and hustled out to the chopper.

Boo stood on the deck. "You ready?"

He nodded, climbed in, and she closed the door behind him.

Moose fired up the chopper, the other Air One bird already lifting off and clearing the area. The blades stirred up a tempest of white as they rose.

He looked out the window, down at the lodge. Not a small place, the lodge rose five stories, with a massive stone fireplace that jutted from the top of the timber building and picture windows that overlooked the surrounding view of the snow-clad Copper Mountain range. It sat in the center of a bowl, the ski runs rising around it, the light of the sun fighting hard to break through the dour clouds.

So much forest. So much snow. "This might be impossible," he said to Boo.

She gave him a grim nod.

The chopper lifted, then followed a ridge toward a semi-frozen river, flowing in some areas, chunks of ice and snow in others. He spotted the hot spring, a stone-clad bath higher up on the cliff with lighting and a path that led back to the lodge. Boo tugged out monoculars and handed Axel one, then Oaken. One for herself.

"Scan the riverbed, but also the shoreline in the woods. It's possible that if they were running from a bear, they might have climbed a tree," Boo said.

Moose flew as low as he could go and skimmed along the riverbank. The world was a wash of gray and brown and white, with some skims of green pine and an ashy river, maybe thirty feet wide, frothy, icy, and wild. Oaken scanned his monocular along the shoreline.

For a long moment, he was back in interior Alaska, running along a river, Mike's death thundering in his mind. That fear had fueled him, kept him alive.

What fear had pushed these ladies into a blizzard and trapped them there?

The river jagged west, and he heard Dodge reporting no joy to Moose when Oaken spotted it—something red amidst the trees.

"Moose—port side," he said.

On the tail of his words, someone ran out of the brush, waving her hands. She wore a parka, a hat, gloves, and boots and jumped along the shoreline, clearly unhurt.

"I see her," Moose said, circling back. "But I have nowhere to put down."

"I'll get her," Oaken said and cast a glance at Boo. She nodded.

"Axel, work the winch. I'll spot Oaken as he goes down."

Oaken sat, working on the harness over his jumpsuit. Boo knelt in front of him. "You know how to do this," she said as she checked his gear, then snapped on the winch line. She also hooked a harness to the winch loop with another carabiner.

Then she met his eyes, and for a second he thought she might kiss him.

Instead, she smiled. "Go get her." She patted him on the shoulder, then opened the chopper door.

Moose fought the sudden onslaught of wind but steadied the chopper. The woman stood below, maybe fifty feet down.

Oaken stepped out onto the skids. Boo, clipped in with her safety line, held on to his harness. "Ready?"

He nodded, and she glanced back at Axel. He gave a thumbs-up.

The winch started to lower him, and he pushed away from the strut slowly, then caught it with his hand and eased himself down.

Almost like a pro.

The wind caught him, turned him, but he kept his focus on the woman and then motioned her away from him as he touched down.

He stood on the beach, his feet planted, waiting for slack, then waved her over.

She'd been crying. Puffy, reddened eyes, her face chapped.

"My name is Oaken! I'm here with the Air One Rescue team. What's your name?"

"Lydia!"

"Anyone else with you, Lydia?"

"We got separated. I don't . . . I think they went back to the lodge. I got lost."

She had to be hypothermic, although the temperatures hadn't dropped much below freezing despite the storm. Still, so much exposure . . . "How did you survive?"

"I took a survival course in college—I made a snow cave and holed up in there."

Smart. "Let's get you into this harness." He held out the leg straps, then helped her into the waist and arm straps. Then he grabbed the front of her harness, the other hand on her belt. "I got you."

He looked up and gave Boo a thumbs-up, along with a "Take us up" into his coms.

The winch lifted them, and he held Lydia even as the line twisted, her eyes widening.

"It's okay," he said as they reached the strut. He put his foot on it and let Boo grab his harness and bring Lydia into the chopper. He stood on the strut while Boo hooked her into a safety line and unhooked her from the winch.

He leaned over to Boo. "I think we need to go to ground. The women headed back to the lodge. They could be anywhere in the woods."

"We're at least two miles from the lodge," she said. "That's a long way to hike." She turned to Lydia. "Where did they run?"

Oaken held on to the bed of the chopper, the rotor wash muffled, hearing their conversation through his in-helmet coms via Boo's mic.

"I don't know. He was chasing us and we got scared, so we just kept running," Lydia said.

"Who was chasing you?" said Boo.

"A man. He came down the trail after us . . . We took off, but he did too. Chased us down to the river. We kept running, but I fell." She pulled back her arm to reveal scrapes on her hands, her wrists. "When I got up, I just ran into the woods and hid."

Boo sat back. Then she reached for a harness. "Moose, I'd like to go back down with Oaken. I'll take the med and survival pack with us."

"Roger. We'll keep searching the riverbed."

She strapped on a harness and reached for the big survival pack.

Oaken took it from her and put it on. She gave him a look but he ignored her. "Clip in," he said.

She slid close, then clipped her carabiner into the winch hook.

"Did you take a walkie?" he said.

"Yes. Axel, put us down."

The winch started to move, and he grabbed her harness, held her to himself as they dangled from the chopper. The wind tried to grab them again, but he kept his eyes on the ground and landed, steadying her as she also touched down.

She unhooked and then released him. "Bring it up, Axe."

The winch went up.

"I'm going to bring her back to the lodge, but I'll be right back," Moose said. "You two keep the line open."

"Roger," Boo said. She looked at Oaken. "Now where?"

He shook his head. "Lydia said someone was chasing them. If it were me, I'd run into the forest." He looked around at the trek behind him, then a wooden bridge cluttered with snow and ice, some two hundred yards upstream. It led into a dense forest, but more importantly . . . "There's a trail. And according to the map of the resort, I think that leads to a summer equipment hut for the whitewater service."

"Good memory."

Moose had spun out and away and now left them alone on the riverbank. They hiked back up over the slippery stones.

"Who do you think was chasing her?" Oaken said.

"I don't know."

"Reminds me of what you said in the car—about the Midnight Sun Killer. Maybe he's out here."

She looked at him. "I hope you're kidding."

Maybe now wasn't the time, but wow, she was pretty, even in her puffy snowmobile suit, her hair tufted out of her stocking cap. His own words came back to him. *So don't die on me, and . . . we'll continue this little chat when we get back.*

But what was he going to say? That he didn't want to leave?

Maybe. Something about this life, this purpose, tugged at him.

"Hey. Is that a hat?" Boo ran up to something grimy, crushed against the rocks in the water.

Yes, a hat, soggy and soiled. Her eyes widened, and she handed it over to Oaken.

Sewn across the brim were the words *Bride to Be.*

"It could have floated downstream," he said.

She nodded, got up, and headed toward the bridge. He caught up. The bridge spanned the river, maybe ten feet over the rapids, cluttered with snow and ice along the footpath and railings. He held on to the railing, right behind her as they crossed.

On the other side, a new layer of snow obscured any tracks, but indentations suggested recent steps. She plowed through the crusty snow, high stepping, her feet plunging in, breaking through the icy layer. Not as deep here in the woods, the snow was crunchy, the dim light turning the forest into a horror movie.

Moose's voice came through the radio. "Where are you guys?"

Boo lifted her walkie. "We took the bridge. We're on the opposite side, heading to a supply shack on the western edge of the resort."

"I'll meet you there."

She clipped the walkie onto her pack strap. "Funny that no one thought to look out here."

"It's too far away from the beaten path. People only look for the obvious. They found my sister's car only thirty feet off the highway, but because a snowplow had come by and sprayed up a bank, they missed where she went off, and the trees obscured her."

"How awful."

As they moved farther from the river, the wildness started to quiet around them.

"When we didn't hear from her, my mom started to panic, and then my dad and she drove the entire route to Minneapolis. By then it had been over a day, so we alerted the state troopers. It took them another entire day to find her, and even then, they found Maggie and her mother first."

"Maggie, of Maggie's Miracle."

"Yeah." He looked at her. "Maggie will be sixteen and is having a birthday party next month, over Memorial Day weekend."

After a moment, she looked at him. "And?"

"And she wrote to me and invited me to the party."

More silence.

"Oaken?"

He kept walking, scanning the forest. "So, what you don't know is that . . . I've always sort of blamed myself for my sister's accident." For some reason, it didn't hurt quite so much coming out the second time. "We got in a fight right before she left, and I . . .

well, I always thought that maybe if we hadn't, she wouldn't have left and . . ."

"And wouldn't have hit Maggie and paralyzed her. I'm starting to put the pieces together. The fifty thousand isn't just a donation. It's . . . redemption."

He ignored the sharp stab of pain. "Sort of. I guess. The problem is . . . I don't really want . . ."

She stopped. Turned. Looked up at him.

"I don't want the world to think I'm some sort of hero, showing up to play for Maggie's party. Fact is, I donate through a charitable organization Goldie set up—Courageous Hearts. Maggie and her mom don't know that I'm involved." He drew in a breath. "But if I tell her, then . . ."

"Then you have to face the fallout."

"Yeah. I'm either a hero or a villain."

"And if you don't show up, you're sort of a villain too."

"But not if I send her fifty thousand dollars."

"So you're buying your way out of this."

He narrowed his eyes at her. Then, "Yep." He walked past her down the path.

She caught up with him. "Well, I think you're a hero. Just for the record."

"Yeah, a hero who jumped off the stage and beat up a guy because he couldn't face a sixteen-year-old kid with the truth. I'd gotten her letter the day before. And consumed way too much whiskey, and . . . yeah. Only chocolate milk for me from now on."

She laughed.

He didn't. "Truth is, Huxley was right. I am hiding."

Suddenly, he felt her hand take his. "Here's to hiding."

He glanced at her.

She gave him a soft smile, an expression that found his soul. *In her eyes, I see a love that will endure.*

The sound of a chopper thundered, and in a moment, the red bird zoomed overhead.

"There's the cabin," she said and let go of his hand, running through the snow toward it.

He caught up to her.

The door handle was broken, and she pushed it open.

He'd pulled out his flashlight.

Inside, two women sat huddled together on the floor. One had her ankle up on a pile of life jackets.

"We're with the rescue team," said Boo. "Are you with the bridal party?"

One of the women nodded. "Did you find the others? Lydia and Grace and Hannah?"

"We found Lydia," said Oaken.

Boo had come over, looking at the other woman's leg. "Your ankle is pretty swollen."

"I tried to keep ice on it, but then the blizzard got too wild. And . . ." She'd been crying, too, but was clearly not as stricken as her friend in the woods. "We got split up when . . . well, there was a man chasing us. He came after us. I thought Lydia had made it back. And then we lost Grace and Hannah. Ruthie fell, and by the grace of God I found this shack. I wanted to go for help, but I couldn't leave Ruthie."

"It's okay. We'll find them." Boo turned to Oaken. "Tell Moose we got them but we'll need a stretcher."

He swung the pack to the floor, and Boo got up and started to rummage through it. Stepping outside, he radioed Moose.

"We'll have to send down the cable with the stretcher and harness," Moose said.

Oaken went outside to the small clearing, not big enough for the chopper, and caught the cable with the stretcher and harness attached.

He unhooked them and brought them inside. Helped Boo load

200

up the injured woman—Ruthie—and then they carried her out and attached the litter to the winch. Boo hooked herself on and rode up the cable with the woman.

Oaken worked the other woman into the harness.

"What's your name?"

"Caroline." She gripped his jacket. "You have to find them."

"We will."

"No, you don't understand. The last two missing are my sister, Grace, and our ten-year-old cousin, Hannah."

He swallowed. "There's a kid out here?"

She nodded, her eyes glossy.

Boo had come down on the line. "Ready?"

He walked Caroline over to the cable, hooked her in, then drew Boo aside. "The bride and a ten-year-old girl are still out here. We have to keep looking."

Boo met his gaze, then looked up at the fading sunlight. "We're nearly out of sun."

"I know."

She nodded then. "Okay. Get the gear. I'll be back down. We're not going home until we find them."

He didn't know why those words reached to grab a broken place inside, but as she went back up the cable to deposit Caroline, he knew.

He wasn't done here yet.

She'd let her own stupid lies get them killed. "I'm sorry, Oaken," Boo said two hours later as the night descended around them. The wind had started to whip up, whistling through the trees and through her layers.

Moose still hadn't returned from bringing the victims back to the lodge, but Boo feared that the mountains interfered with their signal.

He might be circling in the dark, unable to communicate with them. And then he'd run out of fuel and—

"For what? Wanting to save a little girl?" Oaken's question reached out to her in the semi-darkness. "Um, for the record, me too."

She'd turned on her headlamp, and it pushed back enough of the shadows to reveal untrodden snow. But according to Caroline and Ruthie, they'd separated from the others back on the trail, so she and Oaken had backtracked and found another trail, this one leading into a canyon along the river, southwest, on the other side of the resort. It seemed to be a cross country ski trail of sorts, wide enough for a snowcat, although it hadn't yet been touched.

"This might be fruitless," said Boo. "How would they survive without shelter?"

"Hey." He grabbed her hand, not unlike she had after his story about Maggie. Suddenly, the chocolate milk made sense. He stopped her. "You don't know that. Maybe they're scrappy, like you were in the forest when you were lost."

She stilled. "You remember that story?"

"Of course I do." He frowned, then turned and kept walking, his light casting along trees.

Huh. He'd listened to her. Seen her.

Remembered.

See, this was why Oaken *wasn't* Blake, and she'd stop comparing him *right now.* Because Oaken was honest and kind and exactly the kind of person she'd want on her team.

Maybe even in her life.

"Hannah! Grace!" he shouted.

No answer, and the darkness just seemed to spill in around them. The trees crackled. From a distance, a howl lifted.

She found his hand. He squeezed. "Don't worry. I'd make a much more meaty lunch."

"That's not funny."

"Help!" The word rose, faint, on the wind.

She stilled. "Did you hear that?"

"The wolves, sharpening their knives?"

"Again, not funny. No, *listen.*"

Nothing but the wind shivering the trees. She put her hands to her mouth. "Hannah! Grace!"

A moment, then, "Here! I'm here!"

Not loud, but enough that Oaken nodded. "It sounds like it's coming from nearer the cliff side."

"If I was seeking shelter in a storm, I'd look for a cave, or an inlet." Boo headed off trail in the direction of the voice. "Keep shouting!"

Silence, and for a moment she thought maybe—

"Here! Help!"

Oaken pushed past her and took the lead, plowing through the deeper drifts, balancing on trees, holding them away so she could follow in his steps.

They broke out into a small clearing, tufted with white, and his light shone against a towering cliff wall.

It took a second for the realization to click in. She grabbed his harness and yanked back.

He stopped and snow fell away at his feet.

Then, suddenly, the entire shelf tumbled loose, caving in. He scrambled back, away, nearly on top of her as the ledge dropped, some twenty feet down.

"Crevasse," she said. He scooted back, away from the rip in the snow. "Take off the pack."

He shrugged it away, and she dug inside it and pulled out a rope, extra webbing, and a cord that held carabiners. She got up and fought her way to a sturdy pine. Securing the webbing around it, she clipped on a carabiner, then secured the line to it with a bowline.

She brought the line over to him. "I'm going to rappel down and see if I can find her.

"And if you do, then what?"

Right.

"New plan." She unhooked the belay line from the carabiner, then tied another length of webbing onto a nearby tree and attached her only pulley to it. Running her rope through it, she then secured the bowline knot via a carabiner to his harness. "You'll pull her up."

"And you?"

"You'll throw down the line and then unhook the pulley and belay me while I climb up. Remember how?"

He nodded.

She headed back to the line and clicked her descender onto it, then her harness to the descender.

Then she backed up.

He came up to her then, grabbed the front of her jumpsuit, looked in her eyes and said, "Don't die." Then he kissed her. A cold, brisk kiss, but it heated her all the way through to her bones.

"I won't." She went over the edge.

Her feet slipped on the cliffside—she should have worn crampons. And she had no ice axe. But she let the rope out easy and, thirty feet down, landed on snow.

Please, let it not be a bridge. "Hannah! Grace!"

"Help." The voice sounded nearer, smaller, fragile. And when she turned her lamp, the light fell upon a girl. She lay with her leg at a terrible angle, and even from here, Boo could diagnose a fracture.

"Hey," Boo said, unclipping from the descender. She walked up to her, crouched. "Are you Hannah?"

Frizzy brown hair, glasses, wide eyes, she still wore her hat, the one that said *Junior Bridesmaid,* her parka and snowpants. Probably the ravine had kept her protected, but, "I'll bet you're cold."

Hannah nodded.

"My name is Boo. I'm with a rescue team." She assessed Hannah's leg. The foot splayed out the wrong direction, overextended. "Can you move your leg?"

"Just my knee, but no, not my foot."

"Yeah, it looks like it hurts."

"I can't really feel it anymore."

Oh, not good.

Boo picked her way back over to the edge. "Oaken!"

His light appeared over the side. She held up her hand to shade her eyes.

"Sorry!"

"She's got a broken leg. There's an inflatable splint in the medical bag. Pull up the rope and lower it down."

The rope snaked up and he disappeared. In a moment, the entire medical bag came over the side.

She unclipped it and returned to Hannah. "We need to get that leg immobilized."

She reached for Hannah, but the girl pushed her away.

"What?"

"It's going to hurt!"

"Maybe. Probably. But we need to splint it before we get you up the cliff." She knelt next to her and slid the splint under her leg. Velcroed it shut. "I just need to stabilize it—"

Hannah's scream lifted, broke through the night.

Oh, yes, she could feel that.

"Okay, Hannah. It's okay." She pulled the girl to herself, holding on as she cried. "I know you're scared. But you're safe now."

"He's out there. That man—he was big. And . . . he chased us—"

"Listen." Boo held her away and met her eyes. "I brought my

own big man, and he's up on top of the cliff and he's not going to let anything happen to you, okay?"

"Or you?"

She smiled. "Or me."

"What about Grace?"

She drew in a breath. "We haven't found Grace. Or maybe the rest of my team has, I don't know, but I promise we'll keep looking. We need to take care of you first, okay?"

Hannah nodded.

Boo stood up and started taking off her harness, stepping out of it. "We need to get you up the cliff and back to the lodge, okay?"

Hannah's eyes filled.

Boo reached out to get the harness on her. Hannah cried out, pushed away from her. "No! No!"

"Okay, okay." Boo gripped her hands. "Take a breath." *Now what?*

She tromped back over to where she could see Oaken. "I have some pain meds in my bag I can give her, but even with that, getting the harness on is still going to hurt her."

"Can you get the harness around her shoulders? I can maybe pull her up that way?"

Not a terrible idea. She headed back to Hannah. "Honey. We really need to move you. What if I put the harness around your shoulders and waist?"

Hannah started to cry, but the trooper she was, she nodded.

Boo put the harness around her shoulders, then worked the waist strap around her and tightened it down.

"I need to move you over to the rope so my friend Oaken can pull you up."

"But what about you?"

"I'll come right behind you." Although her brilliant plan seemed not so brilliant after her descent. She'd need crampons and ice axes to climb that wall.

206

She'd cross that bridge after Hannah was up and out.

"Ready to move?"

Hannah nodded and Boo stood up and lifted her by her harness straps. But when she began to pull, Hannah started to thrash, moving down to grab her leg. "Stop, stop—"

And then she jerked right out of Boo's hands.

Boo slipped, her knee crashing down onto the ice—

Pain exploded up her leg, through her body, right to the top of her head. She shouted—maybe even screamed—and fell, gripping her knee.

Oh . . . oh . . . Her breath ripped right out of her as she tried to haul in air.

"Boo!" Oaken shouted from above.

She couldn't see him, her eyes focused on the sky above and trying not to scream again.

"Boo!"

"I'm . . . ah . . . I . . . ah . . . oh no." She rolled onto her side, put her hands on her knee, and a loud moan escaped.

"I'm coming down there."

Oh no—had she taught him how to use the descender? Maybe London had—*ah . . .*

Everything curdled inside her brain.

Hannah just started to cry. "Boo! I'm sorry—I'm so sorry!"

She rolled over and touched Hannah's outstretched hand. "It's okay—it's . . ." She closed her eyes.

Breathe.

She may have passed out, she wasn't sure, but the next time she opened her eyes, Oaken crouched in front of her. He wore the pack.

"How did you—what—"

"Shh. Listen. I tried to get ahold of Moose, but still nothing. The wind is whipping up, and I don't think I can get you both up the cliff. We need to find a place to hunker down."

"Hannah's leg—"

"First thing in the morning, I'll get her out of here. I promise."

"Can't you get her out tonight?"

His face twisted. "I . . . don't know. I don't think I can carry her in this—not with the wind. It's starting to really come down, and the temperatures are dropping. We need to get you both to shelter, either way." His expression hurt even her, so much pain in it. "I don't want to leave you out here alone."

Yeah, well, neither did she, but, "Try Moose again."

"I will. After I get you guys to shelter."

She wanted to argue, really, but instead, she gave a pitiful nod.

He looked at her leg. "Your knee is really swollen. I can tell even through your jumpsuit."

"It's hot and it . . . hurts." An understatement, but he already looked a little freaked out, and she didn't want to scare him.

"Okay. We probably need to put some ice on it." He stood up and shone his light down the ravine. "I think this might be a riverbed. Maybe I can find a cave. Or an overhang." He knelt beside her again. "I will come back."

She lay back in the snow, looking at the stars. "I believe you."

Then he was gone. And all she could do was listen to Hannah whimper.

Or maybe the whimper came from the little girl inside her, alone in the woods. She closed her eyes. Somehow, London's words filled her head. *"We're not supposed to be afraid. Or try to fix everything. Because we're not in control anyway."*

Clearly. But please, God.

Her eyes burned, wettened.

No, she would *not* despair. She rolled over and again found Hannah's outstretched hand. Took it.

"He'll be back."

Hannah turned to her side, her big blue eyes on Boo's.

They stared at each other until Boo heard the crunching of

Oaken's boots. She wanted to weep when he appeared out of the night. "I found a cave about fifty yards away. I'm going to carry Hannah. Then you. I promise I'll be back."

"I believe you."

He smiled, then turned to Hannah. "I promise to be careful."

She put her arms around his neck and he lifted her. And she didn't make a sound.

He disappeared into the darkness.

And then Boo really wanted to cry. Her knee burned, lava, encasing her leg in fire. She'd really hurt herself. Maybe even broken her kneecap.

Again, London walked into her head. *"God very much cares about your soul, your heart, and even how the world looks at you."*

Yeah, but how about how she looked at herself?

And see, that was the problem, wasn't it?

Oaken returned, his feet crunching on the ice. Above him, the wind had started to howl, tiny fragments of ice casting down into the ravine.

He put the pack on, then knelt beside her. "I'll try not to hurt you."

"I know."

But he did anyway as he lifted her under her legs and shoulders, and she turned her face into his coat and bit back words, a whimper, even as tears scraped her eyes.

He walked down the ravine, picking his way on the slippery path. "Hang in there, Boomer."

"What is that?" she whispered, more of a groan. "A new nickname?"

"Trying it out."

Okay, she didn't hate it.

They reached the cave—more of an overhang in the rocky wall, but big enough for him to crouch and then set her down. "Let's get some snow on that knee." He took off the pack, pulled a knife from the medical kit, then used it to open her pants, tearing at them.

The release of pressure made her bite down on her molars, a groan deep inside forcing its way out.

"Okay, yeah, it's bad." He got up and returned in a moment with a handful of ice and snow. "Let's pack this in."

The sudden extreme cold doused the fire burning through her knee. She gasped.

"Better?"

"Forget the chocolate milk. I'll take a whiskey."

He smiled, kissed her forehead. Then he fitted a gauze bandage around her leg, holding on the ice. Picking her up around the armpits, he helped her scoot into the alcove. Inside, she found an opening big enough to sit up in. He shoved the pack in behind her. She dug out a space blanket.

Hannah lay there, and Boo scooted beside her. Settled the blanket over them.

Oaken crouched just outside the opening. "I'm going to get some firewood."

"Look for the dead branches under the canopy of the pine trees, above the snow line. Those should be dry and burn well. "

"Got it. I'll be back."

"I believe you."

He disappeared again. In the glow of her headlamp, she spotted the PLB, snapped onto the backpack.

At least, maybe, after the storm, somebody would find them. She turned it on. Then she flicked off the headlamp.

"Are you okay?" Hannah said.

"Yeah. I think so." She pulled Hannah against her, her arm around her.

"What is his name? Your friend?"

"His name is Oaken."

"Like Thorin Oakenshield."

"Who?" She looked down at the girl.

"He was in *The Hobbit*. A warrior. A hero."

Boo wanted to smile, but it came out in tears. "Yeah, like that." Then she closed her eyes, sinking into the pain, and didn't even hear him until he returned with wood and set it just outside the ledge.

"I'm not a survivalist, Boo, so—"

She looked at the pile. "How many trips did you take?"

"Three."

"That should last us a while. Okay. Here's what you do." She groaned as she sat up, but the ice was helping. "We're going to make a safety fire."

She instructed him how to lay the wood at an angle so that the smoke tunneled out the back, the heat toward them, and then how to fill the pocket underneath with kindling to protect it from the wind.

He was a regular Boy Scout with his fire-construction skills. Badge-worthy.

Then per her instructions, he built, with logs and stone, a windbreak to protect the flames.

It took a couple tries, but he got the fire lit from the survival matches in the pack, holding his hands over the flame until it grabbed on, biting into the kindling, then the wood. A blaze crackled, and heat bloomed in their tiny enclave.

Then he climbed inside and settled himself between the girls, leaning against the wall of the cave and pulling them to himself, his strong arms warm, safe.

"I tried Moose," he said softly to Boo. "No answer, and I don't think he could get out in this wind anyway." He flicked the light of his lamp off. "My batteries are dying."

"You can use mine. I'm not going anywhere."

He didn't laugh at her pitiful attempt at a joke. Instead, his arm tightened around her. "We'll make it, Boo. Now, who wants to hear a cowboy story?"

She didn't know whether to laugh or cry.

Instead, she closed her eyes and just held on.

TWELVE

H E'D PROBABLY KILLED THEM ALL.
Oaken sat in the wan light of the dour morning, a trickle of gray denting the darkness in the cave. The fire glowed, just embers, and he should probably leave their nest and find more kindling, but he didn't want to move.

Didn't want to wake Hannah or Boo and send them spiraling back into pain.

He'd been sitting here for the past six hours, drawing a map in his head of the terrain, listening to the wind howl, and he couldn't escape the voices that said he should have gone for help.

Worse, Moose was also in his head, over and over. *"You can trust that God loves you and that he'll carry you through the storm."*

Oaken hated to admit it, but he wanted to believe it. Needed to believe it.

Because maybe there was no other way to survive.

Moose hung around, too, with his stupid but probably accurate sailing analogy.

"The answer isn't to seek the purpose but to ride the waves, respond to what God is teaching you."

Oaken didn't have a clue what God might be saying to him. But maybe it was enough to consider that God wasn't punishing him, or Boo or little Hannah.

Still, it was a little too loud in his head for sleep, so he'd sat up, debating everything.

Including whether he could walk away from the music. Because as much as this world called to him . . . it wasn't real. But it could be, maybe—

Under his arm, Boo shifted. He liked the nickname he'd given her—Boomer. Like she'd set off some sort of thunderclap in his life.

She lifted her head. Made a noise, deep inside her body.

"You okay?"

She sighed. "If I don't move it, maybe. How's Hannah?"

"She whimpered a bit in her sleep, but I think splinting her leg helped."

"We need to get her to medical care, ASAP."

"I've been thinking about that all night. The wind doesn't seem to be lifting. I'm going to have to carry her out."

"Yeah," Boo said. "Maybe I can . . ." She tried to move then and stiffened. "Shoot. I think I really hurt my leg." She looked up at him. "I'm going to have to stay here."

The words put a fist in his chest.

"I'm sorry, I'm . . . I'm sorry I turned into a burden."

"What?" he said quietly. "What are you talking about?"

"I went from being an asset to being . . . well, I'm sorry—"

"Stop. Right now. You're not a burden. You're injured." He caught her chin. "Why would you say that?"

Her mouth tightened. "Just . . . because."

"Boo?"

She sighed. "My real name is Brontë."

He raised an eyebrow.

"It's after—"

"The Brontë sisters?"

"Yes. My mom was a big fan."

"How'd you get Boo?"

She turned her gaze to Hannah. Finally, "My Marine squad leader, Staff Sergeant Hecktor, gave me the nickname. He was a tough guy, a great leader, and pretty much treated me like one of his men, even though I was a Navy attachment."

"Why'd he call you Boo?"

"He said that I had a way of just showing up out of nowhere."

"Like on the highway, about to run over a guy."

"Who is standing in the middle of the road—"

"Calm down. I'm kidding. But yeah, I see that. You're quiet but fierce, Boo."

She said nothing, and for a moment, he thought maybe he'd hurt her.

"Thanks. It's better than being the tagalong, whiny youngest child."

"Aw, c'mon—"

"Believe me. It wasn't easy being the youngest sibling in my family. My brothers are all hockey players, tough and brutal, and my sister is downright brilliant. She's a humanitarian aid doctor."

"Seems to me you're just as amazing."

"You're already on my good side, Oak. You don't need to—"

"Stop." He reached down and tucked his hand under her chin. Lifted it. "I find you to be amazing, Boo. Brave and smart and—"

"He died because of me."

A beat. "Who?"

"Hecktor."

"What?"

She shook her head, looked away, then leaned back into his jacket.

"Boo . . ."

She drew in a breath. Swallowed. "We were in Kabul, helping with the evacuation, and . . . it was chaos. We'd gone to retrieve a group of Americans secured at the embassy, and there were Taliban everywhere. We were loading people into trucks when one of our men went down. I ran over to take care of him. He was alive but had a leg wound, and I thought if I could get him to the trucks..." She shook her head, her eyes filling. "He was too heavy. I couldn't move him. And then the Taliban closed in on us, and Staff Sergeant Hecktor—they called him Hammer—told me to run, but I was... I was paralyzed. I didn't want to leave my marine, but I also... I was scared. Really scared. We hadn't been deployed into any real combat until then, and I froze."

He nodded.

"Hammer told the other trucks to leave, and he and a couple other guys came to get me. Hammer was killed rescuing me."

She met his eyes. "He was always saying how... scrappy I was. I impressed him during training—I not only kept my pig alive but I had better survival skills than a lot of the guys. He was the real reason I decided to join *Survival Quest*. I wanted to... I don't know... live up to all he thought I was."

Oh, Boo. "I think Hammer would be proud of you."

She looked away. "I don't know."

"Listen. You are tough, and amazing. But you're not a burden."

"Say that again when you're carrying me out."

He smiled. "Okay." And he couldn't stop himself from leaning down to kiss her. Something sweet, and he hoped she felt the promise in it.

He leaned away. "I'm going to try to restart the fire, then I'm going to get Hannah out of here. I've been thinking about how to carry her—I think I can make a sling for her with the backpack and carry her that way."

Boo nodded.

"I remember the map—I think if I keep going south it will connect with the river, and maybe I can get ahold of Moose. If not, then I'll hike up the river back to the lodge."

He caught her face again. "But I will come back for you."

"I believe you," she said.

The fourth time she'd said it, and again it reached in and hooked him, held him fast.

He might love this woman.

The thought rushed through him, latched to his bones.

Yes. Yes, he might *love* this woman.

Okay, just calm down. Get back to civilization and then ...

Then figure out what the future might hold.

Easing Hannah off his shoulder, he held her as Boo dragged herself over and took her in her arms. Hannah stirred and opened her eyes just as he left.

The wind howled above the cut of the ravine. Securing them in the cleft of the rock had surely protected them from exposure. Snow tumbled through the air but had died to just flurries.

He retraced his steps from last night, climbing up and out of the crevasse via a tumble of slippery rocks. Then he found more pine branches, broke them off, dropped them into the space, and climbed back down.

At the cave, he stirred the fire to life, blowing on it, building it back up, and resetting the windbreak with more sticks. The fire crackled, growing.

He crept into the space. Hannah was awake, her face pale and drawn.

Emptying the pack, he found a couple protein bars and gave them to Hannah and Boo.

Boo insisted on sharing hers with him. *Fine.*

Then he loosened the straps on the pack. "Okay, Hannah, we're getting out of here. I'm going to put you on my back and carry you out. I'll do my best not to jostle your leg."

She nodded, her eyes wide.

Then he worked the backpack straps over Hannah's legs so that the pack was to her back. He knelt in front of the cave, ducking to meet Boo's eyes. "I'll hurry."

"Just stay alive," Boo said.

"That's the plan." He dearly hoped God agreed.

Then he sat on the ground in front of Hannah, scooted back, and slipped his arms into the straps. The pack also had a hip strap, and now he angled that underneath Hannah's body and drew it around him, loosening it, then snapping it in place.

Hopefully her body would settle into the pouch of the empty bag. She put her arms around his neck.

"Okay, here we go." He gripped her thighs, holding her legs up as he moved one leg under him, rose, then pushed up.

She whimpered but hung on.

Then he put his head down and headed south.

As they walked, Hannah nestled her head against him.

Moose stepped back in his head. *You can trust that God loves you and that he'll carry you through the storm.*

He walked for an hour, the visibility short, narrow. Ice formed on his eyelashes, and for the first time, he truly appreciated the face mask. The ravine flattened out, the shoreline morphing from cliffs to banks, and finally he emerged out to the river.

It was so violent and frigid he didn't have a hope of crossing it with Hannah on his back. He pulled out his walkie and tried it, but nothing.

"Okay, Hannah. Hang on."

Nothing.

"Hannah?"

He looked over his shoulder, but he couldn't get a glimpse of her. She'd stopped singing, though, and he couldn't remember when.

If he put her down, he might not be able to get her back up. He turned and started hiking along the shoreline, his heart thundering. "Moose. Come in!"

Nothing, but he kept trying every few minutes even as he hiked up the shore. He guessed he might be a few, maybe more, miles downstream.

The wind bit at him, tried to sweep his feet out from under him, but he kept his head down, kept moving.

Started singing his repertoire of songs softly in his head.

His legs burned and he slipped, then again. Sweat burned down his back, his chest.

A tree had fallen across his path, and he stood, breathing hard, debating.

Then he trudged into the woods, around it, fighting the snow and branches until he came out on the other side.

Hannah never made a sound.

Oh, God, please help.

He wasn't sure where the words came from, just sort of squeezed out of him.

And then, as he trekked up the river, a song gathered inside him, a tune and then words. Something new.

On a lonesome road, under skies so gray, I face the storms, come what may.
In the dark, I lost my way, but I have to hope there's a brighter day.

For crying in the dirt, he was turning into a gospel singer. Still, he added a hum to it. And as he spotted the bridge up ahead, he heard another verse.

This one, however, felt like it came from somewhere, someone else.

Help me muster the strength to carry on,
Find the courage in my heart to be strong.
In the storm cloud's rage, let me find peace,
and in God's hand, my fears release.

"Oaken!"

He looked up and nearly stumbled. Light, and then through the fog and flurries, a red jumpsuit.

He stopped, breathing hard as the person came up to him. Although he wore a facemask, Oaken easily placed him when he said, "For Pete's sake, not a great day to go hiking, Oak. Where ya been?"

Axel.

"Who you got there?"

"This is Hannah. Check and see if she's breathing."

Axel stepped around him, and in a moment, "Yes. She's breathing. Unconscious, though. Maybe hypothermic."

"Or shock. She's got a broken leg."

"The walkies aren't working in the storm. Can you carry her up to the lodge? Or do you want me to take her?" Axel said, all joking gone.

"I'm afraid of jostling her. I can make it. But you need to send someone to get Boo. She's hurt."

"Where is she?"

"She's . . . back there. In a ravine. I think she broke her knee."

"All right. Let's get to the lodge and you can show us where. Besides, you need to get out of the elements, pronto."

He wanted to argue, but yes, he might need a cup of something hot. And a map. *Wait.* "What about her PLB? You could find her with that, right?"

Axel looked at him. "Right. We were following it—but . . ." He stepped behind Oaken. In a moment, he came back around, holding the device. It looked like a small walkie-talkie. "Unfortunately, I think this is it."

Oaken stared at the device. Wanted to say a word.

"Let's get you back to the lodge, and then we'll figure out how to get Boo. You left her with food and water, right?"

"And a fire."

Axel nodded. "Boo's scrappy—"

"Boo's hurt!"

"Calm down, Oaken. First rule of rescue—don't panic."

Oaken blew out a breath, but he'd left panic behind long, long ago. "Let's go."

Axel walked ahead of him, pushing away brush, watching to grab his harness should he slip. But something fueled Oaken—maybe the heat of rescue, of lives saved.

"I believe you."

He crossed the bridge, then hiked up the other side of the river, and by the time he reached the icy path up to the hot spring, Moose and Shep met him with a litter.

Hannah didn't rouse even as they eased her onto it, wrapped a blanket around her, and strapped her in.

He and Axel took one end of the litter and led the way with Shep and Moose holding her level as they ascended.

The sky seemed even darker by the time he arrived at the lodge. Ski patrol from the lodge met them on snow mobiles at the top of the trail and strapped her into a sled.

Oaken got on behind one of the patrol, as did the rest of the team, and they headed to the resort's emergency services area.

"Are you okay?" London said as he walked into the EMS area.

The heat hit his face, his body, and suddenly, his legs wanted to give out. He sat on a nearby chair and cast a look at Hannah. "I will be, if she survives."

"Her blood pressure is low, but we'll get her warmed up and in an ambulance for the Copper Mountain hospital. It's too dangerous to drive to Anchorage—"

"And the winds are too high for a chopper," Moose said. He had taken off his face mask, retrieving a cup of coffee for Oaken. "What happened? We tried to contact you—I couldn't go back out after we brought Ruthie and Caroline back."

"We figured that. We followed a ski trail and then heard Hannah calling us. She'd fallen into a ravine. Boo went down to get her, and she fell too." He took a sip of the coffee. "I think she broke her kneecap. It's bad—she can't walk." He handed the coffee back to Moose. "We need to get back out there."

"You're not going anywhere," Moose said. "You need to warm up and get some fluids in you."

Oaken stared at him. "I promised her I'd go back."

Moose nodded. "I know. We'll find her."

He stood up. "Now."

"Settle down, Oaken. We care about her as much as you do— but the weather is turning. I can't fly and I can't risk—"

Oaken pushed past him, grabbing his face mask.

"Oaken!"

He slammed outside. Stood for a moment.

The snowmobiles. He ran for the one with the sled and med kit attached to the seat.

"Oaken! Do not become someone we have to rescue too!" Moose, behind him.

He straddled the machine, fired it up.

Moose came out after him.

He gunned the machine and blew past the man, snow showering his wake.

"Oaken!"

But he didn't care.

He bent over the windshield, out of the pelting snow, and headed out into the blizzard.

Don't fall asleep. *Don't fall asleep.*

The fire had died, the cold curling into her alcove, and Boo's leg had started to ache again, something deep that found her bones, her cells, her mind.

She might not be going into shock, but exposure crept over her, turned her mind sluggish.

Don't. Sleep. Oaken kept his promises. She could trust him.

Outside, the wind howled, the darkness falling like a shroud.

What if he couldn't find his way back?

She closed her eyes. Fatigue swept over her, took her.

Nope. Bad idea.

Forcing her eyes open, she tried to move her legs and only earned a shot of heat and pain into her brain.

She had rationed the water in her bottle, now took a sip. It had formed some ice.

Some rescuer she'd turned out to be.

"God says that he will strengthen you and help you."

London's words, and sure, they sounded pretty and hopeful, but . . .

But there was the off chance that she didn't even register on God's radar.

That she was in this alone.

Her eyes fell closed again, and she realized she'd surrendered to sleep when Blake walked into her brain. When she opened her eyes to the memory of him in the tent, sitting up in his sleeping bag, his fever broken, the night still thick around them. Crickets and night sounds shifting outside.

Inside, they were safe. A team. "Hey, Boo Bear."

No. *Not* his Boo Bear. She knew that even as she smiled at him. She wanted to stop herself from sitting up, from reaching out to him. From believing the smile in his eyes, the things he'd said to her while battling his fever the night before.

"I need you, Boo."

"You're the only reason I'm alive."

Stop.

But no, she let him kiss her. Let herself believe his lies.

Let herself betray . . . well, herself.

She thrashed against the memory. "No—get away from me—"

"Boo?"

The voice—not Blake's. She shook, her entire body trembling as she fought to wake up.

"It's okay, Boo. I got you."

Hands moved over her, and she felt something tucked around her leg, then pressure.

She opened her eyes with a cry.

Gasped.

Oaken crouched over her—at least she thought it was him. It sounded like him. But his face mask was caked with snow and ice.

Then he looked at her, and her breath reeled out. Yes, Oaken, those blue eyes—

"Sorry. I had to get a splint on you before I got you out of here." There he was, and he wore such a tender expression. He pulled up his face mask.

Oh wow, she was in love with him. The sense of it swept through her, and she wanted to weep with the brutality of it. She could not love another man who walked out of her life.

But Oaken wasn't a betrayer. He kept his promises.

"You came back."

"Please," he said. Winked. "I said I would."

She nodded, looked away.

"Okay, listen. We have a long drive back. I got you a sled and a sleeping bag, but it's going to be bumpy. You ready?" He met her eyes. "I got you."

Then he put his arms around her, under hers, and around her torso and pulled her out of the cave. She tried to stabilize her knee and not shout.

He pulled her over to a snowmobile sled. "Where's the snow machine?"

"I couldn't get it into the ravine. But it's not far."

He eased her into the sled, into an open sleeping bag, then

zipped her up. Bungie cords strapped over her held her in place. "Here we go." He lifted the metal bars—he'd strapped another cord on the ends to make a sort of cross strap. This he put around his neck, the bars under his arms, held onto them, and started moving.

She tried to stay awake, but the hush of the sled and the swaying movement kept pitching her into sleep, only to be jarred awake when she hit a snag in the ground.

"Sorry, Boomer. I'm trying here."

His voice felt so far away, but she clung to it. Because yes, she was so far beyond falling for this man.

They finally reached the snow machine, and he hooked up the sled, climbed on. "Okay, we're on the cross-country ski trail. It goes over a bridge not far from here and rounds back to the lodge. I'll have you back soon."

He eased out, and the path seemed less bumpy, the motor's engine and the crisp edge of night urging her to sleep.

She was sitting around the campfire, the night of the vote. Watching Blake meet Misty's eyes and smile, hearing her name called as the castoff.

She saw herself look at Blake, saw the way he looked away from her.

Felt again the punch in her gut, the horror of the betrayal, the rawness that ripped through her entire body.

The sound of the motor opening up caused her to jostle awake. The air briefly fogged with the stench of gasoline, and snow flew up around her in a sheet. Oaken was driving through powder, probably a field. Some of the snow landed on her face, and she licked it off, her throat desperately parched.

Or maybe it was simply the memory of seeing Blake talking with Misty, nodding, as if they'd planned the entire thing.

Hazy lights cast down over her, and she recognized the parking lot of the resort. Oaken drove around the massive lodge—she spotted the windows, lit up like eyes—and along the pathways all the way to the end.

Then, voices.

Shouting. Mostly Oaken, but then Moose, and suddenly Axel and London were there, unstrapping her.

"We got you," London said.

Oaken appeared at her head, holding on to the top of her sleeping bag. Axel took the other end, and they carried her inside a building.

The EMS station. Level five, which meant that they didn't have X-ray machines. Still, they could administer pain relief, the center staffed with a physician and nurse. The warmth of the unit hit her like a bath, and every muscle in her body released.

They moved her to a bed, and a female physician stepped up. "Hello. I'm Dr. Huntley, orthopedics and trauma. Sounds like you had a fall. Can I take a look?"

She unzipped the sleeping bag, but Boo's attention was on Moose, pulling Oaken away into the hallway. He cast his voice low, but his expression sent a sliver into her heart.

What—

And then the doc took off her bandage, and all her attention went to the pain streaming through her. She gasped, lay back, gripped the sides of the bed, breathed. *Oh. Wow.*

"Yeah, this is pretty swollen. Let's get some pain meds going here so we can transfer her." Dr. Huntley turned to her. "The nurse will start your intake, but before I order anything, do you have any allergies?"

"No." Her voice emerged stripped and tight.

A nurse put another ice pack on her knee, and the cold sank in, took the edge off. Boo closed her eyes.

In a moment, Oaken returned. "How are you doing?"

She opened her eyes. "Moose looked mad."

He made a face. "Yeah." He leaned down and kissed her forehead. "All that matters is that you're going to be okay."

A male nurse came in with an IV kit, and Oaken stepped back while he found a vein, then inserted the IV. He attached an IV bag. "That's just fluids, but you're in luck. The doctor ordered you a little pain cocktail." He picked up a needle, then inserted it into a port in the IV. "You should be feeling better in a bit."

"Thanks."

"Anything for our heroes." He patted her shoulder.

The drugs filled her veins, burning a little, but they further loosened the edge off her knee. She turned to Oaken. "How's Hannah?"

"I think they took her to the hospital in Copper Mountain."

"Good." Her voice already sounded slushy. She took a breath. "You okay?"

"I am now."

A voice rose from beyond the curtained area. "You've got to be kidding me!"

Oaken looked at her, frowned, then glanced at Moose, who had come down the hall. He stood just beyond her bed.

The voice came into view. An older man, mid-fifties maybe. "Where's my daughter? You're just going to leave her out there? What is wrong with you people?"

Axel had stepped up behind Moose, a coolness in his expression.

"Listen, Mr. Benton," Moose said. "The weather is not safe for our people—"

"*He* was out in it!" The man pointed at Oaken. "He brought back his girlfriend."

Boo froze. *What?*

"I saw him freak out on you when you brought Hannah in." He turned to Oaken. "And you couldn't stay out there, keep looking for Grace? What kind of rescuer are you?"

Oaken just stood there.

"Don't you even care that she's out there freezing to death?"

"Of course he does," Boo snapped, not sure where the words came from. Maybe she could blame the drugs, but—"He very much cares. His own sister froze to death, so yeah, Oaken is probably the one person who would do anything to find your daughter. But if you haven't noticed, it's a blizzard, and we barely made it back—"

"Maybe you shouldn't have without my daughter!" He looked at Oaken. "You left her to die."

Oaken looked slapped. Flinched.

"And maybe you shouldn't be such a jerk to the people who risked their lives for you," Boo retorted. "Your daughter isn't the only one who could die out there!"

"That's enough," Moose said, putting his hand on the man, glancing at Boo.

The man swiped it away and swung his fist at Moose.

Moose caught it and forced the man back. Shep was behind him and now put his arm around Benton's neck, sleeper hold. But he didn't bear down. "Calm down."

"Let me go!" Benton slapped at his arm.

"Stay calm," Moose said. "Listen, we get it. But I'm not going to risk my people any more than I already have. We're sick about this as much as you are, and I promise, the minute the storm lets up, we'll be back out there. But for now, maybe you should spend more time praying instead of drinking."

Benton shook away from Shep, pushed him back, and stormed away.

Shep raised an eyebrow to Moose.

"That was exciting," Axel said. He turned. "Did you get all that?"

Boo followed his gaze and spotted Beto and Huxley standing in the corridor.

Great. But maybe she didn't care.

And maybe it was the drugs.

She sank into the pillow. Oaken turned to her, the residue of

Benton's words on his face, in his eyes. She wove her hand into his. "Oak. That's part of the gig. You can't save everyone."

His mouth tightened, but he nodded.

"Can you get me some water? I'm so parched."

He kissed her forehead. "I'll be right back."

I believe you, she wanted to say, but he walked away.

Huxley followed him.

Boo closed her eyes.

"Good job, Oaken. That was fantastic. And wow, the way Boo went after that guy . . . rough. Almost cruel. I don't think anyone will call you the bad guy when this airs."

What? She opened her eyes, unable to breathe.

"Hux—that's not—that's not the deal," Oaken said.

Deal? What deal?

The drugs, however, were sweeping her away, taking her under.

No—wait!

"I told you, it's not like that—"

And then blackness washed over her, carrying her away.

THIRTEEN

SHE WAS JUST OVERREACTING.

Boo lay in the hospital bed in the shared room of Alaska Regional Hospital, her leg in a brace, trying to turn the conversation around, skew it so that it didn't cut through her.

"Good job, Oaken. That was fantastic."

What did that even mean?

She leaned against the pillow, the sun finally breaking through the clouds, which had emptied themselves on Anchorage overnight, and glistening on the layer of fresh snow. Through her window, the Alaska Range rose, topped with a frosting of white against a backdrop of blue sky.

The temperatures, however, promised to skyrocket into the forties today, so it wouldn't last long.

Not unlike her little romance with Oaken Fox. What. Had. She. Been *thinking?*

The door to her room opened, and she heard someone come in—maybe the nurse, because she greeted the woman in the bed next to her. "Janice, how is my favorite patient this morning?"

Boo closed her eyes. Her knee throbbed, the pain killer wearing off. But hopefully today she could go home. She'd arrived at the Anchorage hospital last night after a long and harrowing ride in an ambulance from Copper Mountain. Not that she remembered much. She'd awakened a couple times to see London sitting with her.

She hadn't asked about Oaken.

"I'm feeling much better," said Janice. "My daughter should be in to see me soon."

"She's right outside." Rustling beyond the curtain, and the sound of the bed being raised. Then the Velcro rip of a blood pressure cuff. "Your blood pressure seems back to normal."

"I told her it was just angina, not a heart attack."

"The doctor will be in soon with your test results. Breakfast is on the way too."

The nurse then came around the curtain. Warm brown eyes, her dark hair back in braids. "And how's our local rescuer this morning?"

Her name badge said Oolanie.

"I want to go home," Boo said as the woman raised her bed, then checked her current blood pressure. Probably high, given the thoughts circling her brain.

"The doctor will be in soon, but I do have in the notes a possible discharge." She looked up from her tablet. "You have a visitor waiting in the lobby."

And right then, her chest clenched. Half hope, half dread. What would she say to him? Maybe it was best she'd had some time to think, to . . .

"Should we issue her a badge?"

Oh. "Yes," Boo said.

Nurse Oolanie pushed the curtain back a little, just as Janice turned on the television attached to the wall.

The local news flicked on, the woman on the screen updating the local traffic report.

Maybe she should just calm down. But every time she shook away Huxley's voice, Oaken's swept in after it. "*Hux—that's not— that's not the deal.*"

A *deal*.

What kind of deal?

"Such a tragedy," the woman in the next bed said. "Were you with the rescue team?"

She pointed to Boo's red jumpsuit, hanging over the back of a chair.

"Yes, I was."

The scene on the television changed, and the woman popped up the volume. A woman reporter stood outside the chalet at the Copper Mountain ski resort, giving an update to the in-studio hosts.

"You can see behind us that the coroner showed up to transport the body back to the Anchorage police station."

The screen switched to tape of the woman talking with Deke Starr. "We found her this morning while resort plows were cleaning up one of the cross-country trails near the resort. Sadly, she was only some three hundred yards from the chalet. Investigators believe she might have been on her way back and got lost in the storm."

"Then why the coroner?"

"I can't release that information, but we do suspect a possible homicide."

The report cut back to the reporter. "I'm here with one of the victims, a Caroline Schumacher, the woman's sister."

Boo sat up, recognizing the woman from the hut. She'd cleaned up, her dark hair up in a bun, wearing a white puffer jacket. Her eyes were reddened, clearly from crying. "We just wanted to thank the Air One rescue team for everything they did to find her. And especially Oaken Fox, who went back out last night and this morning."

She offered a wan smile. "I couldn't believe it when I saw him on the team, but he's a real hero, and I'm glad he's the one who found her. She was a real fan."

"I'm so sorry for your loss," said the reporter, then turned back to the camera for the out.

Of course he was a hero.

And then, as the reporter threw it back to the studio, the camera caught Caroline walking up to Oaken.

It stayed on them, the reporter even turning to watch, as Oaken embraced her.

Janice's daughter had walked in sometime during the airing and now stood back. "What was Oaken Fox doing at the lodge? I wonder if he was on vacation."

"You should ask her," said Janice, pointing at Boo. "She was with him."

The younger woman looked at her. "You were with him?"

Oh. "I was on the rescue team, so . . ." She couldn't bring herself to offer any more.

"Is he . . . amazing?"

Boo's eyes burned. "Just like you see him on TV."

The door opened, and she wanted to spring from her bed and pull London into an embrace. London wore a pair of leggings, her puffer jacket, and Uggs, and carried a backpack. "Hey, you."

"Hey."

London came up to her, took her hand. "How's your knee?"

"Hurts. Doc said my kneecap is cracked in three places, so that's awesome. No surgery, however, just a long recovery time. Did you go back to Copper Mountain last night?"

"No. The weather wasn't great. But I called up there this morning. They found Grace."

"I just saw the news report."

London's voice fell. "It looks like she might have been murdered."

"The reporter talked with Deke. He said the police were looking into it."

She stuck her hands in her pockets. "I saw Reynolds in the lobby with Seraphina. I think they're waiting for Oaken."

Her eyes widened. "He's coming here?"

London frowned. "Yes. Of course. Moose texted me—they landed a bit ago at the Tooth."

So the report must have been pre-recorded.

"I don't want to see him."

London gave her a look, then reached behind her and pulled the curtain. As if that might protect their conversation. *Whatever.* "Why?"

"Because . . ." Boo closed her eyes, then pressed her hands to her face. "I just . . . oh, London. I think I made a fool out of myself."

London's hands wrapped around her wrists, pulled her hands away. "I don't understand."

Boo sighed, her throat thick. "I think I fell for him."

A beat.

And she could hardly bear to say it. "But I think it was all an act. For ratings."

"No—"

"Yes. I heard Huxley and him talking after I had my little run-of-the-mouth moment with the father of the bride. Something about how he wouldn't be to blame when we broke up—and that he'd kept their deal, or . . . I don't know. I was on drugs."

"Exactly. You were on drugs. How do you know what went down?"

And that was just it, wasn't it? She didn't.

But she couldn't bear to find out. To be *right.* "Let's get out of here."

"What, now?"

"Yes. Get my clothes."

London plopped the backpack on the bed. "I brought you sweatpants and a sweatshirt."

"I love you."

"Yeah, well, I don't love this idea of you breaking out of the hospital."

"I'm fine. I have a brace. The doc is discharging me today. Get a wheelchair."

London took a breath, then nodded and disappeared.

Boo untied her gown, then pulled on the sweatshirt. It was long and oversized. She found her phone in the bottom of the pack too.

Then she swung her legs off the bed, gritted her teeth against the rush of pain to her knee as the blood flowed. But she shoved herself into the sweatpants and was mostly dressed when London reappeared. "I'm going to get into so much trouble for this."

"No one will know."

"I think they'll figure it out when the doc comes in and sees your empty bed." But London helped her into the chair.

"I'll call him later." She looked out the window to the parking lot. "I think that's Moose's truck pulling in. Hit it."

London got behind her, pulled her away from the bed and toward the door.

"Are you leaving?" Janice said.

"Live long and prosper," said Boo and held the door for London as she pushed her out into the hallway.

"Just ignore Nurse Oolanie," she said as London hustled her down the hall. But a glance at the empty nurses's desk loosened the grip on her chest.

London knuckled the elevator button. "I feel like I'm party to a jail break. You should just talk to him."

The doors opened and London wheeled her inside. "No. I mean . . . yes, I know, but . . ." She looked up at London as the doors closed. "It's so embarrassing. I do this stupid thing where I fall for guys just because they're a little nice to me—"

"Oaken was more than a little nice to you, Boo. You two . . . you two clicked."

"Yeah, I thought I clicked with Blake too—"

"Stop thinking about Blake. This is about you and Oaken—"

"No, this is about Blake and the fact that I can't trust myself with anyone. And Oaken and his big life is too . . . dangerous. And I should have figured that out. I got caught in the crazy idea that he wanted . . . I don't know . . . this life, maybe. I'm such an idiot."

The doors opened.

Oh no. Press. They congregated in the lobby of the hospital. "Why are they here?"

"I don't know."

And then, *wait,* she figured it out. Huxley stood talking to one of the reporters. Who knew what she was saying, but Boo wasn't going to stick around. "Cut around to the side exit," she said to London, who wheeled her past the group and down the hallway to the other exit.

"For the record, he does know where you live."

"But the press doesn't. And the last thing I want is some sort of painful showdown for the world to see." She gritted her teeth, painfully close to her throat closing up. "I just want this to go away. For *him* to go away."

"Let me go get the car."

Boo searched the hallway. So far, empty. "Hurry."

London pressed out of the doors, then lit out into a jog. The woman was quickly becoming Boo's best friend.

She pulled out her phone and turned it on. Two missed calls, and she recognized Blake's number.

Great, just great.

Noise behind her made her look up.

The press had moved toward the elevator, and she stiffened, seeing Oaken holding up his hand, moving toward the elevator bank with Moose.

She ducked her head. *Hurry up, London.*

London's Subaru pulled up. She parked at the side entrance and got out, jogged around the car. Boo had already hit the button for the automatic doors. Then she got up on her brace. What she needed was crutches, but London caught her and helped her out, then into the back, her leg up across the back seat.

"Let's get out of here."

London got into the front. "Now I'm the getaway driver."

"Just drive, baby."

She pulled away, and Boo ducked down into the seat. The roads still bore the onslaught of the spring storm, much of the snow debris now shoved to the snowbanks, the roads wet and grimy.

"The blizzard broke early this morning," London said. "I shoveled before I came in."

"How is little Hannah?"

"I don't know. I think she might still be up at the Copper Mountain clinic. Moose was really worried that you'd need surgery, so he made the ambulance bring you here."

"Four weeks in a brace, then PT. So that'll be super fun."

They drove along the shoreline, the inlet still throwing waves against the rocks. Boo's stomach growled.

"What do I say when Oaken shows up at our doorstep?" London asked.

"Maybe he won't."

"And maybe you'll suddenly get up and run. C'mon," London said, glancing in the rearview mirror. "Hiding only makes things worse. You need to talk to him. This could be a simple misunderstanding."

"Or talking could make things worse," Boo said. "He could say the things I am hearing in my head and make them real. Trust me on this."

London pursed her mouth but said nothing, her gaze back to the road.

They pulled up to the house, and Boo stilled to see a rental car in the lot.

Oh no.

"Seems like he beat us here."

That couldn't be, but she nearly told London to put the car in reverse. Then she spotted a man standing on the deck, staring out at the sound. Tall, wide-shouldered, dark hair, wearing a black jacket, boots.

Not Oaken.

All the same, everything tightened inside her. Especially when he turned, spotted them, and came off the deck, walking along the shoveled path to the driveway.

He opened her door and crouched. "Wow. That doesn't look fun."

"What are you doing here, Doyle?"

He made a thin line with his mouth. Then, "Dodge called Dad and told him you were missing and to pray we found you. Austen then made me get on a plane. It took me forty-eight hours to get here, and by the time I landed, Moose said they'd found you but you were injured." He eyed the brace. "Broken leg?"

"Broken kneecap."

He grimaced. "Okay. Well, let's get you inside and packed."

She was scooting toward him but stopped. "Packed?"

"It's time for you to come home, little sis."

"I'm not sure what I did," Oaken said. He stood at the window of the Alaska Regional Hospital, staring out at the thawing parking lot, the sun high and strong.

Twenty-four hours after he'd returned from Copper Mountain, after he'd landed at the Air One HQ, rushed over to the hospital . . .

"She just . . . left?" The question came from Seraphina, who held coffee and stared at him from where she sat next to Mike's bed. He'd been transferred, finally, to the med-surg ward, his leg still in traction, still on O$_2$, although his stats were rising.

And he was managing to be awake for longer periods of time. He still looked wan and thin and diminished, however.

Now he slept, his eyes opening occasionally.

"Walked right out of the hospital without being checked out," Oaken said. "I walked through a crowd of press—thank you, Huxley—and went up to her room, and her roommate said she'd escaped. Like a prison break."

"Maybe she was just tired of hospitals," Seraphina said. "I am." She put her hand on Mike's arm. "But also grateful for everything they've done for Mike."

"I don't think that was the problem," he said quietly. He walked over to the other chair, sank down in it. "After I came up to see you, I went back to the Tooth with Moose, got my car, and Moose gave me her address. I went over to her house." He looked at his coffee. "She was gone. Went to the airport with her brother."

Silence.

He looked up.

"Well, I can't say that I'm that upset."

His mouth opened.

"She's . . . Huxley showed me the video of her telling off that poor man—"

"Who tried to hit Moose! The guy was upset—I get that. I was upset. We all were. And we'd done our best to find the woman, but it was dangerous outside. As it was, I stuck around and we went out as soon as the blizzard lifted. I'm not sure we would have found her without the cat plowing her up."

"That's so gross."

"It is. And . . . she was . . . well, for sure she'd been killed. How, we're not sure, but it looked like an assault, and that she'd been shot . . ." He shook his head against the memory.

The dark side of rescue.

"Her sister was grateful." Seraphina smiled.

He stared at her. "Yes." He didn't love the fact that the camera caught her embrace, but what was he going to do—push her away?

"And the social media is fantastic." She picked up her phone from the nearby cart, opened an app, and flashed him a picture. Caroline hugging him, with hearts and a #countrymusichero hashtag across the picture. "And there are a lot more." She put the phone down. "I think you're finally the darling of country music again. No more state fair memes."

A sourness sat in his stomach. "I don't care what social media says." He got up. "I need to talk to Boo. But she won't take my calls, either." He finished his coffee, dropped it in the basket. "All I can think is that maybe she overheard what Huxley said about me faking our relationship for the camera."

Seraphina raised an eyebrow.

"But certainly she would have heard me tell Huxley that wasn't true—we practically got into a shouting match right there in the clinic."

"I know. She told us about it when she stopped by yesterday, after you left."

He shook his head. "I'm done with this reality television business."

"Don't say that." The voice that emerged from Mike trembled, weak. He opened his eyes, blinked, and looked over at Oaken. "You did great."

He held up his hand, trembling, a fist for Oaken to bump.

Oaken met it. "Glad to see you awake, Mike. You had us all scared."

Mike gave a wry smile. "Drama for the camera."

"Right. Listen. You get well." Oaken thumped him on the shoulder. "I'm heading out today to the lower forty-eight."

"How did your songwriting go?" Seraphina asked.

He stopped at the end of the bed. "Actually, after Boo left, I hung around in the lobby. It was pretty late, but there's a piano there. I worked out some lyrics."

More than some. He'd let himself stir up the words he'd found on his hike with Hannah.

"I can't wait to hear the song." She got up and went over to him. Hugged him. Then caught his face in her hands. "You're the real deal, Oaken. Don't let anyone tell you anything else."

He offered her a smile. Nodded.

"Oh, Oak," Mike said as Seraphina stepped away. "Did you ever find out about my chute?"

Oaken frowned. "You mean was your chute tampered with?"

Mike shook his head. "The pack I used—it wasn't mine."

Oaken stilled. "Wait. How did you know which one to give me?"

"I didn't. I just grabbed one."

Oaken went hollow. "Are you saying... Wait. I could have been the one who slammed into the ground?"

All the air seemed to leave the room.

"Moose has the chute," Oaken finally said. "He said he was sending it to a friend in the police department. I'll ask him about it."

Mike nodded. "Be careful. Live big, live wild."

"Thanks, Mike." Oaken exited the room.

Reynolds stood in the hallway, reading his phone. He wore a pair of khaki pants, a sweater, boots. Hollywood goes to Alaska. He looked up. "Heading out?"

"Yeah."

"You did your final interview with Huxley?"

Short, and he'd had to sort of grind out his smile, but, "Yes. It's in the can."

The executive producer held out his hand. "Thanks for every-thing, Oaken. Really. Without you . . ." His mouth tightened.

Oaken nodded again. "Take care of them."

He headed down the hall, into the elevator, and outside.

To his surprise, Moose was in the lobby. For a second he hoped . . . but no, Boo had left.

Without saying goodbye. Without letting him explain.

"Hey, buddy. We wanted to catch you before you left."

We? Oaken looked over and spotted the rest of the Air One crew sitting in chairs. Now London, Shep, and Axel got up. Walked over to him. Axel held out a coin. "This is the Air One challenge coin. It'll get you nothing but respect. Or drinks down at the Tenderfoot. I suppose that might include chocolate milk."

He took it. Heavy, it felt a little like a medal and bore the Air One Rescue logo on the front, the state of Alaska map on the back with a chopper etched over it.

"Don't lose it or you'll owe us a round of drinks next time you're in town," said Shep. "*Not* chocolate milk."

"I'd drink chocolate milk," Moose said, smiling.

"Thanks, guys." And now Oaken's throat did thicken. He gave London a hug, then held out his hand to Shep, Axel, and Moose. Moose pulled him in for a back slap.

"You know this means we can call you when we're in trouble," said Moose.

"Anytime."

Silence, and he wanted to say it—*say goodbye to Boo for me.*

"So, back to Nashville?"

"Montana. I rented an Airbnb in Mercy Falls, near my record label. I need to finish up the songs for the movie I'm working on."

"Cool."

"Then Goldie has me slotted on some late-night shows, repping the television show. They are releasing it soon—I think they've got it slotted for some cable channel."

"Reynolds said he'd let us know," Moose said.

"Can't wait to be a big star," said Axel.

Yeah, well, it wasn't all that the world made it. But, "The ladies will go crazy," Oaken said. He flipped the coin. Held it in his grip.

"Let me walk you out," Moose said.

"Now you're in trouble," Axel said and lifted a hand.

Oaken waved back and headed outside, Moose on his tail.

"So, that's it?"

Oaken rounded, walking backwards. "What do you mean, that's it?"

"You're just leaving, just like that."

"Not just like that—the show is over."

"That's all this was? A show?"

He stared at him. "Since when am I the villain here?"

Moose stopped, shoved his hands into his pockets. "Since you made me a promise not to hurt Boo."

He cocked his head. "I didn't hurt Boo. She . . . left. I don't know why."

"You can't figure it out?"

He opened his mouth. Closed it. "I might have an idea. But the fact is, she didn't give me a chance to explain. She just left."

"Sort of like your sister didn't give you a chance to explain."

He looked away.

"Listen. I know there is all sorts of hurt and anger and grief tangled up with your sister's death. And Boo isn't your sister. But right now, I have a feeling you're listening to something that isn't true."

Oaken looked at him. *Like?*

"I know you said you're not the villain, Oak. But my guess is that that is *exactly* what you fear. That the social-media memes are true and that you don't deserve your fame, or even happiness."

"That's an easy diagnosis—I told you what happened after Hollie died—"

"Yeah. I've been turning that over. What if this was all meant to be?"

He stilled.

"What if God took that dark moment and turned it to light. Gave you a career. A platform."

Oaken drew in a breath and could barely believe his own words. "It doesn't feel like light."

"Because you've been carrying it on your own. You believe this is all up to you. But what if that's just what you told yourself to justify the good that came from the bad?"

"What good?"

"Well, you saved a couple lives this weekend, even if we don't count Mike's. And the fact is, God will do amazing things with someone who is willing to let him. John the Baptist came to make Jesus known. His fame didn't belong to him. Psalm 23 says that God leads us on paths of righteousness for his name's sake." He walked up to Oaken and put his hand on his shoulder. "You don't have to prove that you deserve this, Oaken. God already has. Now let him use that worth."

Overhead, the sun had come out, warm on Oaken's shoulders.

"By the way, Boo is visiting her family in Minnesota."

Oaken's mouth opened.

"I'm not sure your purposes here are over." Moose squeezed his shoulder, then let go. "Stay out of trouble."

Then Moose headed back toward the doors.

And for some reason, all Oaken heard were the words to his song.

On a lonesome road, under skies so gray, I face the storms, come what may.

In the dark, I lost my way, but I have to hope there's a brighter day.

Maybe. He took out his keys, heading to his rental.
Back to his life, his music, his world.
The kingdom of Oaken Fox.

FOURTEEN

S O MAYBE IT HADN'T BEEN A TERRIBLE IDEA
to go home.

Boo sat on the back steps of her family home turned inn, a three-story Victorian-style home built in the late 1800s, telling herself to just . . . go down the stairs.

Down. Usually bad foot first, but after a month, the doctor—a.k.a. her sister, Austen—told her she could try bending her knee.

Terrifying.

The sun hung just above the horizon, spilling golden light between the cottonwood and birch trees on the distant shore and gilding Duck Lake. The Canada geese had returned and now bobbed in the reeds by the shoreline, the foam and debris of winter having been cleaned by Doyle last weekend.

Today, he planned on putting the dock out, just in time for the fishing opener in a week. Now, the metal dock lay in sections onshore, covered in a tarp.

Her stomach curled at the scent of fresh Saskatoon berry muffins, the berries frozen from last summer's harvest of their massive bush near the house, probably planted by great-great-grandpa Bing Kingston, former newspaper man and general rabble rouser. But his wife Clare had settled him down, and he'd grown a conglomerate from his starter nest egg. He'd eventually built his wife the home of her dreams.

He'd also built homes for his three sons. One now belonged to Boo's brother, Doyle. Her parents lived in the updated carriage house, where she'd grown up. Together, her father and Doyle ran the big house as a bed and breakfast, under the watch of her mother, the chef and hostess.

Her father had spent the better part of a decade restoring the place one room at a time after renovating the carriage house into a place for his family.

Boo had never wanted a hand in the business—spent too much of her childhood cleaning rooms and serving guests—but now she didn't mind the three-course breakfasts that her mother served in the oak-paneled dining room, light casting in from the stained-glass windows.

In fact, the entire place felt like something out of time, with the parquet floors, the stamped metal ceiling tiles, leaded bay windows in the parlor, the gorgeous tiled fireplace, and the tall turret with the winding staircase that led to a bedroom suite. The upstairs billiards room now served as a gathering place, with white overstuffed chairs overlooking a view of the lake. The five second-floor bedrooms all boasted their own fireplaces, with a massive hearth opening on the third-floor ballroom turned conference room.

The perfect place for weddings, corporate events, and family reunions, according to the website.

And the perfect place for a little girl to feel forgotten amidst all the activity.

Just go down the stairs. She blew out a breath, held on to the railing, and eased herself down.

Pain shot through her body, right into her brain, crippling her.

Nope. Not yet.

"That doesn't look fun."

The voice came from her brother Doyle, who'd come outside into the bright, sunny day with a cup of coffee and a fresh muffin. He wore canvas work pants, a sweatshirt, his cap on backwards, his brown hair sticking out the front and back.

"It's a blast," Boo said, limping over to a nearby chair. The air carried enough crisp to settle a fog over the lake. A few geese sounded, then landed on the lake.

A mother waddled along the shoreline, followed by goslings.

Boo sat on the chair, then eased her knee up slowly. The pain gathered, and she slowly straightened it.

"Only about two hundred more of those."

"I don't need your help."

He held up a hand. "Grumpy."

She sighed. "Sorry. I'm just . . . I need to get back to Alaska. I'm not sure why I let you talk me into this."

He came over, leaned his muscled shoulder against a column on the covered porch. Took a sip of his coffee. Grinned.

"What?"

"Nothing. Just, I had dinner with Ranger and Noemi last night." He took another sip of coffee. "Wanna tell me about Oaken Fox?"

Her mouth opened. "What? How—"

"Dodge told Ranger that he saw Axel in Copper Mountain, who asked about you and then mentioned something about Fox, and I got the whole story."

Not the *whole* story. Not the part where Oaken had completely eviscerated her—or was about to—on national television. Maybe she just wanted to keep hiding until after the show aired.

And then move to Iceland.

"So what's the deal? A month you've been here, and you haven't mentioned him once."

"What's to talk about? He worked with us."

"He nearly got into a fistfight with your boss about rescuing you in some blizzard."

She froze.

"Hmm. By the look on your face, you didn't know that, did you?"

She looked away, massaging her knee. "It was his job."

Another sip of coffee, this time loud.

"Fine. Listen." She looked at him. "I clearly haven't learned my lesson about falling for teammates, okay? I might have . . . cared about him. More than I should. But he . . . well, he didn't feel the same way." She took a breath. "But fool me twice . . . It won't happen again. There is nothing between us."

His mouth made a grim line. "You've got this whole thing wrong, sis."

She cocked her head at him.

"Any guy who is lucky enough to be loved by Brontë Kingston is a fool to walk away from her."

Oh. Her throat tightened. She looked away.

"I don't care who this guy is—you need me and Conrad and Jack to take a little visit to Fox's doorstep—"

She held up her hand, looked at him. "Thanks, but no." But she smiled.

He smiled back.

The porch door opened. "Doyle, I need you to get some fresh eggs." Her mother came out, dressed in her apron, her hair back in a net. Her nearly sixty-five years had barely etched a wrinkle in her face, her hands still strong, her eyes still clear. If Boo could be like anyone, maybe it would be her mother.

Except for the judgment.

Her mother handed Doyle a basket.

He took it and headed off the porch out to the garden area.

Her mother stuck her hands into her pockets. "He's right, you know."

Boo frowned. "What?"

She sat on the chair next to Boo. "I think there's a conversation we never got to finish."

"I think it's finished, Mom. You told me what you thought about the show—"

"No. You told me what you thought I thought. You never let me speak."

"Your silence spoke volumes."

"My silence was pain for what you went through. For the hurt you endured. And my biggest concern wasn't what happened between you and Blake. It was what you carried away from it." She reached out and touched Boo's hand. "I feared that again you'd feel like you didn't matter. That you were easily forgotten. And that now, Brontë, it was worse—because you could give yourself a reason for that."

What was this, therapy hour?

She sighed. "Mom, my name is Boo."

Her mother shook her head. "No. Your name is Brontë. It's a great name. A beautiful name. A name that means thunder. You were the smallest of my babies. But I knew you'd make an impact."

Boomer. Aw. Maybe the man knew her better than she thought. But, "Mom, I—"

"Wait. Still my turn," her mother said.

Boo closed her mouth.

"I know that you always felt different. You weren't the student like Austen. Or into sports like your brothers. The minute you returned from that adventure camp in Deep Haven, I knew you wanted a life outside the borders of Duck Lake. A life of adventure and challenge, and maybe a little to prove that you were every bit as capable as your siblings."

Boo said nothing.

"But in being so capable and not a burden, you've also decided

SUSAN MAY WARREN

that you are on your own. That you have to fight your own battles and bear your own burdens, endure your losses on your own."

She lifted a shoulder. "If I get lost, it's on me to find my way back."

"That's a lie."

She frowned.

"The world says that. And yes, we need to take responsibility for our actions, but even in that God says he lifts us out of the darkness. That he is our light and our hope and our salvation. That whatever we've done, whatever darkness we find ourselves in, he can set us free."

"I don't even know what that means, Mom." She shook away her tone.

"It means 'Fear not, for I am with you; be not dismayed, for I am your God; I will strengthen you, I will help you, I will uphold you with my righteous right hand.' There are no conditions in that verse. Not—I'll save you if you prove yourself or if you are strong enough to come to me, or even if you love me enough . . . Just, I am with you. That's Jesus running after the lost lamb, just because she needs him."

Her mother squeezed her hand. "What you don't realize, Brontë, is you are like that shepherd. Going after the lost. Rescuing someone who doesn't deserve your love. And you know a little what it feels like to be left behind, too. Could be that Jesus is wondering where his little lamb went."

Doyle had appeared, carrying the basket. "Mom. Your stupid chickens hate me."

She laughed. "Doyle, they love you." Standing up, she took the basket from Doyle. Turned again to Boo. "Could be that the person you've been trying to rescue all this time is you, Boo. Maybe it's time to let someone else do the rescuing." She stood at the door. "As for Oaken Fox, well, Doyle's right. He's the idiot." Her mom winked and went inside.

251

Doyle picked up his coffee where he'd left it on the railing. "Uh-oh. You okay?"

"Yeah." She sighed. Got up. Then she walked over to the stairs. Held on to the railing.

Eased her good leg down, bending her knee.

Pain, but it didn't encompass her body.

Maybe, with movement and time . . .

Sort of like how she'd get over Oaken.

"Brontë!" Her mother came to the door. "Get. In. Here."

Doyle looked at her, raised an eyebrow. Boo limped over to the door, came inside.

Her mother stood at the center island, holding the remote, popping up the volume on the flatscreen.

Boo froze.

Oaken Fox sat in the high-top chair across from Katie Riley and Mike Cortas, the hosts of *Live with Katie and Mike*.

Oh, he looked good. All that sandy-brown hair tousled, the way he smiled, his blue eyes twinkling for the audience.

Such a charmer.

Oh, she was a fool.

He wore a pair of faded jeans, cowboy boots, and a denim blue snap-button shirt, the cuffs rolled up over his strong forearms. A guitar leaned against his chair.

Katie, her long blonde hair spilling around her petite shoulders, leaned back, one elbow hooked over her chair, clearly enjoying her guest. "So, you were really on a rescue team?"

Oh no.

"Yep." He sat, his boots hooked into the lower rung of the chair, his hands folded. A little golden-brown scruff layered his perfect chin. "It was part of a new reality show by Grizz Productions. I joined Air One Rescue out of Alaska for three weeks, and learned how to rappel and rescue someone on a chopper cable, and even some survival skills."

"In the teaser, it shows you rescuing a little girl from a blizzard," said Mike, leaning forward.

"It was the entire team, really. I just happened to be the one on camera. Really, she owes her life to my partner, Boo Kingston. She's the one who found her."

Her mom looked at her, winked.

Boo swallowed.

And then, yep, just as she feared—"Wait. Boo Kingston, from Blake and Boo fame?" Mike said.

"Boo Hoo Kingston?" Katie added.

Perfect. If she could, she'd run from the room. Because here it came—the part where he laughed along, maybe even added to the nickname for the pleasure of the audience. Or, best case scenario, he just shrugged and said he knew her and . . .

"I actually take some offense to that nickname, Katie. Because Boo—and I call her Boomer—is an amazing rescuer. It's a very good thing that Blake had her as a teammate, because he might not have survived without her. And any guy who betrays the woman who kept him alive doesn't deserve any platform." He leaned back. "I think Boo deserves an apology."

Silence, and Katie looked at Mike, then back to Oaken with a tight smile. "Really."

"Yep," Oaken said. "In fact, she inspired a song that I wrote for an upcoming Winchester Marshall movie." He reached for his guitar. "Would you like to hear it?"

The audience erupted.

He grinned, got down from the chair, and slung the guitar over his shoulder. Walked over to a mic, stage left.

The band had already fired up the intro, and he took the mic.

Boo couldn't move, his tenor thrumming through her . . .

"In the dust of a heartbreak, I'm standin' tall.
Lost the girl I love, and I took the fall.

Her love slipped away like a river's flow.
Now I'm left here wonderin' if I'll ever know."

What?
"Well, well," said Doyle.

"Oh, the nights are long, and the days are cold.
Regret's a heavy burden that I can't seem to hold.
I'm prayin' for a chance, a glimmer of hope,
But deep down inside, I fear I'll never cope."

"Sounds like you made an impression," said her mother.
Boo slid onto a bench. "This can't be right . . ."
The camera panned in, close up, and Oaken stared at it like he
might be staring into her soul.

"I see her in my dreams, dancin' in the rain.
Her laughter echoes, drivin' me insane.
I wish I could turn back time, change the past,
But all that's left are memories fadin' fast."

"There was no dancing in the rain," Boo said.
Her mother slid her a cup of coffee as he sang the bridge.

"I reach out to the stars, beggin' for a sign,
Hopin' she'll hear this broken heart of mine.
If only I could find the words to say,
Maybe she'd come back to me one day."

The door opened and shut, and her father said, "What's going
on?"
Boo glanced at him. He wore a jean jacket, a gimme cap, his

white hair full and curling out of it. He'd shaved and smelled like
Old Spice.

"That's Oaken," said Doyle. "He's singing about Boo."

"He is not," Boo said, but stopped talking to hear the next verse.

"As the sun sets on this lonely town,
I'll keep searchin' for her, though she's not around.
Maybe fate will lead her back to me.
Until then, I'll live in this bittersweet melody."

"Wow," her father said. "Left an impression, huh, Brontë?"

She gave her father a look.

He glanced at Doyle, then her mother. "It's about time a man
figured out what he lost." He reached for a muffin. "Although,
I would think a decent guy would talk to her father about his
intentions before singing her love songs on national television."

Oh brother.

Oaken finished the chorus again, and now Katie walked over
to him, along with Mike, applauding. "When will the series air,
Oaken?"

"I think it comes out in a couple weeks. And the movie—it's
filming this summer, in Montana."

"What's next for you?" Mike said.

Oaken looked at the camera. Smiled. "As Mike Grizz would
say, the best is yet to come."

Please.

She reached for the remote and turned it off.

Silence filled the kitchen.

"It's just for show," she said. "Really."

"Hmm," her mother said and grabbed hot pads to open the
oven.

From the table in the kitchen, a phone rang.

Oh great. Now it would be Oaken. Or maybe London. Or . . .

She stared at the screen, her heart in her throat. *Blake?*

"It's raining men," Doyle said, walking past her as she hung up.

Oaken blamed his producer for why he'd ended up on a horse in the middle of a spring-swept prairie, the sun high, the air smelling of fescue and bluegrass, the prairie rolling as far as his eye could see.

In the distance, nestled into a valley, sat the Fox Ranch two-story homestead house, the big white barn, and the pens for cattle.

His father's house, a smaller version of his grandparents' home, sat on a hill less than a half mile away.

"How you doing, Oak?" His father sat on Scout, a quarter horse, and turned in the saddle.

"Sore."

"Figured. A couple more days and you'll be as broke in as Rio there."

Oaken shifted in the saddle, his legs and back burning. So maybe he'd idealized his childhood on the ranch a little, following cattle around as they drove them to a new pasture. Or rode fence.

His father rode back to him. Arie Fox had John Dutton written all over him—strong, quiet, thinking. He wore jeans, a canvas jacket, a black Stetson, and boots, and sat in the saddle as if he'd been born there. "Stick around a few more days and you can help with branding."

"I dunno, Pop," Oaken said, laughing. "I just needed to air out my brain. Not get kicked in the head."

His dad nodded, smiling. "Well, I'm just glad to see you, son. The land gets lonely out here sometimes."

Oh. Well.

"I'm going to check on that last stretch of fence—we've had some wolves find a way in of late. There's a couple of mamas in the closer herd about to drop. Can you bring them into the pen near the house?"

"Yep," Oaken said and urged Rio down to the herd in the nearby field.

So much for the conversation Ben King had sent him out to South Dakota to have.

Oaken should have packed up his guitar and left right then, in Ben King's home office-slash-studio, after he'd played the producer the songs he'd written for the Western. Ben had sat on his sofa, his ankle propped on his knee, listening, bobbing his head, one arm up on the back of the worn leather sofa. Behind him, through tall picture windows, arched the frosted white mountains of Glacier National Park, the grasslands of Ben's ranch heavy with the blooms of spring. Winter treaded lightly in this Flathead Valley of Montana, where Ben had set up his recording label. Not the usual place for a label, but then again, Ben had shaken off the dust from Nashville when he'd returned home to discover that he had a daughter with the woman he loved waiting for him.

Now, so many years later, he'd become a wildly successful record producer. And when Goldie had talked Oaken into signing with him, the partnership had felt right. Mostly because Ben had been Hollie's partner in her early years.

But Ben also had a knack for songwriting and knew talent when he saw it.

"Great song," he'd finally said when Oaken finished with the last song, "The Lonely Road." "I like them all. 'The Showdown' is perfect. And you know I love 'Come Back to Me.'"

Oaken still had "Storm Song" rattling around his brain, wanting music, but he hadn't dug down into it.

It just felt easier to focus on the movie.

"Good idea to tease it on Katie and Mike," Ben said. "It's already trending."

"I'm staying off social media," Oaken said.

Ben raised an eyebrow. "Well, me too, but I can tell you there are people asking questions about your friend Boo."

He had questions too.

Silence, and Ben raised an eyebrow. "Okay, I see. So she didn't call you after the show, beg you to forgive her for walking away."

"I'm not sure Boo is the begging type."

Ben smiled. "I understand. My wife and Boo would get along." He got up, walked to the window, stared outside. "You probably don't know my story, but I didn't know my daughter, Audrey, for the first decade of her life." He took a breath. "I walked out on Kacey—she was just my high school girlfriend then—the night Audrey was born. I thought Kacey was going to give her up for adoption, so . . . I didn't look back. And I had my reasons—thought they were good ones too. I thought Kacey didn't want me, and her Dad sort of threatened me . . . It's a long story. But most of all, I was angry."

He turned. "I was angry that I didn't fight for her. And that made me hate myself a little. And I was mad at her, too, after I found out about Audrey. But you know, anger leads to pride, which leads to broken relationships and unhappy endings."

"I'm not angry."

"Of course you are. You like this girl. And she walked away from you."

Oaken had gotten up, put his guitar away. Pictures of Ben with country music stars crowded the walls.

"I like your chorus," Ben said. "That part about regret being a heavy burden? There's only one way to get rid of it."

"How's that?"

"You need to forgive her for hurting you. Only then can you get rid of the pride that's standing in your way."

"It's not like that. I do forgive her. And actually, I think the song is only partly about her."

Ben raised an eyebrow.

"Hollie."

"Oh." Ben shoved his hands into his pockets. "I see."

"You know the story."

"You told me most of it."

Oaken walked to the window, stood beside him. "I just . . . I hate the fact that I didn't go after her. I knew she was angry and that there was a blizzard coming . . ."

"So you're angry at her. And yourself. Anyone else?"

Oaken looked at him. "Okay, yeah. I'm angry at my mom for leaving my dad for Nashville. And my dad for not going after her—"

Ben raised an eyebrow. "So this not going after someone you love—otherwise known as pride—runs in the family."

Oaken drew in a breath. Stared past him. "I guess . . . I hadn't . . ."

"That's what my father might call a generational curse, Oak. Anger and pride being passed down, father to son. I think it's time to break that."

Oaken made a face.

"What?"

"You're going to tell me I have to forgive my father too."

"Nope. It's worse. I'm going to tell you to forgive him to his face. Set you both free."

Aw.

Which was why Oaken now found himself on the back of a horse, grimy and sore, separating the handful of heavily pregnant cows from the herd.

He pulled out a rope and started to whoop, sending them walking toward the barn as he tried to figure out how, exactly, to have that conversation.

He did, however, find a tune to "Storm Song," let it run through his mind.

When the dark clouds gathered and tears fell like rain,

I found comfort in his shelter, where I'd remain.
In the trials I faced, I learned to hold on,
And in the toughest moments, I grew strong.

He moved the cows into the pen, then closed it and latched it and climbed down from Rio.

The sound of horse's hooves made him turn. His father, riding into the yard. He slowed to a walk, let the horse cool down.

Oaken took Rio and walked him around the yard too.

His father finally caught up. "Let's put up the horses, then I think there's some coffee waiting for us at the house." He pulled his foot from the stirrup, swung his leg over, and hopped down. Still spry at sixty-five.

They led the horses into the barn and removed their tack.

His father filled the water tank, the water lukewarm, and they stood there in silence, listening to the animals drink.

Now. Tell him now. The urge swelled through him . . . "Hey, Pop—"

"Get the bucket and let's wipe these guys down."

Right. He found the bucket, and his father filled it with warm water. Oaken led Rio over to his stall, tied him to the door, and ran the thick sponge over him, wiping him down. He checked Rio's legs for any cuts and his hooves for stones or damage.

Then he followed his father and his horse with Rio for a final walk around the barn before leading the horse to his stall.

"Thanks, buddy," he said to Rio and caught up to his father, walking toward his truck.

They got in, and silence filled the cab. *Now. . .*

"Pop, I need to talk to you."

"Me too, son. Something I need to tell you." Arie looked askance at him. "Let's get some coffee."

And now Oaken's gut tightened. He was ten again and in trouble for scaring the chickens.

They went inside his father's house, the one Arie had moved to after his family had moved out of the big house. A simple house, two chairs resting on the front porch, now dirty from winter. Inside, the place felt homey, with a small kitchen, a round table with today's paper folded by an empty cup of coffee. Attached to it was a small living room, his father's recliner worn and facing the flatscreen. Three bedrooms down the hall, one of them converted to an office.

Oaken had slept in his old room, on a twin bed.

His father went into the kitchen and grabbed his empty cup off the table. Then he emptied the coffeepot and started a new brew.

"So who goes first?" His father folded his arms, leaning against the counter.

"Me," said Oaken, mostly because, well, who knew what might come out of his father's mouth, and . . . "Pop. I'm here to tell you that . . . I'm angry with you."

His father raised an eyebrow. "Are you?"

"Yep. Or at least, I was. Or maybe I still am—I don't know. I just . . . why didn't you go after us when Mom took us to Nashville?"

His father's mouth opened. And then he let out a laugh. "Oh. Okay. I thought—" He shook his head. "Never mind." He drew in a breath, took off his hat, and set it on the table. "Well, son, truth is, I was selfish."

Oaken just blinked at him. "What?"

"It started with me being angry. And then, honestly, I was scared. I'd only known ranching, and . . ." He shook his head. "I didn't know what I could do down there in Nashville, and I just saw your mother leaving me and me ending up with nothing. So I thought only about myself." He made a wry face. "I guess that's how it ended up anyway. But I always sort of thought she'd come back to me. You know, after Hollie didn't make it."

"But Hollie did make it."

"Yep. And then I was too ashamed of myself to show up at your mom's door with my hat in hand. So . . ." He lifted a shoulder. "Again, selfish."

Anger. Fear. Pride. And yes, selfishness.

The coffee had stopped brewing, and he filled his mug, then Oaken's.

"I remember the fight. Right before we left . . ." Oaken looked at the coffee. "She called you selfish. And then she called *me* selfish because I didn't want to go either."

"Well, she was right. And maybe she was a little selfish too. Because fear is at the root of selfishness, son. It's that fear that God won't provide for you or protect you, so you take control back. That's why God says so many times, 'Do not fear.' Because fear leads to anger, which leads to selfishness . . . which leads to being alone. Most of all, people who fear end up doing stupid things. They hurt people. Destroy lives. Like I did to you and your sister."

Huh. And with those words, Moose toed into Oaken's mind. *"So you let anger get a root inside you and tell you lies."*

He took the mug his father held out to him. "I didn't know that you and God had . . . well, that you two were talking."

His father slid onto a chair. "A lot happened after Hollie died. You started singing. Your mom moved to Florida, and I . . . I got real lonely. Started getting to know my friend Jim."

Arie drew in a breath. "And then one night, I was just broken. And I wanted it to be over."

Oaken's eyes widened. "What? Why didn't you call me?"

Arie lifted a shoulder. "Pride? Shame? Your uncle found me . . . and he was angry too—real angry. And of course, that was fear too. And he got in my face and told me that I was my own worst enemy. That I could spend my life angry and afraid and alone . . . or I could realize that God loved me. Even in my pitiful state. Like the prodigal son in the Bible, mucking about with the pigs. His father saw him coming a long way off and ran to him. Because he'd been waiting for him."

He took a sip of coffee. "See, God doesn't wait for us to come to him. He comes after us. He moves first, Oaken. Even when it feels like we're the ones running to him. He's already out there, searching for us. And that just . . . it just broke me." He looked away, swallowed, searching for his composure as sunlight filled the tiny kitchen.

And for a moment, Moose filled in the space, his words echoing in Oaken's mind. *"God is not content leaving us in our lies. He wants to set us free, and he'll keep running after us, in every storm, trying to get our attention."*

His father turned back toward him, his composure tucked back in.

"God put me back together. Told me I was safe. And loved. And forgiven. And that all I had to do was . . . trust." He met Oaken's eyes. "So, that's a long answer to a short question. I'm sorry I didn't come after you, son." His eyes had turned glossy. "More than you can know."

Oaken swallowed. Met his eyes. *Now.* "Pop. I forgive you."

Oh. Oh. A terrible rush filled him, swept through him, as if something dark and snarled exited his entire being. He drew in a breath, and . . . it was whole, and freeing.

His father smiled. "Feels good, doesn't it."

"I . . ."

"That's the feeling of perfect love, son. It casts out all fear."

Oaken pressed a hand to his chest.

His father took another sip of coffee. "So, now, let's talk about the girl."

"What?"

"'I reach out to the stars, beggin' for a sign, hopin' she'll hear this broken heart of mine.'"

"You . . . what? How do you know that?"

"I saw the show."

"You saw Katie and Mike?"

"Yeah. Your mom likes to watch it, and she was really excited, so she called me into the kitchen and there you were, on the screen, singing."

"Yeah. I wrote it for this girl named Boo."

"The rescue girl."

He just couldn't . . . then, "Wait . . . what do you mean you *went into the kitchen*?"

His father nodded, his eyes shining. "I was in Florida until just a few days ago."

Nothing. Oaken had nothing.

"Your Mom and I never stopped loving each other. And she doesn't want to live here, so . . . I'm going to figure it out. The fact is, she gave me two amazing children, and I should have given her my provision and protection. And I regret that. But maybe it's not too late. She still needs me."

"*I* still need you, Pop." And just saying it made his throat ache.

"Yep," his father said. "So, what are you going to do about the girl?"

He stared at his coffee. "I don't know. Maybe nothing."

"Oak."

"She doesn't want me."

His father's mouth made a grim line and he nodded.

"What?"

"Sounds an awful lot like fear."

"I'm not . . ."

His father raised an eyebrow.

"Fear. Anger. Pride. It's all selfish. The only remedy for that is repentance, Oaken."

"And then what? God magically fixes everything? Hardly."

A loud sip. Then, "You're under the illusion that your happy ending is up to you. You've been bought by love, son. And that love wants to do amazing things through you. It already is, if I'm seeing things right. So, yes, actually. But, you know, you gotta let go. Push yourself out of the plane."

Oaken shook his head. "People get hurt that way."

"Only if they're depending on themselves to fly."

"You don't happen to watch *Wild with Grizz,* do you?"

"Live big, live wild?" He took a final sip. "Your mom told me about the show."

"I called her before I went to Alaska."

"How is your friend Mike?"

"In rehab, still in Anchorage. But he's getting better."

His father pushed up from the table. "He starts all his shows with jumping out of a chopper. That's crazy right there."

Oaken laughed.

And then, weirdly, his father's words came back to him. *"People who fear end up doing stupid things. They hurt people. Destroy lives."*

He got up and went to his room, found his cell phone. Then he texted Moose.

Oaken

Any news about Mike's chute?

No answer. Maybe Moose was out on a call.

His father was waiting in the kitchen, making a couple sandwiches. "Daylight's burning, son. I hope you're still handy with a wrench."

"I've never been handy with a wrench, Pop."

"That's not true, son. You have a mind like a trap. Always marveled at the way you could look at something once and remember it forever. And you're the most adaptable, handy guy I've met. Never seen you tackle something you weren't fantastic at. Roping, herding cattle, baseball, music . . . Seemed to me sometimes like you were born sixteen and burnin' to change the world." He handed Oaken the ham sandwich. "Follow me out to the barn."

Oaken ate the sandwich, his father's words settling inside as he walked down to the shed on his father's property. Inside, his father's old 1962 Ford sat up on blocks.

"I need to bleed the brake line. Get in the cab."

Felt like old times. Especially when his father turned on the radio. Or maybe it was an old boom box, because his sister's voice emerged, young and timeless.

He sat there, his throat tightening when his father walked up, put a hand on his arm.

"I know you miss your sister. I do too. But you can't look at your life as the consolation prize. God's love is perfect, even in the dark times." He squeezed Oaken's arm. "I'm proud of you, son. Now, pump the brakes and don't stop until I tell you to."

"I'm not sure what sort of shake to offer you with that face."

Moose looked up at Tillie and found a smile. "Yeah. I dunno."

"Bad callout?" She leaned a hip against the booth.

He hadn't forgotten about his pitiful attempt to ask her out a month ago, but he'd largely put it in the back of his mind, what with Boo's injury, the blizzard, and the fallout from the frozen bride.

"No. Snow is gone, and except for a couple fishermen caught in rapids and one missing hunter, it's been quiet."

She slid into the booth. He frowned.

"I heard about that girl in the news, the one you tried to rescue." She hesitated as if she might actually reach out, touch his hand or something. Then, "I'm sorry, Moose. I know . . . well, I remember you telling me about your cousin missing, and I would guess that hit a little close to home."

He stared at her. "You remember that?"

"You remember the mayo?"

"It's my favorite now."

"Of course it is." She got up. "I remember every conversation we have. So, mocha shake?"

He had nothing, his breath stripped. She remembered every conversation? He shrugged.

She winked. "I got this." Then she walked away.

Pulling out his phone, he read a text from Dodge.

Dodge

Heard from Boo.

Looks like rehab might be another week or so.

Great. She'd called in last week with the news, but he'd been hoping for a sooner recovery. He didn't want to replace her, not after everything she'd done to earn her keep. Wasn't easy to put together a crew that worked well together.

He had even started to wonder if Oaken might stick around. Seemed like Oaken might have been thinking about it for a while.

A tall glass came down into his view and then a straw and long spoon. He looked up to see Tillie standing there. "It's strawberry-chocolate and you'll love it. It's my—" Her breath caught. "It's a fan favorite."

"Thanks." He put down his phone. Sighed.

"You okay, Moose? Feels like something more than the rescue is egging you."

She stood there, so much concern on her face—

"The woman at the ski hill—the bride—she was *murdered*."

Maybe he shouldn't have said it like that, and the investigation had only started, but he had his suspicions. "She was shot. By a hunting rifle." And that was probably enough. He looked away. "Sorry. It just . . ."

She sank into the seat across from him.

"My cousin Aren was murdered too. By a hunting rifle."

"You think—"

"I don't know." He looked at her. "But it's sort of stirred up everything and . . ." He sighed. "Thanks for the shake."

She nodded. "I put down some chicken for you too."

His throat tightened. Oh, he liked this woman. "Will you go out with me?"

Oh. Oh no. How did that come out?

Worse, her breath caught and she swallowed. Then she closed her eyes tight, making a face, as if his words had stung.

Shoot. They'd sort of stung him too.

She opened her eyes. Gave him a soft smile. Opened her mouth, and for a second—

"I'm sorry, Moose. I . . . you . . ." She sighed. "I would love to say yes, but . . . I can't." She shook her head. "I'm sorry."

Then she got up and headed to the kitchen.

He ran his hands down his face. What kind of idiot was he?

The strawberry-chocolate shake was delicious, of course, but he couldn't finish it. Especially after she delivered his order of chicken, not meeting his eyes. Yeah, he'd lost his appetite. "Can I get a box?"

She nodded. Tore off his check and left it at the table. Returned with a box, picking up the twenty he dropped on the check.

"Moose—"

"Keep the change, Tillie."

She pocketed it. "I—"

"Nope. It's all good." He forced a smile. "Thanks for the shake." Then he pushed out of the booth, carrying his midnight chicken, and headed outside into the sunny Alaska night.

He'd forgotten his pie. But it didn't matter.

He'd have to find a new late-night diner anyway.

FIFTEEN

WE'RE GLAD TO HAVE YOU BACK, BOO. THE team seemed like a three-legged dog without you." Moose stood at the briefing board at the Tooth, talking through today's training outside in the sound.

Which she wouldn't take part in, thanks to her stupid knee.

"Glad to be back," she said from where she sat at the table. Across from her, sitting in for today's briefing, Dodge winked. His wife, Echo, had an appointment later today for an ultrasound.

"How's the knee?" Axel said.

"I can walk on it, but doc says no running quite yet." Could be a month, actually, although in the few days she'd been back, she'd started taking walks on the Kincaid Trail.

Of course, that also conjured up that happenstance meeting with Oaken so long ago. Her mind just wouldn't let him go, despite her efforts to quit him.

Or to get his stupid song out of her head.

"The gear room desperately needs your touch," Moose said. "Would you mind digging in while we're out today?"

"No problem."

She listened half-heartedly as Moose explained today's train-ing—a rope rescue from an overturned boat in the sound. "Axel, you're in the water. Shep, you're on winch, and London, you're the spotter."

Boo wanted to offer, but she'd probably lose her balance and just re-crack her knee.

"Dodge will copilot, and we'll run it twice, him at the controls for the second run."

Dodge gave him a thumbs-up.

"We'll be working with the local sheriff's office for this one—they'll have the boat in the water and will provide dummies for the haul out. With more boats heading out for recreation and fishing, there's no doubt we'll get more callouts, and we all need to be ready."

Already the sun had started to dominate the day with nearly eighteen hours of daylight. No wonder Boo felt a buzz under her skin, an adrenaline that had kept her awake since returning to Alaska.

Had nothing at all to do with the recent promotion of *The Sizeup: A Grizz Production*. And shots of Oaken dangling from a chopper, along with a couple of close-up interviews with Moose and Oaken. One shot with a voiceover even showed them eating midnight chicken at the Skyport, Tillie serving them shakes.

Maybe she should leave the country—

Around her, the others had started to get up, heading for the door. Dodge came over to her. "Echo is at the motel. She's coming by later, after her appointment. I know she can't wait to see you."

Sweet. Boo rose, needing coffee, her knee already aching. Maybe she'd put too much into PT this morning.

"Boo." Moose stopped her with his voice, and she rounded back to him.

"'Sup?"

He looked a little tired today, wore a bit of scruff on his face.

"We still have Mike's gear from when we picked him up. Reynolds wants to come by and get it. He's stopping by to pick it up later today. Can you grab it from the gear room for him?"

And again Oaken walked into her head, sat down. Maybe she'd never escape him.

"On it, boss."

Moose grinned. "I know you're itching to get back out there, Boo. Give it time."

"Yep." She turned to walk out when—

"Have you heard from Oaken?"

She stopped at the door. Glanced back at him. "Nope."

"Even with the song—"

"I swear, if you break out into singing—"

He held up his hands. "Sorry. It's just . . . he was pretty upset when you left. And then London played me that song and, well, I was hoping you two had figured it out."

"Figured what out?"

He gave her a look.

"Listen." And then her chest tightened, her throat burning. "I . . . we . . . it was just for the show."

"No, it wasn't, Boo."

"Yeah, well, you don't see him gearing up for any rescues with Air One, do you?"

He closed his mouth, and she turned and walked out, trying not to limp. Maybe that wasn't fair, but . . .

No, it wasn't fair at all. Oaken had a life. A big life. She didn't expect him to give it up for her. So what *had* she expected?

He'd even stuck up for her on national television.

She probably needed to forgive him.

And maybe it was hearing London's voice emerging from the locker room where the team gathered, but her words from long ago swept through her. *"You can't let Blake and your anger for him get inside your heart. It'll do all sorts of destructive things, like make you afraid and controlling and bitter . . . Anger is the root of so much tyranny in our lives."*

Maybe.

Boo grabbed a fresh cup of coffee in her mug and headed back to the gear room.

Oy. Ropes lay on the floor, some of them wound tight, others loosely bound. Carabiners hung on numerous webbing loops, clearly clipped on with no regard to type and count, along with descenders and rope clamps and pulleys and figure eights, as well as harnesses, a few tangled even as they hung from hooks.

She propped up the rescue dummy and set the coffee in front of him. "I guess it's just you and me, pal."

Rescue Ronny.

And there was Oaken, laughing, teasing as she clipped him into his harness.

Shoot.

She picked up a backpack and recognized it as the one Oaken had used to rescue Hannah. Heard his words, deep inside. *"I'll be back."*

And then her own. *"I believe you."*

She *had* believed him. Had trusted him. And then promptly hadn't given him the benefit of the doubt the moment . . . well, the moment she simply overheard something.

Yeah, lies had done a number on her.

She hung up the pack, then picked up a coil of rope, re-coiling it, tying it, and hanging it on the rope rack.

Oaken deserved better from her.

"Boo, we're out of here," Shep said, sticking his head into the room. "We'll be back in a few hours."

"I'm making chili."

He gave her a thumbs-up. "Glad you're back. You were missed."

"Yeah, well, I wish I were out there with you."

"It's enough that you're here." He tapped the doorframe and headed out.

Yeah, lies had created chaos in her life. Made her believe she had to do more, be more.

And now she was humming that stupid song.

I reach out to the stars, beggin' for a sign,
Hopin' she'll hear this broken heart of mine.
If only I could find the words to say,
Maybe she'd come back to me one day.

Aw. She finished re-coiling the ropes and reorganizing the tech on the webbing. Then she went to the gear in the corner. A parachute pack, and inside, the broken chute. Mike's gear.

She pulled out the chute and brought it to the chute room to lay on the long table and refold.

The chutes had been repacked since her last time in here, the packs all neatly hung on hooks. Now, Mike's silk fluttered out as she laid it on the table.

The cut ran down one of the sections, and she picked it up to examine it. Frayed edges, jagged, torn from the violence of the wind. So, just an accident.

Except, as she ran her fingers along the tattered edge, the rip became less ragged, smoother.

As if it had been cut. Or at least ripped with something sharp. Like a knife.

Huh.

She folded the chute up and put it into the pack, zipping it up. It was then she noticed the PLB clipped to the webbing, and once again, Oaken was in her head.

"That would have been nice to have when I was out with Mike."

Yeah, he was a real hero. The kind worth waiting for. *"First rule of rescue—don't panic. Use your resources."*

She should start listening to herself.

She carried the pack to the main area.

Two hours. She should get the chili going.

Her cell phone buzzed on the table, so she went over and picked it up.

Drew in a breath. *Blake.*

No. Never.

She hovered her thumb over to swipe it away, except . . . well, *you gotta find a way to forgive him.*

Maybe that was the first step in stepping away from the chaos.

She answered. "What?"

A beat. "Boo?"

His voice rippled through her, old memories, old emotions. She shook them away. *Forgive.* "Yes." She sighed. "What do you want, Blake?" Okay, so it might take a minute.

Another beat. "Thanks for answering. I've been trying to get ahold of you."

"I know."

Now he sighed. "Boo . . . I broke up with Misty."

"I know. It was all over the internet."

"Yeah, what she said. But not what I said to her."

She closed her eyes, ran her finger and thumb against them. "Blake, I don't care—"

"I'm sorry, Boo. I'm so sorry for what I did to you."

Her eyes opened. "What?"

He exhaled hard. "I was a jerk. During the show and after the show and . . . I'm so sorry."

She had nothing.

"What you don't know is that . . . well, everything we did, everything I said—I meant it."

Oh boy. "Blake, this is—"

"I'm not done. I was in love with you, Boo. Truly. And then . . . then the producer came to me and said that they had projected

Misty to win and that if I wanted second place, I needed to support her."

She went cold. "What are you saying, Blake?"

"The entire show was rigged. Misty was a better fit for their after-show social media, and . . . they cut so many of my words out, changed them around."

"You called me Boo Hoo. You said I was the weak link. You . . . we . . ." She blew out her breath. "I believed you when you said you loved me."

"I *did* love you. And then it all got . . . messy. I should have never listened to Reynolds. He lied. Said that they'd keep our night out of it—"

"They replayed your body cam image of us kissing!"

"I know."

Silence.

Then, "Wait. Did you say that Reynolds Gray was the producer?"

"Yeah. *Survivor Quest* is a Mike Grizz production. Didn't you know that?"

She swallowed. Drew in a breath.

Yeah, she was really an idiot. "Blake. I forgive you."

She expected some sort of fanfare from heaven, maybe a rush of emotions. But it felt like she'd simply swept away the last of the debris from her heart.

Clean.

"You forgive me?"

"Yep. We all do things . . . well, that we regret. But I can't live in that regret, and neither can you. Let it go, Blake. And in case anything Misty said was right . . . let me go."

She could almost see him, those sad brown eyes that had torn at her heart, that devastating smile, the swallow he gave before making a decision.

"Thank you, Boo." He took another breath. "You're . . . well, I know what social media is saying about you and Oaken Fox, and I just want to say—ignore them. He's a lucky guy."

For a second, her body seized up.

But it didn't matter what anonymous people on social media said about her. She smiled. "Yes. Yes, he is, Blake. Take care of yourself and be happy."

She hung up. Set her phone down.

Blew out a breath.

Yeah, that felt good. Good enough, maybe, to call Oaken. To apologize. Because if Reynolds had orchestrated everything behind the scenes, even to the point of rigging the outcome—who knew what he had done with their show?

And then she heard it—*"That's not the deal."*

Oaken deserved for her to get to the bottom of that, at the very least. Maybe even for her to tell him that they could give this one last shot.

Tonight. After the chili, maybe.

She walked over to the refrigerator and opened it. Pulled out the meat.

Behind her, the door opened and she startled. Turned.

Echo Kingston walked into the Tooth, seven months pregnant. "Hey, Boo."

"Echo. Dodge said you were coming by. You okay?"

"Yeah. Just an ultrasound. I have two long months to go. My mom wanted the ultrasound—she's hovering a little."

"That's what happens when your mom is an ob-gyn. Can I get you something to eat?"

Echo slid onto a chair at the table. "I'd kill for a ham sandwich."

Boo laughed. "I'm on it." She opened the fridge and retrieved mayo, ham, and bread. "Moose always keeps the fixin's on hand."

"They're still out training?"

"Yeah." She set the ingredients on the counter.

"Someone forget their bag?" Echo had pushed the parachute bag to the end of the table.

"It belongs to Mike Grizz. His producer, Reynolds"—*the jerk*—"is picking it up."

"Yeah, I met him the day they dropped Mike and Oaken from the chopper. We were down for an appointment, and I met him here at Air One. He asked Dodge to drop off Mike Grizz on our way back to Copper Mountain. He and his cameraperson took Oaken Fox up early to get shots of the area before they dropped off Oaken and their gear."

She stilled. "Reynolds dropped off their gear."

"Yeah." She got up. "I go to the bathroom every fifteen minutes, I think. Be right back." She waddled into the locker room.

If Reynolds had dropped off the chutes . . .

Naw. He wouldn't . . . That was just her anger talking.

Except, hadn't Oaken said that finances were in the tank over at Grizz Productions? Certainly, as his partner, Reynolds had insurance on Mike.

Her gut tightened.

Especially when a car pulled up outside and Reynolds Gray got out.

She set down her butter knife as he walked inside.

"Hey, Boo," he said. "I didn't realize you were back."

"Yes," she said quietly. She walked over to the table, met him there, her hand on the pack. "How's Mike?"

Reynolds looked as Hollywood as always in pressed dress pants, an oxford, his hair slicked back, aviator sunglasses on his head. "Good. Better. I just came from the rehab center. He's up and starting to walk. With help, of course. It'll be a while before he's out with any more celebrities, but thankfully we have *The Sizeup*. And lots of good buzz." He winked and reached for the pack.

She was too late to grab it back.

He turned to go outside, and she followed him. *Stop.*

But she couldn't limp fast enough.

He was outside, the trunk open to put the pack in by the time she made it through the doors. Panic, maybe anger, pushed the words out. "I know it was you."

He looked at her, lowered his glasses. "What?"

Okay, slow down. Because suddenly, this might be a bad idea, standing out here in the parking lot, alone. "I mean . . . I know what you did on *Survivor Quest.*"

He cocked his head. "What did I do?"

"You rigged it. You made Misty win."

He raised an eyebrow. "That's a sore loser talking, Boo Hoo Kingston."

Her mouth gaped. "Yeah, well . . . I know about the parachute too." And why that came out of her mouth, she didn't know.

Especially when he took a breath, his mouth a tight line. "Is that so."

She swallowed. *C'mon, Echo, be done in the bathroom.*

"You won't get away with it," she said.

"I already have, Boo," he said. Then he grabbed her arm. And she had to blame her knee and the fact that she had zero balance and still hurt, and frankly, he'd simply surprised her.

But just like that, he pushed her into the trunk, swept up her legs and rolled her in.

Shut the trunk door.

Blackness. And it happened so fast, even her scream was a beat behind.

And here he was, at it again. Oaken stood outside Mike Grizz's rehab room, letting Huxley adjust his mic under his shirt.

"Walk into the room one more time, Oaken, and just smile at

him. You're old friends, and you saved his life. We want to capture the happy ending."

Oaken had really thought the whole malarkey was over. He'd finished shooting, the show in the can. And then Goldie had called him and said they wanted a final shot for *Go Wild with Grizz*.

Even then he might not have gotten on a plane, but . . . well, his dad's words kept rolling around his head, the part about trusting God for the happy ending.

So yes. Here he stood, outside Mike's room at Premier One Rehab in Anchorage, his thoughts on when they might wrap up so he could head over to Air One.

Surprise them all.

Mostly, surprise Boo.

Please let her be there.

"Anytime you're ready," Hux said and put on her headphones. She went inside the room.

He took a couple breaths. Inside waited Seraphina with her two children, along with Huxley, and Beto on camera.

Smile. He pushed inside the rehab room.

They'd closed the curtains to control the light, and Seraphina sat on a chair beside the bed. Mike sat up, fully dressed in a pair of sweatpants over his cast and a black T-shirt that suggested he'd been working out at least his upper body over the past few weeks since his discharge from the hospital. He bore signs of health in his color, the bruises nearly gone now, his eyes bright as Oaken walked in.

"Oaken Fox! What a surprise," Mike said.

Yeah, yeah. Whatever. But Oaken held out his hand. "Mike. Wow, it's good to see you."

Mike shook his hand. "You've met my wife, Seraphina."

Oaken bent and gave her a hug.

"Thank you," she said quietly into his ear.

"And this is Jasmine and Liam."

"Hey," Liam said, nodding his head.

Jasmine grabbed Oaken's hand. "I remember you!"

He grinned. So much for that. "Yeah, I was here after the accident, while your dad was still sleeping."

He turned to Mike, Jasmine still holding onto him. "So, I see you're up and running around. Causing trouble."

Mike laughed, then grimaced.

"Ribs still sore?"

"A little. It'll be a while before I jump out of any more choppers."

Oaken laughed. "Me too, pal."

"How's the music industry?"

"Busy. I'm writing songs for a new album"—there, he'd checked that off Goldie's list of things to mention—"and heading out to do some promo for the movie I'm working on."

"Any more thought to joining the Air One Rescue team?" Mike raised an eyebrow.

Oaken laughed. "I think rescuing you was enough fun for one lifetime."

Mike clasped his hand again. "Don't forget—Live big! Live wild!"

Oaken pointed at him. "The best is yet to come!"

They laughed together.

"And, cut," Huxley said. "That's in the can, Oaken. Good job, and thank you." She took off her earphones. "Too bad Reynolds didn't stick around to see that."

"Reynolds was here?"

"Yeah, he left a couple hours ago. Said he had some errands to run before he caught his flight back to L.A.," Seraphina said. "But Huxley showed us the first episode of the show—they're doing an intro with the footage before Mike's fall. You on the beach and then whatever they could grab from your GoPro."

"They got GoPro footage?"

Huxley looked up from where she was watching Beto play back

the video they'd just taken. "Yeah. Quite a lot. It's a great setup for joining Air One. First episode ends with you agreeing to join Air One. This will be a nice finale piece."

He debated for a moment, then, "Do you want to talk to the police about your suspicions about the parachute?"

Mike frowned. "What suspicions?"

She looked at Jasmine, then Liam. "Liam, can you take your sister down to the cafeteria? Get her some ice cream?"

"Ice cream!" Jasmine shouted.

Liam took his sister's hand. *Good kid.* Had to be hard to see his dad broken.

Oaken's thoughts briefly went back to his father, telling the story about how God had saved him. *"God put me back together. Told me I was safe. And loved. And forgiven. And that all I had to do was . . . trust."*

Yes, God very much had Oaken's attention.

Liam left with his sister, and Seraphina turned to her husband. "When you woke up from the coma—you said someone had tried to kill you."

Silence in the room.

"I did?"

"See, this is why I didn't bring it up again." She looked at Oaken. "He was probably just confused."

"You don't remember?" Oaken asked.

"I don't remember anything from the day before to . . . well, just a few weeks ago. After I woke up in my hospital room."

"None of the ICU?" Oaken said. "Or my dragging you across the Alaskan wilderness?"

"Just what Huxley showed me on tape."

"You said that you thought someone tampered with your parachute," Oaken said now, quietly.

He lifted a shoulder. "Maybe I dreamed it up, woke up saying it."

"We talked about it right after you got out of ICU. You seemed lucid."

Mike made a face. "Some things are still spotty. My memory drops in and out, like bad reception."

Okay. "Hang in there, Mike. And if you guys need any backstage passes—"

"We'll call Goldie," Mike said.

Oaken laughed. "Take care." He pushed out the door into the hallway.

"Oaken, wait."

He turned, and Huxley came up to him, her satchel slung over her shoulder. "I forgot—Reynolds dropped this off for you." She pulled out an envelope. "Said he'd send it to Goldie but he didn't want her to take a cut out of it." She grinned, but he wasn't sure she was kidding.

She handed it over and he looked inside. A check for fifty thousand dollars made out to Maggie's Miracle.

"You more than earned it."

As if someone could earn redemption. But, "Thanks, Hux."

She caught his arm. "Um, I'm not sure how to say this but . . . I'm sorry."

He frowned.

"It was Reynolds's idea to involve Boo in the . . . romantic charade. I didn't mean . . . I mean, I didn't know you had actual feelings for her. I hope I didn't mess that up too much."

He frowned at her.

"The song? And the way she looked when I confronted you at the clinic. Beto captured it. But—we're not using it. I promise."

Everything inside him turned dark. "I want to see it."

"Oh . . . uh . . ." She made a face. "Okay." She reached into her satchel and pulled out her tablet. Opened up a file and scrolled through it. Then opened the file and clicked on a clip.

It opened on the screen. She'd kept the volume low, but he still heard her words, his retort— *"Hux—that's not—we had a deal."*

On the tail end of her words, Boo's eyes widened. She gasped. *Aw.*

"I told you, it's not like that—"

She put her hand over her mouth, blinking hard. Tears.

And then she closed her eyes.

Huxley looked at him. "Sorry."

"Yeah. I sort of figured she heard us." But watching it put a fist in his chest.

She closed the file. On the screen was his face, another shot still open. "Is that the footage we did on the shore, right before Mike's accident?"

"Yeah."

He reached out for the tablet, stared at himself. And then the man behind him.

Reynolds.

He pushed play. Ignored his words about hoping to live through it and focused on Reynolds Gray setting a couple packs on the ground.

"People who fear end up doing stupid things. They hurt people. Destroy lives."

"Did Reynolds pack Mike's chute?" He stopped the video and handed the tablet back to Huxley.

"I don't know. He was at Air One when I arrived, talking with Moose. It's possible—although Mike usually packs his own chute as well as the guest's chute. Or gets them professionally packed. But Reynolds has packed a chute before, so maybe."

"He skydives?"

"Oh yeah. He used to be in the military along with Mike, way back when they were young. Paratroopers. Mike got him into the television business, and they've been partners ever since."

"Right into bankruptcy," Oaken said, mostly under his breath.

"Oh no, we're doing great. Lots of ad offers after the teaser came out." She pointed at the envelope. "Hence the check."

Right.

"Although, Reynolds did record some footage of Mike jumping, and later, your interview about rescuing him, as well as some of the family in the hospital for the sponsors."

"He has footage of Mike jumping?"

"Yeah. From your GoPro and the chopper cam. We're not using it for the show. Or we weren't. Don't know now. Reynolds makes those decisions."

"Where is Reynolds now?"

"He went to pick up Mike's gear from Air One."

"I'll bet he did." He turned and nearly ran down the hallway.

And maybe—probably—he was overreacting.

Still, he got into his rental and dialed Boo.

No answer—voicemail. He called Moose next.

Voicemail.

Perfect.

Despite the late hour, the sun still hung high in the sky, above the Alaska Range, as he drove to the Tooth. He pulled up beside Moose's truck and got out.

Went inside.

A thousand memories washed over him, most of them with Boo, but she wasn't at the table, now crowded with the rest of the Air One team. They wore their red jumpsuits as if they'd just returned from a callout.

Or were on their way out. Except then they'd be in the briefing room.

Something . . .

They looked up at him as he came in. "Oaken," said Axel. He wore a thread of tension in his expression, and that slowed Oaken down.

"What are you doing here?" Moose said.

"Hi to you too," Oaken said.

"Sorry," Shep said. "But we have a bit of a situation here."

And he knew, just *knew*—"Boo."

London stared at him. "How—"

"Just a gut feeling. Because if someone was in trouble, Boo would be at the center of trying to save them. The fact that she's not—"

"We're not jumping to conclusions here," started Moose.

"Oh yes we are," said a woman with dark hair in braids, visibly pregnant. He recognized her—*oh, wait.* "Echo, right? We met—"

"Yeah, yeah. We met." She walked over to him. "Have you heard from her?"

He glanced at Moose. "Now I really am jumping to conclusions."

"When we left for training six hours ago, she was here. She was organizing the gear room. And then Echo showed up."

"About three hours ago," Echo said. "She was making me a sandwich, and I had to go to the bathroom. When I came out, she was gone."

A beat. "What do you mean *gone*?" Oaken said.

"I mean gone. And so was the pack on the table."

"What pack?" asked Axel.

"It was a parachute that Reynolds Gray was picking up—" Moose started.

"Mike's parachute, from the accident," Oaken said.

"Yeah." Moose stepped away from the table, folded his arms. In the center was a tablet with a GPS overlay of the area and a general search grid.

"What's this?"

"The LUT system picked up this signal about two hours ago. Usually the Coast Guard would handle it, but the signal is not at sea, per se, so they sent it to the sheriff's office. All their people are still out on the Knik Arm doing drills, so dispatch sent it to us."

"What kind of signal is it?" Shep asked.

Moose looked at Shep. "It's a PLB signal."

"Personal Locator Beacon," Oaken said.

"Yep," Shep said. He looked at Oaken. "Do you know if Mike had one?"

"I don't. Boo mentioned that he might have, but..." He looked at them. "Does it matter? Is someone in trouble?"

"Maybe. The Coast Guard is checking if there is a second homing frequency—a backup. If so, it's a ship and not our territory."

"And if not?"

Moose leaned over the table. "If not, then it's a boat. Or a person. In distress."

He paused.

"And... where is this person?"

"In the Turnagain mudflats," Moose said, tension in his tone.

"I don't get it," Oaken said. "What are the Turnagain mudflats?"

"It's the runoff of the glacier field," said Shep. "It's sort of an illusion—people think they can walk on it, but really it's quicksand. Or quick cement. You go in, but you can't get out. And then the tide comes in and..."

London wrapped her arms around herself.

Moose looked at Oaken. "You drown."

Shep stepped back. "And there's a bore tide heading in tonight."

"What's *that*?" Oaken said.

Shep shook his head, then headed for the locker room.

Axel followed him.

"It's a ten-foot wave, in from the ocean. Even if she isn't stuck in the mud, if she doesn't get out before the tide gets there..." Dodge looked at Moose. "So we go in by air."

Moose nodded and looked at Oaken. "Do you think... would Reynolds..." He appeared stripped.

"Yes," Oaken said and followed Axel into the locker room. "Let's go."

286

SIXTEEN

AT LEAST SHE'D DIE WITH A VIEW. BOO climbed in the back seat after kicking out the panel from the trunk. She was sweating despite the chill in the air. The sun had fallen just behind the faraway Alaska Range—or maybe it was the closer mountains in the Lake Clark National Preserve.

Whatever. The tufted clouds had turned a glorious orange and periwinkle, the sky above darkening. No moon tonight—not that she kept track of the lunar cycle, but last night a sliver of a thumbnail had hung in the sky as she'd stepped outside onto the deck, breathing in the crisp Alaskan air, glad to be back.

Now, maybe not so much. And she might be getting a little punchy, but it had taken her the better part of three hours to kick out the inner seat panel between her and the trunk. Everything hurt, her body spent.

But there was nowhere to go.

How Reynolds had stranded the car in the middle of the mudflats, she had no idea, but she suspected he'd simply put a brick to the gas and let it drive off the road, down the embankment—she'd felt that—and into the mud, the glacial runoff firm until it was so agitated that it gave way.

And turned to cement.

She sat about a hundred feet from shore now, the wheels implanted in the mud. And the tide filling in around the car. Cold and lethal, but the height of stupidity would be venturing out onto the quicksand.

She should get on the roof, see if she could wave down help.

But the last—*very last*—thing she wanted was some passersby to unknowingly think they could save her, venture out onto the mudflats, get stuck, and drown.

Even EMS personnel.

Worse, the car sat too far from land for anyone to throw out a buoy and pull her in.

But it was all moot anyway, because she didn't spot one car along the faraway road, which probably meant Reynolds had taken her on one of the side roads.

He'd probably then joined one of the many hitchhikers along the stretches of highway in Alaska.

Maybe with the tide coming in, she could swim to shore. If it was deep enough. And if she didn't pull a Jack from *Titanic* and die of hypothermia, encrusted with ice before she hit the shore.

Please let the PLB be working. She had hit that on as soon as the car stopped moving and the silence closed in around her. It was then that she'd realized that Reynolds had left. Until then, she'd braced herself against the sides of the car, trying to protect her knee as he wove through the city.

So, not the safest place to ride, the trunk. Cramped and hot. Probably Reynolds hoped the mudflats would swallow the car whole, taking her and the chute with it. And if that didn't do it, then the sea would finish the job, maybe washing her into the sound.

Out the back window, the long stretch of glacier and mud ran into the faraway glacier spill, the landscape like the moon, cratered, rippled, and bleak.

The front window, however, betrayed a much different view—the ocean headed in on a rising tide of water. It slapped against the bottom of the car doors, but so far hadn't made it inside. Although, by the view of her horizon, it seemed she'd sunk farther into the mud.

Of course Reynolds couldn't rent an SUV or something practical like that. No, she'd die in a Ford Taurus. At least it was clean.

On the inside.

She gave herself about ten minutes before the tide reached the windows and she'd have to climb out.

Ten more and the water would find the roof.

And then there was the bore tide. The wall of water scheduled to crest along the arm tonight. She'd watched it come in last month, the rumble so loud that it had burrowed through her and trembled her bones with the power of it.

Breathe.

Please, PLB, be working.

Of course, she'd left her phone at the Tooth, and that thought burned through her entire body.

He'd never know. Oaken would never know that she regretted running. Never know that he'd . . . well, he'd restored her trust in humankind, or perhaps just her belief in love. Never know that yes, she wanted to run back to him.

I love you, Oaken. That thought had been running around her head for a while and now simply sat down and wouldn't budge.

She loved his laughter, the way he believed in her, and the fact that he'd written a song about her for the entire world. Oaken was truth and laughter and food fights and stories and . . .

And she wanted to be his girl. Just like in the song.

Thunder sounded and she sat up, listening.

The bore tide, coming closer.

She barely glimpsed it, a line of foamy white in the epic distance, but the sound rose, a growl on the horizon.

Don't. Panic.

Her own words to Oaken rose, and she closed her eyes. Heard his song from so many weeks ago at the Tenderfoot.

"Through stormy nights and sunny days,
She's the anchor that keeps me from drifting away."

Her eyes filled. *Okay.* She had to figure this out. *Breathe.*

The water nearly lipped the window, so she put the chute on her back and climbed out. The water spilled inside the car.

She sat on the roof, holding the pack.

Okay, how cold could it be, really? She reached over, put her hand in.

Yanked it out.

But she was a strong swimmer.

She put the pack down. Stood up.

And strangely, her mom appeared in her head. *"Could be that the person you've been trying to rescue all this time is you, Boo. Maybe it's time to let someone else do the rescuing."*

Yeah, well, no one's coming, Mom. Not Oaken, not Air One, not . . . God.

And then, with that thought, the words *Fear not* swept over her. Like a wave. Or a gust of wind.

"Fear not. For I am with you."

She looked up, around, wrapped her arms around herself. Studied the water. Listened to her mother's words. *"That's Jesus running after the lost lamb, just because she needs him."*

Yeah, okay. Okay! "I need you. I really need you, God. And I'm sorry I tried to do this on my own, but anytime you want to show up to rescue me"—she closed her eyes, her jaw tight—"I'd be grateful."

The bore tide's thunder increased, and she stared at it, weak. Even now, it seemed to pick up speed, louder and—

Over the trees came the rhythm of chopper blades slicing the air. She waved her arms. "Here! I'm here!" A red bird—Air One Rescue.

She kept waving even as the chopper came close, hovered over her. She crouched, fighting the burn in her knee as the water around her turned to chop, as the wash ripped up droplets onto her face and neck.

Yeah, she wouldn't have survived five minutes in the soup.

But they'd better hurry, because the bore tide was rolling in fast.

The door opened and a man in a red suit, wearing a helmet, leaned out and waved at her.

Axel. Another rescue tech clipped into a safety line, looking out the door. Probably London, spotting.

Axel stepped out onto the skid, then leaned back and let the winch lower him down. A rescue harness dangled from the winch clamp. He held on to the line, one-handed, a real pro as he descended.

The bore tide rushed toward her, and the car jostled with the wind and churning of the water. The line started to twist, but Axel kept his attention on her, unmoving, and landed neatly on the car.

"Let's get this harness on you!" he shouted over the roar.

She looked past him to the tide. The water rose, cresting over the roof, wetting her feet.

"No time!" She grabbed the center strap of the chute pack, hooked it across her chest, then stepped up to the winch and clipped it to the carabiner.

Then she wrapped her arms around Axel and held on. "Let's go!"

He didn't even hesitate—just put his arm around her, clamping her to himself, and suddenly the chopper whisked them off the car.

Shep didn't even bother to winch them up, and the chopper

simply whisked them up as the bore wave crashed over the car, burying it in a wall of frigid water and ice.

She held on, her arms burning, not sure the strap could bear all her weight. But Axel gripped her around the waist with both arms now, the chopper ferrying them to shore.

It lowered them onto a rocky cliff overlooking the flats. Her feet touched the ground, and in a moment, she unclipped herself.

Axel did the same.

The bird veered off.

She turned and searched for the car.

Nothing but murky, swirling water.

Her knees started to buckle.

"Gotcha," said a voice, his arms going around her.

She turned, grabbing his arms. Holding on, then staring up at him.

Not. Axel.

He'd taken off his helmet, dropped it onto the ground, and now stared down at her. Those blue eyes took her in, held her, careened through her, past all her disbelief and even the parts of her that wanted to run.

"You found me."

He touched her face, curled his arm around her neck. "I'll always find you, Boo."

Oaken.

"You really scared me," he said quietly. "Tell me . . . it's not too late. That we have another shot at this."

She smiled. "Yeah. One last shot."

Then he pulled her to himself, his mouth on hers, hard, drawing her in, taking possession, telling her everything she needed to know.

No, she wasn't lost. She was found.

She wrapped her arms around his waist and kissed him back,

surrendering to the rush of his desire and hers, sinking into the safety, the sense of knowing exactly where she belonged.

No more running. Or hiding.

He leaned away, met her eyes. "I'm sorry. I know what you heard—I never—"

"I know." She touched his face.

He closed his eyes, met her forehead with his. Drew in a breath. Then he simply gathered her into his arms and held her.

And she held him back. "Thank you for rescuing me."

"Oh, baby," he said quietly. "Let's not get confused about who the real rescuer is in the family."

She laughed and lifted her head. "It was Reynolds, by the way."

"I know," he said. "I figured it out. Too late. But we'll get him."

A car pulled up on the lonely road, and Oaken looked up. Then back at her.

Dodge got out and headed toward them, almost at a run. "Boo, are you all right?"

"Yeah. We probably need to alert the authorities about Reynolds."

Dodge glanced at Oaken, back at Boo. "We already found him. He was stuck in the mudflats near the shore, down by where you went in. He probably rigged the car to drive in, then got stuck heading back."

She stilled, and Oaken did too. "Wait. Are you saying he orchestrated his own demise?"

"The chopper couldn't get to him before the tide came in." Dodge shook his head. "Axel did try, but . . . yeah. He sabotaged himself."

"There's a metaphor there, but I'm too tired to work it out," Oaken said as he walked to the truck and climbed in beside Boo in the back. Echo sat in the front and reached over to Boo. She'd clearly been crying.

"Let's get her to the hospital, make sure she's okay," Echo said.

"I'm fine."

"Humor us," Dodge said.

Boo wasn't sure who'd called ahead to warn the press, but a small army met them at the hospital ER when they pulled up.

Moose was there, inside, with the rest of the Air One team.

As was Mike, in a wheelchair, flanked by his very beautiful wife.

Mike rolled up. "You had us pretty scared, Oaken." He held out his hand. "And you." He looked at Boo. "Not sure we've met."

"Boo Kingston," she said. She glanced at Seraphina.

"Nice to meet you, Boo," Mike said.

Huxley came over, carrying a couple cups of coffee. "Heard about the harrowing rescue."

"Too bad you didn't get it on tape," Axel said. "It was cool."

She didn't miss Oaken's grin.

"So does that mean you're officially joining Air One Rescue?" asked London.

Boo looked at her, then Oaken. "I don't think—"

"Keep me on the roster," he said, slipping his hand into Boo's.

Moose came down the hallway with a wheelchair. "The police need a statement, but let's get you checked out first."

"I'm not getting in that," she said, despite her knee.

"Whatever," Oaken said and picked her up, right there, in his arms.

Oh, for the love—

But she hung on.

Because why not? Every girl needed a good rescue at least once in her life.

Oaken carried her inside the room. Planted himself beside her bed even when the ER nurse came in and tried to shoo him out. "I'm not going anywhere without Boo," he said and took her hand.

And she believed him.

Such a beautiful day to bare his soul . . . Hopefully he wouldn't end up burned.

So here went nothing.

Oaken pulled up to the curb of Maggie Bloom's ranch home, seated at the end of a cul-de-sac. Balloons fluttered from the mailbox, tied with ribbons, a sweet sixteen sign in the yard.

Cars jammed the driveway to the house, lined the circle, and spilled out along the street. A pretty home, modest, with a van in the driveway and hostas lining the front walk.

Boo reached over and took his hand, squeezing. He glanced at her. Sometimes the sight of her simply swept his breath away. She wore her hair down today, a jean jacket over a black T-shirt, a pair of faded jeans, and pink Converse tennis shoes.

Pink. That was unexpected. But Boo had stepped out of herself over the past few weeks. He couldn't believe it when she sat with a reporter and unreeled the story of her kidnapping, along with Reynolds's rigging of *Survivor Quest*.

She let Oaken take pictures of them together and let him send them to Goldie's marketing team.

And didn't, not once, look at social media.

He drew in a breath. "I haven't been this nervous since my first gig. I stood there in the wings as the band spun up my first song and thought, *What am I doing?*"

She turned in the seat. "You're doing the right thing."

He wanted to believe her. "I should have just sent the check."

"You're giving a teenage girl the thrill of her life."

"Yeah. Then why do I feel like I'm walking in naked?"

"Oak. You feel naked because this isn't a performance. This is your heart. You're about to be the real you, the guy who cares about others. For too long you've stood in the shadow of your sister, at

least in your own mind. Today, Oaken Fox steps into the light."
She touched his face, her hand warm. "You need this as much as
she does—probably more."

Then she leaned over and kissed him. Gently, sweetly. Pulled
back and met his eyes.

"There you go, rescuing me again."

"Just go in there and play some music, tough guy."

Okay, yes. He blew out his breath, then got out and opened the
back door, retrieving his guitar.

Spring fragranced the Minnesota air, and the scent of something
grilling suggested a beautiful summer day. Memorial Day weekend
seemed the right day for this event . . . Saying thank you to the
past, embracing the hope of the future.

Boo waited for him on the sidewalk, then took his hand as
they walked to the door. Tightened her grip as he rang the bell
and waited.

Kept him from running back to the car, his heart slamming
against his ribs.

The door opened. He recognized Maggie's mother, Stella, from
her pictures on the website, although they'd never personally met.

Now he offered a smile.

Stella wore her brown hair back and up, a trim woman, although
stress was etched around her eyes. She stared at Oaken, glanced at
Boo, then back to Oaken. "I . . ."

"We've never met," said Oaken as he let go of Boo's hand and
held his out. "Oaken Fox."

"Yes. I know who you are." She frowned, glanced over her shoulder, then back to Oaken. "I never . . . I can't believe you're here."

He sighed, swallowed. *Do this already.* "Maggie wrote to me
and asked me to play for her birthday."

Stella's eyes widened, and her mouth opened. "Oh my. I'd forgotten that . . . I . . . *really?* You came all the way from Nashville
for my daughter's birthday party?"

Actually, he'd most recently been here in Minnesota, having a face-to-face with Boo's father about his intentions. Which felt weird and yet somehow right. And he liked her family, despite her rather intimidating brothers. They'd all arrived for a birthday party for her mother, and seeing them together harkened back to old times with his family. Before.

And maybe again, now that his father had moved to Florida.

"Yes, and ... can we talk?"

Stella nodded, confusion in her expression, and stepped aside for him to enter.

The room opened into a kitchen, and through a sliding glass door, he spotted a pool, smoke billowing from a barbeque.

A cake sat on the kitchen island, along with a stack of plastic cups and plates, a bowl of potato salad, and cut-up watermelon.

He set down the guitar and dug an envelope out of his pocket. Handed it to Stella.

She took it, frowned, and opened it.

Her mouth opened as she drew out the check. "I don't ... Wait. This is ..." She looked up. "Wait. This is from Courageous Hearts."

"Yeah. That's ... me."

A beat.

"I don't understand."

"I'm Hollie Montgomery's brother."

She nodded. "I know that."

"And, well, I ... you see, that night that Hollie hit your car, she was fresh off a family argument with me and—"

She held up her hand. "I can't take this."

"What?"

"Oaken." She gave him a soft smile. "Hollie's already been forgiven. It was an accident. A terrible accident. But God uses all the darkness for good."

Words hung in his head ... *Love wants to do amazing things through you.*

"Yes. He does. And part of that is my ability to help Maggie's Miracles."

She considered the check, her mouth tightening. When she looked up again, tears glistened. "Have you been held hostage all this time?"

Oh.

Boo took his hand and squeezed.

"Oaken Fox, whatever went down between you and your sister, whatever blame you feel in this . . . you're forgiven." Then Stella stepped forward and put her arms around his neck.

His throat burned, but he managed to put one arm around her.

Boo had stepped away and now grinned at him.

Stella finally let go. Put her hands on his shoulders. "I think Maggie is going to lose her mind." She winked.

So this was what a full breath, what wholeness, felt like.

"Ready?" he said to Boo. "Because you know this is going on social media."

She held up her fist and he bumped it. He took out his guitar from the case, slung it over his shoulder, and followed Stella to the sliding door, pausing as she stepped outside and got Maggie's attention.

Maggie sat in a wheelchair, dressed in a pink sundress, her hair up, laughing with a group of friends. Her mother walked over. Bent and whispered something into Maggie's ear.

He could guess her words, at least in part, when Maggie turned and her eyes rounded.

"Let's go, hero," Boo said and practically pushed him out the door.

"Are you kidding me?" Maggie said, rolling her chair toward him. "I . . . What is happening?" She covered her face with her hands.

"Hey, Maggie," he said, ignoring the phones. "Thank you for inviting me to your swanky party."

She started laughing, crying, looking at her friends. "I . . . Seriously?"

"Seriously," he said. Then he leaned in and gave her a hug.

She wrapped her arms around him. "This is ridiculous!" Her laughter swept through him.

He laughed too, then pulled away. "How about a song?"

Cheers, and he looked back at Boo, who winked.

"I've been working on this for the last couple weeks. It's going on my new album, but I thought I'd try it out here first. Ready?"

He pulled up the guitar, strummed out the intro, then dove in.

"Out on the open road, I've been searching high and low
For a love that's true, a heart that knows.
Through dusty towns and city lights, I roamed,
Seeking a love that felt like coming home."

He smiled down at Maggie. Yeah, this was why he sang. For the light he found in the eyes of others.

"But then you walked into my life, like a sunrise over fields.
I saw forever in your eyes, and all the past wounds healed.
Now I know, deep in my soul, I'm the luckiest guy alive,
For in your love, darlin', I've found my guiding light."

He took a step back, moving into the chorus, watching people bob their heads.

"I've walked through valleys, climbed mountains high,
But it all led me to you, under this infinite sky.
With your hand in mine, I face every storm,
Because of you, my love, I've truly been reborn."

He looked at Boo. She nodded, swaying with his song.

"In the tapestry of time, our paths aligned.
You're the answer to my prayers, the love I've pined.
Through every trial, every twist and turn,
With you by my side, I've come to learn—"

He turned back to Maggie, a glance at Stella, then to heaven.
Closed his eyes.

"You're the missin' piece, the melody to my song.
With you, I've found where I truly belong.
Underneath the stars, hand in hand, side by side,
In your embrace, I'm living a blessed, forgiven life."

The last of the song faded, and he opened his eyes to cheers,
clapping.

"Now, how about a Happy Birthday song?"

He did a fancy lick, then settled into the song, the friends singing along.

Maggie beamed.

Her mom disappeared and in a moment, headed back with the
cake, candles burning.

She set it on the table, and Maggie rolled up, blew out the candles.

Cheering, and he gave her a high five, then stepped back as
Stella cut the cake.

Boo slid her hand into his. "That's a future number-one single."

He glanced at her. "At least now I know who I wrote it for."
He winked.

"Are you putting that in your album notes?"

"Maybe I'll reveal it on Fallon."

She shook her head. "Perfect."

"Hey . . . are you . . . are you Boo Hoo?"

He stilled even as Boo's smile faded. She looked past him to Maggie, who held a piece of cake on her lap.

"I was," she said.

Maggie's mouth opened. "Oh my—Mom! Mom—do you know who this is?"

Oh no. Oaken glanced at Boo. "Should we leave?"

Boo, however, had found a brave smile.

Stella came over.

"Mom, this is Boo. Boo Hoo. You know, from *Survivor Quest*?"

Recognition flashed over Stella's face. "Wow. This is a real treat. I . . ." She looked at Maggie. "Should we show them your room?"

Oaken raised an eyebrow.

"Oh," Maggie said. She wrinkled her nose.

"Okay," Stella said and turned back to them. "Maggie is a huge fan. She used to watch the show during PT, right after they put in her spinal stimulator, when they were trying to get her legs to move."

"Yeah. It worked too," Maggie said. She handed her mom the cake.

And then Oaken's hand tightened in Boo's as Maggie pushed herself up from the chair. Grabbed onto her mom, who'd put the cake down too.

She stood there and grinned at them. "And I'm getting stronger every day. I can do five steps on my own now."

"Let's not try it out here on the concrete, shall we, honey?" her mom said.

But Oaken just . . . couldn't move. And beside him, Boo seemed to be equally undone.

Maggie lowered herself back into her chair. "I'll never forget the episode where you hung on to that belay of Blake's for nearly two hours as he tried to climb the X-treme Apex Ascent."

"So much pain," Boo said, suddenly breaking free from her silence.

"And then you ran ten miles—like, at top speed."

"We had to beat the other teams."

"It was boss," Maggie said. She held up her fist.

Boo met it.

"I hate Blake." Maggie said. "What a jerk."

Boo knelt next to her chair. "Aw. You know that was for the show, right? Ratings. Blake's a good guy. He just needs to start listening to his own voice instead of the world's comments, right?"

Maggie nodded. "You're cool, Boo."

"Actually, the name is Brontë."

Maggie smiled. "That's a killer name."

"Yeah, it is," Boo said.

Oaken put his hand on her shoulder, squeezed. Boo got up.

"Any cake for me?" Oaken said.

Maggie laughed and Stella went to retrieve him a piece.

But Boo turned to him. Put her hands on his chest. And then she kissed him.

"Oh, I want a picture!" Maggie said.

A few other friends had grabbed their phones.

Boo glanced at her, then grinned. "Alrighty. You asked for it."

Then she put her arms around him and pulled him into her embrace, mouth on his.

He could do this all day.

Phones clicked, and then he poked her and she started to laugh, and more phones grabbed the shot of him leaning over her, chasing a kiss while she threw her head back and laughed.

He caught her kiss, then pulled her back up, his eyes on hers. "That'll go viral."

"Good," she said, winking. "Because the world needs to see that you're a good man, Oaken. A hero."

"The only person who needs to believe that is you, babe."

"Oh, I believe," she said, meeting his eyes, her hands on his chest. "I believe."

And finally . . . he did too.

Get the next book in the series and
continue the adventure!

ONE LAST

ALASKA AIR ONE RESCUE | BOOK TWO

CHANCE

BESTSELLING AUTHOR

SUSAN MAY
WARREN

The voice on the radio saved his life.
But when he discovers who she is . . .
it just might cost him everything.

Axel Mulligan was built to be a Coast Guard rescue swimmer. He could swim faster, endure longer and became a miracle for those in peril in the sea. Until a tragedy destroyed him and sent him home, to Alaska.

Now, three years later, he's not going to let the past repeat itself, so as an Air One rescue swimmer, he'll do anything to save lives. Including lose his own—which is what he expects when he goes into the icy waters of the Bering Sea, trying to rescue a cruise group of tourists. But for the voice on the other end of the Ham radio, he might have given up, let hypothermia win.

But it didn't. Now he'll do anything to find the voice and thank her.

Except the voice—Flynn Turnquist—is not who he thinks. A national wildlife researcher, she's deep in the bush, tracking wolf pack patterns. Or is she? In fact, she's a former cop, tracking down a serial killer. And she's close enough to see his handiwork in the trail of bodies. She nearly had him—until he escaped into the Bering Sea. But she just knows he's still alive . . . and she's sure she's on his trail . . .

When Axel finds Flynn . . . and what she's really up to, it stirs up a terrible nightmare he's been dodging for years—the kidnapping and death of his own cousin. Worse, he's led the killer right to her doorstep. Now, it's a race through Alaska to stay alive . . . and when tragedy strikes again, he must choose between rescue or redemption . . .

An exhilarating adventure through the Alaskan Wilderness!

Note to Reader

Thank you again for reading One Last Shot. I hope you enjoyed the story! There's more to come...!

If you did enjoy One Last Shot, would you be willing to do me a favor? Head over to the product page and leave a review. It doesn't have to be long—just a few words to help other readers know what they're getting. (But no spoilers! We don't want to wreck the fun!)

I want to shout out a big thank you to the following people for helping me put together this story –

Rachel Hauck (of course!) and Sarah Erredge who always answer the phone and put up with my endless brainstorming questions. (And my husband, Andrew, for his technical help with all things mechanical!) The amazing Anne Horch for her editing, and Emilie Haney for her beautiful cover designs. Tari Faris for the way she makes the interior shine, and Rel Mollet for ALL THE THINGS. A thanks to Katie Donovan and Sara Shull for their last minute proofing help. I have an amazing team—and it does take a team to make this all happen. I'm so grateful for all of you! My deepest gratitude goes out to Andrea Doering and the excellent team at Revell, also, for partnering with me on this story. I'd love to hear from you—not only about this story, but about any characters or stories you'd like to read in the future. Write to me at: susan@susanmaywarren.com. And if you'd like to see what's ahead, stop by www.susanmaywarren.com.

If you enjoy news on upcoming releases, freebies and sneak peeks, sign up for my weekly email at susanmaywarren.com, or scan the QR code below.

XO!
Susie May

More Books by Susan May Warren

The Marshall Family Saga

The Minnesota Marshalls

Fraser
Jonas
Ned
Iris
Creed

The Epic Story of RJ and York

Out of the Night
I Will Find You
No Matter the Cost

The Montana Marshalls

Knox
Tate
Ford
Wyatt
Ruby Jane

Also by Susan May Warren

Sky King Ranch

Sunrise
Sunburst
Sundown

Global Search and Rescue

The Way of the Brave
The Heart of a Hero
The Price of Valor

Montana Fire

Where There's Smoke (Summer of Fire)
Playing with Fire (Summer of Fire)
Burnin' For You (Summer of Fire)
Oh, The Weather Outside is Frightful (Christmas novella)
I'll be There (Montana Fire/Deep Haven crossover)

Light My Fire (Summer of the Burning Sky)
The Heat is On (Summer of the Burning Sky)
Some Like it Hot (Summer of the Burning Sky)
You Don't Have to Be a Star (Montana Fire spin-off)

MONTANA RESCUE

If Ever I Would Leave You (novella prequel)
Wild Montana Skies
Rescue Me
A Matter of Trust
Crossfire (novella)
Troubled Waters
Storm Front
Wait for Me

A complete list of Susan's novels can be found at
susanmaywarren.com/novels/bibliography/.

About the Author

With nearly 2 million books sold, critically acclaimed novelist **Susan May Warren** is the USA Today bestselling author of over 95 novels, including the Global Search and Rescue and Montana Rescue series. Winner of a RITA Award and multiple Christy and Carol Awards, as well as the HOLT Medallion and numerous Readers' Choice Awards, her compelling plots and unforgettable characters have won acclaim with readers and reviewers alike. The mother of four grown children, and married to her real-life hero for 35 years, she loves travelling and telling stories about life, adventure and faith.

For exciting updates on her new releases, previous books, and more, visit her website at www.susanmaywarren.com.